CHILDISH DREAMS

a superstardom novel

I0668562

MALORIE VERDANT

For Chantal,
Whose talents are limitless and who inspired me to follow my dreams.

CHILDISH
DREAMS

PROLOGUE

Are you going to answer the boy?

Billie

The spotlight was blinding me, the collective gasp of the audience freaking me the f*ck out. The colors that had filled the theater stage moments ago hid in the shadows, gleefully waiting for my response.

I shut my eyes to stop the pounding in my head. I desperately wanted to run and hide from everyone's eager facial expressions. Over seven thousand people sat in the dark staring at me—at *us*—and I didn't have the words.

I willed the band to start up again. I wished to hear the first notes of the song that was meant to launch my career. I knew I hadn't hit my mark at the front of the stage and my body was too far away from the conductor. However, I was prepared to start singing, with my eyes closed and my back to the audience. I hated the fact that the glittery fringe swaying back and forth from my blue sequin dress was the only thing making music. My singing career was like a forgotten tumbleweed blowing away.

I prayed that if I stood still for long enough, with my eyes closed hard enough, at least one of the producers would step in to end this madness.

It was live television, after all.

I knew we were already over time, and I couldn't imagine a nonresponsive contestant was great for their ratings. Connor must have repeated the phrase "Live television doesn't do overtime, children" twelve times during each rehearsal. They would have to step in. Connor would come out with his disgustingly charming smile and his perfectly styled hair and talk to the audience. He would encourage everyone to laugh about this as if it were the best practical joke in the history of the series. He'd then remind them that the moment they had all been waiting for would happen after a very short ad break.

They couldn't possibly expect me to answer on national television. They surely had better things they needed me to do, like sing to thousands of viewers. Viewers who had been watching eagerly and spending their money on getting to this very moment. Surely no one wanted to watch *this*.

After seconds ticked into minutes, I wondered if I needed to remind the people in charge to get on stage. They must have been as shocked as I was, and unsure of what to do next. If I made eye contact, maybe it would spur them into action.

I tentatively opened my blue eyes and quickly turned my head to look at Steve , the stage manager, standing by the control box. I tucked a loose blonde curl behind my left ear, my cue for him to come on stage—a subtle prompt to handle this problem, just like he handled any and all production issues in the past. When he just answered by smiling, giving me a thumbs-up in congratulations, I was left speechless. Again.

"So are you going to answer the boy?" Russell asked from the judges' bench, chuckling. I turned to stare at them in confusion.

Is no one going to stop this from happening?

"Maybe she needs to hear him repeat the question." Claudia laughed. "Girl's having a big night."

Before I could reply with how unnecessary that was, the most beautiful guy I'd ever met touched my shoulder. For the second time this evening, he looked deeply into my eyes and asked softly, "Billie Bishop, will you make me the happiest man in the world and marry me?"

CHAPTER
ONE

Superstardom

Billie

Five Months Earlier

"You're going to kill it," Zach told me as he spun around in my desk chair, his voice fading as he yawned. "Your audition is going to be on YouTube's trending list for weeks."

"You can't say that. It'll jinx everything," I whispered while I continued to pack. I already had my favorite pair of black jeans and a few white T-shirts in a duffel bag. It was more than enough for a quick two-day trip, but I kept deciding I needed more. "Darn it, where are my ankle boots?"

I looked around my bedroom at the Miranda Lambert posters hanging above my bed, the large bookshelf filled with old records that took up the entire left wall, and my small desk that was tucked into the corner. As my eyes passed the small piles of belongings I had scattered around the room, I tried to imagine what else I might need. "Do you think I should bring my hair straightener?" I asked quietly with a pained expression on my face.

"I thought you were going to keep it casual, jeans and T-shirts? Won't straightening your hair look like you're trying really hard if they ask to see baby photos for your backstory and realize that your hair is actually a crazy mess?" Zach muttered, raising an eyebrow at me.

"That's right, that was the plan. Why do I keep forgetting about the plan? Casual means curls," I exhaled. "It also means I can go straight to the auditions and won't need to find a hotel. It's not like I'll be the first to audition with a crazy mane of curls. That guy from Austin who won in season two had crazy curls, yeah?"

"I think he did. I think he even had curls when he won that Grammy last year for debut album," Zach reassured, winking at me. "Which brings me to why I came here at this god-awful hour. I really think you need to let me come. When you take me to all those award ceremonies, I want to be able to say that I was there from the very beginning."

"I thought you came to make sure I didn't chicken out or make up some excuse about why I missed the bus? But if you came over just to try and convince me to let you join, I'll repeat my mantra. You aren't coming with me," I reminded him. "It's not happening."

"I won't even talk to the all-important *Connor Graves* or the infamous *Jax Bone*," he told me, pouting. Zach then posed, resting his elbows on his knees and letting his blond hair fall in front of his dark blue eyes. "You won't even know I'm there. I promise I'll be as quiet as a mouse," he pleaded.

"Don't try and pull that seducing-the-cheerleader face on me, Zachary James Montgomery. It won't work. We've already discussed this. The deal was I would go to the auditions if they were held only a short bus ride away from here. And if you kept your word and didn't come, didn't tell either of our families and make me even more nervous than I am," I responded firmly.

"It was a stupid deal," he complained as he went back to spinning in my chair and yawning again, his broad shoulders scraping the bookcase with each rotation. "And you know our mommas are going to go crazy when they see you on television, then find out I knew and didn't tell them. You know they're addicted to *Superstardom*. They'll see it all go down."

"Well, if you let me back out of the deal, I'll stop packing and you can stop worrying about the wrath of our mommas. Hell, at this hour, if you stop trying to destroy my bookcase, we could head over to Lucy's Diner and get the best table for breakfast," I said with a sneaky smile.

"I built this bookcase in shop class; it won't fall apart with a few knocks. And you aren't getting out of going to Charleston. It's not even the worst deal we've ever made, so you aren't bailing, B." Laughing, he looked at some of the photos I had scattered across my desk documenting our past adventures. He held up the picture of when we were ten by the creek. We were both in matching overalls holding fishing rods, and my wild blonde curls were hidden by a red polka-dot bandana. "Remember the time you agreed to eat a snail from the creek if I let you go fishing with me?"

"Don't remind me. I believe my momma made me brush my teeth twelve times that day when she found out. My gums are still scarred. Although, it was still better than that stupid deal I made so you would try out for the basketball team," I groaned.

Zach burst out laughing. "Oh yeah, why isn't there a photo of your attempt at joining the cheerleading team?" He ducked when I threw my pillow at him.

"Keep your voice down. It's because my poor coordination and inability to show team spirit in synchronized arm movements didn't need to be documented. At least it got you on the team," I replied smugly. "There were what, two scouts at the last game? And how many letters have USC and Clemson sent you?"

"Yeah, yeah. If I make it to the NBA, I'll owe all my success to you. Although, after your audition, when you're sitting beside Jay-Z and Beyoncé, I'm going to make sure everyone knows you got there because of me."

"Zach, don't get too excited. They only give out five passes to go to the Las Vegas auditions in each town, and literally thousands of people audition. The likelihood that they'll give a ticket to an eighteen-year-old girl who predominately sings to her best friend's dog is very small."

"B, Rocket is a fabulous judge of singing talent. Have you not seen him run and hide when I try to do my best 'Take Back Home Girl' karaoke routine?

Picturing Zach's large golden labradoodle huddling behind his couch had me forgetting my anxiety and smiling at his exaggerated disgruntled expression. "He really does have excellent survival instincts. But all jokes aside, you really think I can do this? Audition for a singing competition that airs around the country when I don't even have a YouTube channel? Shouldn't I try that first? Wait, are you encouraging this so I end up as one of those bad auditions that gets played on loop for the world to laugh at? Is this just material for a future stand-up comedy career?"

"How long have we been friends?"

"Since birth. Our mommas are basically sisters—"

"Exactly. And in all these painful years, we agreed to two deals a year. And none of those deals were ever meant to humiliate each other."

"The cheerleading one—"

"Was your idea." He laughed. "I was just a victim like everyone else."

"Ha ha. You're lucky I know you're right. Well, if you're not going to let me get out of our deal, then at least help me find my shoes and take me to the bus station before I change my mind."

"Sure. Just so you know, our deal didn't mean I couldn't send you hundreds of messages throughout the day. I'm going to be messaging you nonstop until you tell me how much they loved you."

"You can message. Just don't hold your breath."

It was a thirty-minute bus ride next to a guy named Dylan, who snored like a tractor the entire trip into the city. It would have been torture if Zach hadn't been sending me sad selfies. As his photos became more and more ridiculous, I actually laughed out loud and feared I'd wake my bus companion. When the bus finally pulled into the terminal, I decided to go straight from the station to the convention center. This whole painful experience needed to be treated like removing a Band-Aid. I wasn't going to go find a hotel room and obsess about which T-shirt I was going to wear or how I would style my hair for an hour. I would keep my casual travel clothes on, and just risk disappointing the judges.

When I finally reached where they were hosting the open call auditions, I stood and gaped at the number of people I was up against.

People had clearly camped out all night. Their multicolored portable chairs, flashlights, and sleeping bags were confined between the fenced-in sections that started only a few feet away from the steps of the building. The kaleidoscope of clothes from all the people crammed in beside one another was as beautiful as it was intimidating.

I decided to get in line and watch silently as people woke up and began packing away their sleeping gear, smiling and chatting about the day ahead. A big group of family and friends supporting the youngest boy in their pack joined the line behind me. When they tried calming his nerves by excitedly talking about all his experience at performing in front of crowds, my nerves began to intensify. I was about to text Zach with a serious *what have you gotten me into* message when my phone beeped.

You've got this. Proud of you. Z

Seeing those small words, I sighed, then stopped listening to the chatter around me and tried to relax. I kept thinking about the song I needed to decide upon. I was a country girl at heart, but I didn't want to go in there and be viewed as a pathetic imitation of the current 'it' girls in country music. I wasn't going to destroy one of their greatest hits by performing it in my first audition. I wanted the judges to see that singing wasn't about my desperate wish to turn into one of my idols. It was about emotion. It was about dreams and happiness and escape. It was about me getting to be me.

I narrowed my song choice down to two when an energy seemed to spread through the crowd. Bodies began shifting to the right, and through the gaps I was able to see what everyone was staring at—a short woman with bright purple hair wearing a commanding pinstripe suit.

She carried a microphone as she walked up the stairs of a podium. When she reached the top and looked out at the line of people that seemed to be growing longer and longer with each second, she began talking.

"Hey, y'all, my name's Danielle, and I'm the casting producer here in Charleston. Thank you so much for coming all the way out here to be a part of *Superstardom*. In just a moment, we are going to start checking your registration paperwork, handing out audition numbers, and inviting you to come inside the coliseum to wait until your number is called. Please don't lose your number, because you won't be able to meet the judges without it. I also wanted to let y'all know that camera crews will be circling the lines and asking a few of you to do some quick interviews before everyone is inside. Don't worry if they don't interview you; these interviews are not a guarantee that you'll make it through to Las Vegas or that you won't. Now good luck, and break a leg!"

As the crowd roared and cheered in response to the start of the audition process, I watched her disappear amongst the numerous camera people and those holding clipboards and wearing headsets. My nerves were back.

This was really happening. I was really here and about to sing in front of that woman and the judges who had been on billboards all around the country for the past couple of months.

As I began hyperventilating, I watched as a camera crew started to make their way toward me. I felt my heart jump into my throat. I wasn't ready to be on camera. I needed to decide on my song, needed to look in a mirror and check that sleeping Dylan hadn't accidentally drooled in my hair. When the cameramen walked right past me and smiled at the family waving their signs and pushing the fourteen-year-old boy to the front, I got my sh*t together.

They didn't want me.

They wanted the experienced fourteen-year-old.

Good Lord, that was a close one.

I clasped my hands together tightly and looked away to ensure I didn't catch any of the cameramen's eyes as they asked the kid about his hopes and dreams. I could hear the excitement in his voice when he talked about his passion for performing for others. When the kid broke into song and the camera crew started clapping, I was suddenly jealous of his confidence. I knew I would face them eventually, and I never chickened out of a deal, but I wasn't sure my eyes wouldn't be wide or filled with terror.

Excitement was unlikely.

Three hours later I had my ticket number and was ushered through the entrance with the thousands of other hopeful contestants like cattle being rounded up and put on a semi. Everyone quickly took a seat beside their loved ones, still cheering and clapping. When Connor Graves, the host of *Superstardom*, walked into the arena with microphone in hand, the noise amplified.

I always thought that Connor Graves, the gatekeeper to the judges, was paid by everyone who wanted to audition with attention and love to ensure their safe passage into the land of hopes and dreams. Even when their eyes suggested they didn't like him all that much, they still lavished him with praise. I watched in fascination as he kept talking to the camera crew about how glad he was to be there. I gawked as he continued raking his hand through his coiffed brown hair and displaying his famous television personality by jumping up and down, doing tricks for the audience, and singing a few bars of past contestants' latest hits. He then shifted his attention from the camera to ask the crowd to shout the show's catchphrase—that we were all "looking for *Superstardom*"—three times. As swiftly as Connor Graves came into the center of the arena, he passed his microphone to the nearest producer and moved to the side to talk to the girl with the bright purple hair. When his body slumped to the side and his head tilted back and forth, he reminded me of the waitresses at Lucy's Diner, entertaining everyone for tips but unable to hold the smile for that long, because it was just a job and a lousy one at that. He was an entertainer like everyone in this room, but maybe he hated being the gatekeeper to a world he also wished to live inside of.

When they brought up the first wannabe superstar, a fifteen-year-old girl with red curls in pigtails, and he led her behind the curtain followed closely by the camera crews, I felt my breath catch. When she walked out again crying, I felt the bottom of my stomach drop. Two hours disappeared while my eyes were glued on the curtains that led to the judges' rooms, watching the people leave the auditorium to audition with smiles and exit with tears. After a forty-year-old man left with his two little daughters trailing him, streaks running down all of their faces, I told myself I needed a distraction.

I couldn't keep watching the heartbroken.

My nerves weren't going away.

My heart pounded in my chest, and my legs were shaking. I needed to focus on something that didn't make me want to run away and never look back.

I decided to watch the other people sitting in the audience and the camera crew. After examining the room, I realized that observing the effects of crushed dreams was causing many individuals in the room to snap under the pressure. The cameramen were like police dogs, sniffing out the ticking time bombs before they exploded.

My legs almost stopped shaking completely after I saw the camera spin and capture two girls pulling at each other's identical tank tops and blue leather skirts, screaming ,"I picked this outfit first!" and "If you were really my sister, you wouldn't have worn the same outfit as me!" When the camera then shifted and zoomed in on a guy with a pot belly and yellow teeth yelling at his girlfriend to go home and not interfere with his chances of being a sex symbol, I actually giggled.

"This is crazy, huh?" a girl sitting beside me asked cheerfully. She had silky black hair hanging loosely down her back, wore thick-rimmed glasses, and had her guitar resting against her knees. She was clearly the cool singer-songwriter, and I knew I must pale in comparison.

"It's not what I expected," I muttered.

"Some people are just a hot mess under the pressure," she continued. "One year I watched a pair of identical twin brothers doing synchronized dance moves fall down and start hitting each other. Blood sprayed everywhere, and it was a little scary to watch. But Mr. Sex Symbol up there, that is definitely a first."

"You've done this a lot?"

"Oh, I've auditioned for the last four seasons. The moment I turned fourteen, I flew to the nearest audition center and gave it my shot."

"Is it always like this?"

"People bringing a massive entourage, glittering signs, matching T-shirts, and those special few who yell and blame their family if they walk out without a star ticket? More often than I care to remember."

"Number 1201," called a voice from the speakers. "Please make your way down to the casting producer."

"What number are you?" the cool girl asked.

"1203."

"Wow, you're going to be called really soon. It's only been what, like three hours? That's amazing. Are you ready?"

"I don't think so."

"That's good. It's always best to be a little nervous and naive. The producers are more inclined to let you sing in front of the celebrity judges if you're pretty, nervous and likely to break down in tears in front of them. It's good television watching pretty girls cry."

"Are you serious? Doesn't everyone get to sing in front of the judges?"

"Definitely not. We're lucky though. Some shows make you go through, like, three sets of auditions before you even get to the celebrity judges, girl. At least *Superstardom* just runs this thing for two days in each city, and most of us fools find out quickly if we should pack our stuff up and go home. They send you behind that curtain and you find out if you're performing for producers or the real superstars. If you're really good or really bad in front of the producers, they might ask you to come back tomorrow and film again in front of the celebrity judges. But the lucky few get to do the golden walk to the fancy room with the fancy judges the first time."

"How many times have you gotten to sing in front of the celebrity judges?" I asked in shock, unsure if I wanted to be one of those lucky few.

"Twice. I'm a couple sizes larger than their typical favorite *Superstardom* poster girls, so usually they always send me to a producer first. But that doesn't bother me, because they always say really nice things about how I sing even when I don't make it into the top fifty. Although this year, I'm desperate to get in front of the judges."

"Why?"

"Why do you think? Jax Bone, that stunning tall drink of water."

"I'm not a fan."

"Girl, have you seen his posters?"

"The ones where he's playing his guitar and sweating on the crowd? Yeah, it's sort of... icky."

"It's hot. And he's written, like, the last ten number one songs in the country, and he's only nineteen. Even when he isn't singing, he's casting spells on people. I heard celebrities pay Jax's agent for his number. I can't believe they even got him to agree to judge this season. I'm just hoping to shake his hand. I want some of Jax Bone's magic touch to rub off on me before I sing."

"I doubt you're the only girl in this room who wants Jax's Bone to *rub* on them. I should ask him how many girls he plans on sleeping with on the show."

The cool girl laughed. "Honey, I hope you make it into that room with those judges. I'd tune in to see you asking Jax Bone questions like that on television. Although, if you make it that far, it's usually good to ask the judges for advice rather than tease them about their known promiscuity. Might as well get something out of the hours you spend here, right? Last year, Russell told me I needed to bring my guitar to all my auditions because it was clear I wasn't comfortable singing without it. He was right."

"Number 1202, please make your way down toward the casting producer," crackled from the speakers.

"Good Lord," I exclaimed.

"Don't start freaking out now. We don't want that camera finding you just yet. How about we take some photos together? If I make it, you can tell everyone how you met Faith Randall first, and if you make it—"

"You can tell everyone you knew Billie Bishop when."

"Exactly. Now pose and tell me, what are you looking for?" Laughing, she held up her camera phone and pulled me close beside her.

"*Superstardom.*"

CHAPTER
TWO

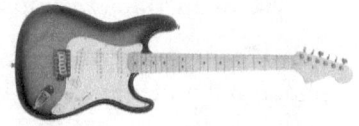

I just like to sing

Jax

"**D**onny, I told you I'd do it and I'm here, aren't I?" I growled into the speaker. "So why don't you just let me get back in the room and get this thing done. Stop blowing up my phone every five f*cking minutes."

"I just wanted to remind you what's at stake here, Jax. This show is meant to be about promoting your new image. The record label didn't like the tabloid article that came out this morning about you trashing your last hotel room," Donny explained.

"I didn't trash that damn hotel room," I grunted. "We were in town for less than two days, and I was stuck in a small room listening to bad singers pretending to be me. I didn't even have a chance to go to the bar, let alone drink myself stupid and smash everything made out of glass in that damn room. The housekeepers were just trying to get a payday by making that mess and photographing it."

"It doesn't really matter what happened," Donny sighed. "The label is forgetting that you're their golden boy, but this show is loved by everyone—moms, dads, brothers, and sisters. You get the nation to believe you're the son they all wish they had and I can guarantee when you sign that new contract on your birthday, there will be a few extra zeros added in. We try and rework your contract now and we're going to be holding our family jewels after their lawyers finish screwing with us."

"So the fact that nearly every song played on the radio is one of mine means nothing? And that I've got messages from the biggest names in the industry asking if I have anything new they can record is worthless?"

"The label execs are arguing that you're on drugs and soon won't be able to sign your own name, let alone write another hit."

I scoffed. "You've got to be kidding me. I've never touched the stuff. My father died because some a**hole was driving while high, for Christ's sake."

"I know, Jax, and they know it to. But with the tabloids reporting about the trashed rooms and brawls in bars, people will start wondering if you're too young for this life. Even Graham can't convince them that you're still the same kid from when you first signed with him. They're arguing that the women and celebrity life have changed you—"

"You know that's bullsh*t."

"I know that and you know that, which is why we need to let this show film you 24-7. Everyone will see that you're not high every day and you have a brain and talent that no one can compare to."

"They'll twist my image on this show, Don. I'm not an idiot. They paid me to do this show because they want the drama. Their costume director has got me dressed in leather pants day in and day out. I'm sitting for hours. I should be in my damn jeans or sweatpants."

"They want the rock star from the posters. Can't blame them. They still let you wear your favorite white T-shirt and Converses, boy, so don't complain. They also can't create drama from nothing. We put that in the contract. Just don't give them anything they can use against you."

"I'm guessing I'm not allowed to be truthful, then, when these contestants sing like sh*t?"

"F*ck no. Boy, leave that hard judge act to someone else. Be the nice one," he said pleadingly.

"I'll do the best I can."

"You never do make this easy for me, kid."

I chuckled. "That's why I let you take your huge cut."

"Ain't that the truth? Okay, go in. Sit down. Smile for the cameras, flirt with the gorgeous Claudia. Let Russell, Nashville's favorite country boy, become your best friend. The woman's a pop princess, so it won't be hard to convince viewers that there's some chemistry between you two, and I hear Russ is great to go to the bar with any day of the week. And if you can manage it, applaud the kids that walk through the door and give a couple of standing ovations. It wouldn't be the worst thing in the world."

"Donny, I know how to sit at the goddamn table and act. I don't live under a rock. I have seen the show before."

"Good. Remember, in ten more months, it'll all be over and we can celebrate the way I know you like to."

"I'll remind you of that."

"Great. Oh, and Jax? Don't break the judges' glass table, yeah?" He laughed.

"Wiseass."

I strode back into the room the show had arranged for the celebrity judges, ignoring the personal assistants and makeup artists trailing behind me. There was always someone trying to fix my hair and have me look like I was a superhuman who didn't sweat or appear tired. I shook them off, smiled, and sat in my assigned seat at the end of the table.

"Sorry, everyone. My agent is more of a diva than I am. If I hadn't taken his call, he would have shown up here himself, demanded bottled water, and terrified the assistants," I explained. "I'm ready for the next audition when everyone else is."

Claudia and Russell Conway laughed, well aware of the reputation of my agent. Meanwhile the others in the room gave me skeptical looks, obviously reserving judgment on my actions due to my rumored bad boy status. Thankfully, everyone's attention quickly returned to the director and the camera crew, and with the spotlight off my every move, I reached for the pen and paper engraved with the show's name on the top that the judges were provided with. I just needed to write down the lyrics I had formed in my mind about breaking glass.

"I'm ready for the next one," Russell announced as he reclined in his seat.

"Me too," Claudia purred in her signature sultry tone.

"Connor, go get the next one," Linda Kramer, this season's director, dismissively muttered before checking her own buzzing phone. "Now I've got a damn phone call from the executive producers I have to take. Let's just keep filming. You all know what to do by now."

I kept writing, not looking up when Linda exited or when the door opened again and tentative footsteps could be heard drawing closer. I wanted to get the emotions I was feeling on paper and fast. It was always the same: a conversation about what it was I should or shouldn't be doing and inspiration hit.

"Come closer, sweetheart. We won't bite," Claudia encouraged from her spot at the other end of the judges' table.

"You want me to sing to this table, really?" I heard a soft feminine voice whisper to a production crew member. "Maybe I should go to the other room. You should definitely check if I'm going to waste their time."

"No way. We want to see you sing, girl," Russell hollered.

I was two words away from having a completed chorus when Russell nudged me with his elbow. At first I thought it was to remind me to get my head in the game, but when I looked up, I knew his nudging had nothing to do with me.

We had seen good-looking girls come audition over the last few days.

We had seen a lot of very pretty girls covered in too much makeup come audition, trying to look spectacular.

We hadn't seen a supermodel on her day off walk in this room and offer to sing for us.

The girl was standing in front of us in a simple pair of ripped black jeans, brown cowboy boots, and a loose white T-shirt with her blonde curls a chaotic shower over her shoulders. She didn't have a lot of jewelry or makeup on, but she was the most stunning thing to have walked into a judging room since the start of this whole damn process. Her big blue eyes revealed every emotion. There wasn't a doubt in our mind as to why she managed to land a spot in front of us.

I was afraid that even if she couldn't sing, those with the real power on this show were going to make us bring her back tomorrow and vote her through. Although, staring at her each judging day wouldn't be the worst thing I had to do over the course of this show.

"Just stand on the marker on the floor," Connor barked from the side of the room, always the jealous prick. His true nature showed a little more whenever Linda wasn't in the room.

"Hi, sweetie. What's your name, and how old are you?" Claudia asked the gorgeous girl standing before us. Always the sickly sweet one until she decided to show people how sharp her claws really were.

"I'm Billie Bishop, and I'm eighteen years old," the girl murmured, her battle to calm her nerves and get back in control of her voice evident.

"That's a damn cool name," Russell replied. "You want to be a superstar, Billie Bishop?"

"I just like to sing," she responded with a little more steel in her voice.

"Who's your favorite musician?" I asked, knowing I needed to contribute at some point and partially curious about what music she listened to, if my name would roll off her tongue.

"Do I lose points if I don't say your name?" she queried, looking me straight in the eyes, finding her spine.

The others burst out laughing, and I couldn't help but grin. The response was a refreshing one compared to all the other fangirls. "I won't kick you off the show. Yet," I told her.

"If I'm honest, Miranda Lambert and Martina McBride are my favorite artists at the moment, but my taste tends to change with my mood."

"My mood always changes my taste too," Claudia agreed. "Will you be singing one of their songs today?"

"No, ma'am, I'm going to be singing Jewel's 'Foolish Games.'"

"Okay, then, let's hear it," Russell encouraged.

With her hands laced and rested against her stomach, she began the song softly. The moment she started singing, everyone put on their prepared listening faces. Our expressions were part of the façade of the show, to ensure viewers knew we were taking every singer seriously, though it wasn't long before each of us usually dropped the act to roll our eyes or smile encouragingly or grin at each other.

However, there weren't grins or eye rolling with Billie's voice, a whisper hanging in the air like a cloud shocking us with its perfect pitch. When she hit the chorus, she had an almost guttural growl that acted like thunder ripping apart the perfect cloud and drenching us in her feelings. The anger and the pain of each lyric reached inside of me and squeezed something in my chest. My heart, my lungs, I had no f*cking clue.

Damn. We were stunned by how beautiful she was, but her singing was something else.

When she finished the song, there was silence at the judges' table.

There weren't words for what we had just witnessed.

"Do you have anything a little more upbeat?" Claudia choked out. Every person in the room looked at her like she'd just grown horns.

Another song? She seriously needs the girl to sing some upbeat pop to vote her in?

I was about to interrupt by doing what Donny asked of me and giving the girl a standing ovation, turning into the nice judge by telling everyone in the room that they would be crazy not to send this girl straight to the finale.

Then she muttered, "Sure," and began singing Lady Antebellum's "Downtown." With a few twists of her hips and flicks of her hair, she transformed in front of us. She wasn't just keeping her emotions under control anymore, she was owning them and everyone in the entire room. She was laughing and making eye contact with each of us as if we were all the best of friends.

When she finished, Russell beat me to the standing ovation. "I don't care what these fools think. You're going to Las Vegas if I have to put you in my carry-on luggage."

"That's unnecessary, Russ." Claudia laughed. "We all saw how diverse and talented the girl is, unless Jax has something else to say."

While they were giving her compliments, her anxiety returned. The confident girl who was swinging her hips moments ago began tapping her foot nervously, her hands shaking. Another surprise, because usually when someone auditioned and killed it and the judges started praising them, they became obnoxiously cocky. They didn't regress.

"Who's here with you?" I asked bluntly, wondering if someone needed to hold her hand as we began to change her life.

"No one," she muttered, looking directly at me, her blue eyes capturing mine. It was like everyone else disappeared and we were just having a conversation without a table separating us, an audience listening in, and a film crew capturing every twitch. "But it was my best friend's idea that I come audition," she said, smiling slightly.

"How come they didn't join you to see you go through?" I asked with a hint of annoyance in my voice.

"I made him promise not to. I know that sounds weird, but if he came, then our mothers would have known we were missing and would have chased after us. It would have been a whole ordeal. It's better that he stayed behind."

"Although, if they had chased after you, they all could have been here to see you perform. They all would have been so proud of your kickass performance," I told her.

"My momma isn't a huge fan of my singing."

"Is she deaf?" I scoffed.

"No, she's incredible. A single mom at sixteen who was kicked out of home, abandoned by her boyfriend, and worked three jobs to support us. She just thinks chasing childish dreams isn't how I should spend my time. I should be studying and focusing on going to college."

"Sure, college is great, but it's not for everyone, and it's also not going anywhere. She won't be thinking you're doing anything childish when she sees you in Las Vegas," I said as I grabbed the star-shaped ticket from the table.

Her mouth dropped open as she saw what was in my hand. Instead of just handing it to her over the table, I decided to stand up, walk around the glass separating us, and reach for her wrist with my left hand. I put her palm facing upward and then placed the ticket in it. "Some people are going to want different things for you, but you've got to be prepared to grab on to what you want and not let go."

I watched as her hand curled around the ticket.

"I want it."

"You wouldn't be here if you didn't," I quietly replied.

"I'm scrunching it up," she stated anxiously.

"I'll get you a new one if they carry on about the scrunches. It's also not the real ticket to Vegas anyway. They'll give that to you downstairs."

"Vegas," she whispered with wonder.

I grinned. "Yeah, Vegas."

"Wasn't that sweet?" Claudia laughed as the makeup artists came back into the room to touch up her lipstick and prepare for the next audition. "The executive producers are going to love it. No doubt that's going to be in all the promos. Timid girl turned rock star turned dream chaser. The public is going to eat it up. Linda will be furious she missed it."

"They won't want to show her singing too often in the promos or it'll lose its impact," I muttered as I took a sip from the water bottle the assistants brought me, still standing where I'd handed the sweet Southern girl her ticket to this crazy train. I waved off my own hair stylist wanting to adjust the strands around my ears. "But you're not wrong. She'll be a hot contender."

"I just hope she ain't a two-trick pony. It's going to be awful hard to go back to nowhere South Carolina after Jax Bone puts your dreams in your hand while looking at you like he wanted to screw your brains out." Russell laughed, taking a couple of swigs from the small flask in his suit pocket. "And she's got weeks of singing to go if she can't bring herself to sing her idols' hits. I hope she can at least sing 'Billie Jean.' That'll make a hell of an episode. Billie singing 'Billie Jean.'"

"I bet Billie can do those country songs she loves," I told the group, picturing her singing on stage at the Country Music Awards.

"I give her two weeks before her true colors show and she's sleeping with the entire crew," Connor muttered from the sidelines like a snake slithering into our conversation as if he were one of us. "The timid sh*t is just an act. Wannabes always have a sob story thinking it'll increase their chances, and a teen mom ain't anything compared to the ones I'll no doubt have to listen to and pretend I care about. She'll see that, if she wants to get attention, she might have to do more with her mouth than just whine about her absentee father. All that hair over my trailer couch, I'd definitely be willing to do some one-on-one coaching."

When he laughed, no one joined in.

Connors smile turned into a sneer as he noticed everyone looking at him in disgust.

"You're revolting," Claudia told him with contempt in her eyes. "You talk like that again and you'll be fired. I'll see to it personally."

"Dude, this industry is getting so uptight these days." Connor rolled his eyes. "It was a damn joke. Get off your high horse. And I've been the face of this competition for nearly ten years. They'll replace you guys before they replace me. You're just a celebrity judge. There's a ton of celebrities out there who'll sit in those chairs, but I'm the one and only Connor f*cking Graves. Do your worst."

I took four steps from the center of the auditioning room and wrapped my empty hand around Connor's throat, holding him against the wall as I squeezed.

"If you threaten or joke about threatening any of the women in this competition, or f*ck, you even *think* about touching any of the women, it won't matter whether or not you're the face of this damn show because you won't be able to talk or sing. And everyone here knows you. You think we don't notice how you try to grab attention during every audition. Singing past contestants' latest hits for the cameras, hanging around during auditions to talk about each person like you have a say. Dude, you suck. You're the wannabe. You've got pretty hair and a face that people think is reassuring enough for their television screen. Don't get delusional that it's more than that."

"Jax," Russell warned.

I let go of Connor's throat, watched him have a coughing fit and stare daggers at me.

"F*ck you," Connor growled as he continued to dramatically wheeze.

When I looked around the room, I saw the cameras trained on me, their little red lights blinking rapidly. I didn't regret what I just did, but Donny was going to be *pissed*.

"I need to call my agent and get some fresh air. Send someone outside to get me when this a**hole has gotten his act together and you need me back desperately. Linda has a problem with it, she can take it up with Donny herself."

Claudia nodded and then turned to the young female assistant staring with wonder at me. With acid dripping from each word, she said, "Cindy, be a dear and run to my darling girlfriend Danielle. She's got the bright purple hair. Let her know that Connor can wait at the door from now on with the parents. We don't want the distraction of his beautiful face in here. And if you see Linda, let her know what just occurred."

CHAPTER
THREE

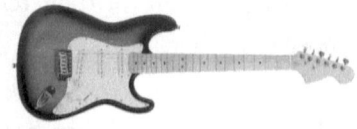

Friends

Billie

When I felt my phone vibrate in my pocket, alerting me to Zach's latest text, I ran to the nearest trash can outside the convention center and emptied the contents of my stomach. I pictured my mother's face as she watched me tell the nation that she didn't support me, and my stomach heaved again.

"You okay?"

Bent over the trash and yet I still knew who was asking the question. His voice was like smooth whiskey, unmistakable and incomparable. It broke hearts and won awards. And, from its volume right above my head, was likely unavoidable.

Damn it. I really didn't want to pull my head up.

I wiped my mouth with the back of my hand and slowly raised my head to look into the dark brown eyes of Jax Bone.

"I just threw up," I told him, completely mortified.

"I noticed."

"This is really embarrassing."

"Don't sweat it. It could have been worse," he replied, chuckling. He looked like he should be posing for *Rolling Stone*, not casually standing beside a trash can next to me. His thick brown hair fell stylishly over his forehead, his white singlet exposed the tattoo of a lion growling at his enemies that wrapped around his right shoulder, and his black leather pants just helped define his thick muscled legs.

"How could this possibly be worse?" I asked him, trapped in his chocolate-coated irises like I was during the auditions. Lost to reality. Confessing things I should never have been confessing. Transfixed by something he exuded that was intangible and more powerful than his devastating good looks and chiseled jawline.

"Well, there could be a camera crew here, and you could have thrown up *on* me." Jax smirked.

With the mention of a camera crew, I shuddered and took a look around. When I noticed that we were in fact alone, I exhaled and turned my attention back to Jax. He left me speechless. No one should look that good in leather pants this early in the morning.

"Good point. That would have been worse," I managed to choke out.

"Water?" he said while offering his bottle to me.

"Huh?" I was still distracted by his leather pants.

"To rinse?"

"That would be amazing. Thank you so much," I replied and took a quick mouthful from his water bottle. I'd swirled it around my mouth and was just about to spit into the trash can, when I realized I couldn't spit in front of him. It would look like I was puking. Again. Spitting in front of him was also like bad innuendo waiting to happen. If Zach were here, I knew he would be talking about how girls only swallow around Jax Bone.

Good Lord.

"You know, the whole point in rinsing is to spit it out again." Jax laughed.

Damn it. I spat the water into the trash and wiped my mouth again. "Thanks. I'm all good now. You can, you know, get back to work," I told him, wishing desperately for this moment to end.

"I'm not rushing back to anything." He laughed again. "I've got an assistant running to get me when they need me, and I was going to call my agent even though I don't want to. I think I'll just hang with you until he calls me. He usually can't last twenty minutes without talking to me, so I shouldn't have to wait long."

"Hang with me?" I asked. "Why would you want to do that?"

"Well, we just met, you told me personal stuff about yourself, and I guess I figure that makes us friends," Jax said, smiling. "And I have a feeling we're going to be seeing a lot of each other while I'm on this show."

"I told the whole world some really personal stuff about myself today," I said softly, feeling my stomach rumble again. "And I'm not sure I'll make it past the week in Vegas ."

"Would it feel better if I told you the embarrassing things I did when I first started doing this gig professionally?"

I scoffed. "You, Jax Bone, international rock god and musical prodigy, have made embarrassing mistakes?"

"Two years ago, after my first recording session for my dream record company, I threw up in the car they had given me as a signing bonus. Totally gross. Way worse than you. My stomach was already freaking out about the celebrities who were in the studio, and it only got worse when my idols were looking at me like I was one of them. I was a street grifter turned sure thing in their eyes, and I wasn't sure I was any good, so I flipped out. Of course, people had also been giving me shots to celebrate between takes, and when I left, taking my new car seemed like a good idea. I hadn't even put the keys in the ignition before I was destroying the leather passenger seats."

"Oh my Lord."

"That's not all. After watching my recording session and talking to some of the labels execs, Donny, my agent—though this was before he was my agent—raced after me and climbed into my car all full of self-confidence to tell me I needed him to help my career. He sat right in all my puke."

"Sat in it?"

"Yep."

I was laughing so hard that Jax's smile turned into a wide grin. "What did you say?"

"Nothing. He worked it out pretty quickly and just said, 'First order of business, I'll get you a new car and a driver to take you home.'"

"That easy?"

"A week later I had a new car and an agent who called me constantly."

Imagining this rookie musician with a powerful agent had me completely forgetting my worries and concerns. I stood there smiling at Jax and said, "I can't wait to meet your agent. He must be something else."

"Trust me, he sees you singing on television like you did for us in that room, and with a name like Billie Bishop, he'll sit on your puke too."

His complete sincerity had me burst out laughing again.

"I'm not sure I would want that," I managed once I got myself under control.

"You'll be surprised with what you want at the end of this competition," Jax told me cryptically.

However, before I had a chance to ask him what he meant, we heard an awkward coughing sound behind us.

"I'm sorry to interrupt you both, but Mr. Bone, they need you back in the audition room," Cindy, the assistant, hesitantly said from behind Jax.

Almost as quickly as she appeared, she disappeared like a little mouse back inside the building. The spell that had been cast since the moment we looked into each other's eyes was broken.

"I guess you have to get back." My wide grin relaxed into a small smile.

"This is the second time I've left the room today, so I probably can't put it off for any longer."

"Thank you. For in there and for out here."

"I get it. It's not every day your life changes so damn radically. When you teased me about your favorite artists though, I saw some of that bravado that'll get you through this competition. You'll need every ounce to put up with all of us." He looked at the gold star still clutched in my hand.

"Don't forget to go to the producers and swap that for the real thing. It would suck if this was the last time I saw you." He laughed, raked a hand through his hair, and gave a reluctant look toward the building before murmuring, "I better go. See you in Vegas, Billie Bishop." He then disappeared back into the building to undoubtedly cause some other foolish girl's heart to trip over itself.

I wondered for just a moment if Faith Randall had been right, if Jax's touch was magic. I certainly felt his presence alone was charismatic, and even without shaking his hand, I worried I had suddenly become like all the other fangirls who auditioned today—totally entranced.

I filled out the paperwork. The show now had information on every facet of my life recorded on paper. Those in charge of this portion of the day seemed even more excited than I was that I received one of the sought-after star tickets. It confused me until an angry father shoved his way to the front of the desk and verbally abused them about his daughter's unjust dismissal. Pushing me to the side, he demanded they take his child's information and send her a real ticket. Security quickly escorted him outside the building, but it occurred to me that, with the limited number of star tickets given away at each audition, they likely had to deal with more angry fathers than joyous celebrations.

After the chaos, one of the ladies behind the counter asked if she could announce to the room that I had made it through to the next round, and I nodded. The cheers and crowds that formed around the table in celebration after the words "She's going to Las Vegas" left her lips were deafening. I spent a good portion of the afternoon dodging questions about my audition and taking photographs with complete strangers. In addition to getting on the show themselves, everyone seemed to be on a mission to take a photo of anyone *else* who might become the star of the show.

When I felt like the crowds were too much to handle, I looked at the lady who announced my star ticket dealing with yet another complaining contestant. Then I continued to appease their desires and spread the joy. After an hour of photos and avoiding the more upsetting details of my audition, my cheeks hurt from all the fake smiles and I desperately needed air. With my duffel bag containing the instructions on how to get to the next phase of the competition, and how to ensure I received the real ticket in the mail, I waved goodbye to everyone and headed for the door.

I was going to Vegas. I didn't need to stay the night in Charleston after all. I wasn't required to sing for the producers or the judges again. I was one of the lucky ones; I could go straight home and wait the four weeks before I needed to board a plane paid for by the competition.

This is a good thing.

All the positive thinking in the world didn't make going home less frightening though. Determining exactly what I was going to tell Zach and eventually my mother had my pulse jumping.

I had just pushed open the doors of the building when I heard "You're Billie, right?" The casting producer with purple hair stood behind me with a clipboard and earpiece and looked at me in utter relief. "I've been looking for you since you left the audition room. I went to the sign-up table after your audition, but you weren't there. Then I went outside. I think I kept missing you by seconds. Before you left, I just wanted to check if you completed any interviews before you auditioned or chatted with Connor before you went inside the room?"

I shook my head.

"Do you mind just answering a few questions or speaking with Connor for a little bit, then? Usually we like to have something shot the day of your audition," she told me, smiling. "Plus, if you make it all the way to the end, maybe you'll love having the footage of the start of your career. Discussions about how your journey to *Superstardom* began, your home life and backstory, that sort of thing."

I almost laughed out loud. I hadn't planned on watching any of the footage of me on this show, and that was before I idiotically trashed my mother during my audition. Nor did I believe for a second that I would be in the finale looking back on this day like a Hail Mary football pass.

But I was willing to do anything at that moment for an excuse not to go home without attempting to salvage the day.

I thought I needed air.

An escape.

I really needed a parachute. A chance to save myself from the jump I'd taken earlier when I spoke on camera for the first time. If I were going on camera a second time, I prayed I could redirect the way my comments landed.

I hoped Connor Graves would be willing to help me inflate my parachute and land safely.

He was laughing with a man holding a camera on his shoulder when I walked into the room. When they heard the door close behind me, their laughter abruptly ended, and they both turned to stare at me.

Connor recovered faster than the camera operator and approached me with a big smile across his face.

"Hi, Billie. Thank you so much for agreeing to chat with me. We didn't really get a chance to speak with one another before you wowed the judges," he smoothly told me before running a hand absently across his neck.

He seemed perfectly genuine and kind, except the glint in his eye when he looked at my tank top had me wishing I had a sanitary wipe.

I felt greasy.

"Danielle said she wanted me to talk to you about my backstory?" I asked meekly.

"That would be a great start. I know you talked a little about coming here alone during your audition. We can talk about that a bit more if you want, or we can discuss something else entirely." His sympathetic smile and outstretched hand almost made me feel guilty for distrusting him so quickly.

"Um, I was hoping we could talk about my momma and best friend again, but maybe how they encouraged me to do things outside my comfort zone?"

"Sounds good to me," Connor reassured. "Matt, you ready with the camera?"

"Yep, all good."

"Okay, Billie, I'll need you just to stand in front of the *Superstardom* banner and we'll just have a casual chat, yeah?"

I nodded and moved into position.

The interview went quickly. I discussed the deals Zach and I made with each other every year. I mentioned how my momma was never afraid of anything. I praised how she moved to a small town as a single teenage mom and became one of the best sous-chefs in the state. I feared there weren't enough good stories to prevent the words I'd said earlier from being on everyone's mind, but I hoped that with each comment I expressed how much they meant to me. How I wouldn't have been here without them. How the show *had* to present them in a positive light because I needed them in ways that were more important than just standing beside me while I sang to a panel of strangers.

I had no control over what the people in charge of the show would do with the footage. I had no idea if the questions Connor Graves slipped into our discussion about my love life were for his own curiosity or were being directed from some higher power whispering in his ear. Although I knew it didn't matter, because my answers were all boring. I didn't have any ex-boyfriends who would regret dumping me after they saw the show or a potential love interest who would profess their undying love after seeing me perform.

There was no secret love story for me.

I had friends and family. That was all.

Or at least I did.

CHAPTER
FOUR

Tell me

Zach

"**C**an we please stop talking about me and focus on the fact that you have practice and tryouts next month?" Billie pleaded. I gave her my you've-got-to-be-shitting-me look and examined the way she sat in the passenger seat of my truck, her feet tucked under her legs and her gaze shifting from me to the window. She was in total avoidance mode.

"You leave in three days to fly to Las Vegas to be one of the fifty contestants on *Superstardom*, yet you would prefer we talk about my high school basketball schedule?" I shook my head and turned onto the main street leading to our high school. "You're crazy."

"I hear Chelsea is going to keep cheering this year even though she'll be seven months pregnant by the time the first game starts. I'm thinking about making her a sign. I've never made a sign, and I'm pretty sure I'm not a huge fan of glitter, but she might be my new idol. The girl totally gives zero f*cks about what people think of her."

"B, don't try and change the subject. You met Russell Conway, three-time CMA star of the year. You didn't even tell me if Claudia ever revealed her last name or if Jax Bone is as obnoxious as his name sounds. Although the dude was photographed wearing leather pants to a Wholefoods at their last audition city, so it's not like I really need you to clarify that."

I laughed before pulling into the school's parking lot, then turned and stared at Billie, knowing my green eyes, which always turned a shade darker when I got serious, would likely be almost black right now. "Besides telling me that they made you sing two songs before you were given the ticket and that you met some girl in the coliseum who you hope will make it to Vegas, it's been nearly a month and I haven't gotten all the details. We tell each other everything. I'm not stupid here. I know you left out some major details for a reason. If they were hard on you, you don't need to be embarrassed. If they were raving about your voice like only sane people would and you're trying to be modest, it isn't necessary. This shouldn't be like the time you lost my favorite leather jacket. You should be able to tell me things."

I knew she heard my words—I saw her flinch—but she remained silent. I barely heard her whisper, "I just wanted to live normally for as long as possible before I leave."

I sighed. I didn't believe her, but after years of friendship, I could tell when pushing her would motivate a response and when it would cause her to dig in her heels. It seemed like this was a day for the latter, so I let go of my concerns and curiosity, accepted that she would tell me all about the show when she was ready, and embraced her change of topic. "You're right about Chelsea. Our mothers totally love her more than both of us. They made me bring organic cookies to my last practice to give her. I even heard my momma call her and let her know that if her parents ever did what our moms' parents did to them, she can choose whose house she stays at. I think they secretly wish they could adopt her."

"I love you, Zachary James Montgomery," Billie told me with relief and affection sparkling in her eyes, unaware that her casual words were like throwing stars digging into my chest.

"Don't use the L-word, B. It's weird." I groaned and then chuckled, pretending I didn't wonder what it would be like to hear those words spoken from her lips with a little more than friendship behind them.

When we exited my truck, I casually threw my arm over her shoulder as we walked a few yards toward the gymnasium. Finally she exhaled and shared the one thing I'd been waiting to hear since we'd worked out how long we would be separated for the competition. "I'm not sure what I'm going to do without your company for months."

"That's easy. You'll sing, rehearse, and call me all the time to tell me about the annoying jerks you have to room with until they get voted off the show."

"What if they're all delightful?" She laughed.

"There's only one winner at the end of *Superstardom*, B." I scoffed. "At least in basketball you've got teammates on your side to help defend against the enemy. In your position, everyone is the enemy."

When she burst out laughing, I relaxed and forgot about the things I was always avoiding. When she sat in the stands to watch me practice like usual, pulling out her notebook to write down lyrics while the team ran drills, I could even fool myself into believing that it was all I ever wanted.

When we walked into Billie's house, she was smiling wide. We had stopped discussing the singing competition and instead focused on talking about my upcoming tryouts. She thought after seeing the way I played today, there wasn't a chance in hell I wouldn't be made captain this year. I wasn't so sure; there were a lot of other guys on the team with just as much talent and a few less blonde singing distractions on their minds.

"Billie? Zach?" Billie's mom, Michelle, called from the kitchen.

"Yeah, we were just going to chill and watch some TV before studying. Watching Zach practice is exhausting work," Billie called back, her eyes smiling up at me.

"Sit for a spell with me in the kitchen first."

I saw Billie's face drop, but she quickly recovered and put her usual smile on before waltzing into the kitchen without a care in the world.

Neither Billie's nor my house was very big, only two bedrooms and one bathroom each. They wouldn't be on those home shows any time soon unless someone was gutting every room and redecorating the damn things. They were both located on one of the busiest roads in the whole town, so the rent was cheap. Unlike at my house though, Billie's mom had convinced the owners to remodel their kitchen with crisp white cabinets and porcelain countertops. After spending almost my entire childhood between our two houses, I knew Michelle always gravitated toward the kitchen when she was stressed or sad.

I hung back, letting Billie stride in to talk to her mom as I leaned against the doorframe. I could see that Michelle was chopping up carrots, still in her work clothes but looking like she'd just left a television talk show. Billie's mom was always the best-looking mom I'd ever seen. Even without makeup, she looked like she was barely out of high school and about to walk a runway. If I hadn't grown up around them, I would mistake them for sisters just like every stranger did.

There was only one difference between them, and that was that Billie's hair was like sunshine while her mom's was the color of chocolate. It was that one difference that made Billie unable to see how alike they were, or how pretty she really was. She never covered her entire face with makeup or lip gloss like the other girls in our grade, but in her mind, if her mother was beautiful, she was something else.

One day, I figured I'd try and explain to her how much better being something else made her. Although, from the sound of a clearly angry sous-chef chopping vegetables, I knew today wouldn't be it.

"I got those letters in the mail this morning," Michelle rigidly stated while she continued to chop carrots without looking at either of us.

Billie glanced at the stack of envelopes. I peeked around her to notice the bills and a flyer for the local gardener always begging to fix their lawn before I noticed the two letters separated from the pile. The first had our school emblem in the corner and the other the *Superstardom* logo.

Ah, sh*t.

"They were addressed to me," Michelle informed Billie, still not looking up from her vigorous cutting. "I didn't have a clue why a television show felt they needed to contact me, but apparently I needed to sign a release form if I wanted to join my daughter during the second stage of the audition process or request seats if she makes it through to the live voting—"

"Momma, I meant to tell you—" Billie tried explaining.

"You were going to tell me?" Michelle scoffed. "The school also sent me a note informing me of their approval of the leave I apparently requested and wished you luck in chasing your dreams." After she finished talking, she put down the knife and looked directly at Billie. As far as either of them were concerned, I wasn't there, just furniture in the background. The word disappointment didn't need to fall from Michelle's tongue; it swam in her blue eyes. The exact same eyes Billie had. Ones that never managed to conceal how they were feeling. The Bishop women's curse.

"I'm sorry," Billie whispered.

"You're leaving on Thursday for Las Vegas, is that right?" she softly inquired.

"I was going to leave you a note. I wouldn't have just vanished."

"Ha. A note. Just like your father."

"Not like my father. I'm coming back. I'll likely only be gone for a few days. I'll be back before Zach even has his first game of the season. I just need to see...."

"See what?"

"If I'm any good."

"You have a beautiful voice. Everyone says that. Why you need strangers behind a desk to tell you is ludicrous. Why you need to give up parts of your final year at school to pursue some childish notion of fame is spitting on everything I've ever done to help you have a better start than I did."

I wanted to interject. I wanted to tell Michelle the reasons why I encouraged Billie to audition. How uninterested she was with every-thing at school and how amazing she was when she sang. If there was a better way to make singing a career, I would have found it for her, but Michelle had to know that *Superstardom* was the best option.

But Billie was already telling her mother, "Now who's being ludi-crous? It's a singing competition, Momma. It isn't a show about how to live like a starving artist or give up all other possible future careers. The show doesn't even film for twelve months." I could hear the tears begin-ning to choke her up, even with her back to me.

"People will watch you on that show, Billie, and those people might twist your appearance or portray you as someone you aren't. Future em-ployers might see it and never want to hire you. The time you spend on that show might be just a blip in your life but have devastating effects. Do you know how many restaurants I had to beg to give me a chance? I had no qualifications outside working as a waitress and being the girl who stacked food at the supermarket late at night. I wanted better for you. I don't want you to have to beg people to give you a chance."

"I'm not begging. I'm singing. If you don't like it, then when it comes on TV, don't watch," Billie choked out before she rushed out of the room and didn't look back.

When Michelle looked at me standing there, defeat etched into every line of her usually perfect face, I muttered, "She needs to do this. Her microphone is just like your knife and my basketball. You take it away from her, you'll be like all those restaurants who didn't give you a chance."

"Zachary, you couldn't possibly understand. You're both only eighteen—"

"I know I don't know everything, but I know Billie. She needs this," I softly replied before I turned and headed toward Billie's bedroom.

When I entered, I found her curled up on her bed with tears si-lently falling down her cheeks. We had discussed keeping her Las Vegas plans from both our moms because we knew this was how Michelle would react. However, deep down I secretly hoped that once she found out about Billie making it to the Las Vegas auditions. She would be proud, impressed even, with how well she had done.

"She gave up her childhood for me. The least I can do is give up a silly competition," Billie told me before she curled back up and went to sleep.

"You can't give up Las Vegas. I won't let you," I murmured. "You aren't risking your future career options, you're expanding your horizons. She'll get over it. I'll make sure of it."

Two days went by without Billie or her mom speaking. I kept visiting after school and basketball practice like I always did, hoping to encourage Michelle to say something positive about Billie leaving or at the very least prevent Billie from giving up.

"You should stop coming over until we're back to normal," Billie groaned before opening the kitchen fridge and passing me a can of Coke. "We eat breakfast together and she cooks dinner each night, but she isn't saying anything. She just goes to her bedroom, closes the door, and the house stays silent."

"When you both went through that vegan stage, I still kept coming over, and the things you guys were eating were nasty. Silence I can deal with." I smiled at her, encouraging her to smile back. Her face remained blank though, and I tried not to give in to the urge to shake her. "Plus, your fridge always has way more food than ours."

"That's because you eat it all and then come over here and eat ours," Billie muttered before reaching for her own can of pop.

She had barely lifted her drink to her lips when her mom walked into the kitchen.

It was super awkward. They stared at each other. Billie tried to take a step forward and Michelle took a step backward. Their identical eyes both filled with sadness.

"Momma—" Billie attempted to reach out, and I reacted. I lifted Michelle's favorite knife like I was holding the Olympic torch.

Michelle looked from Billie to the knife and then out the window before retreating into the living room.

Billie turned her head to me and rolled her eyes. "Why are you holding a knife?"

"You guys might have started to have a catfight. Every guy needs to be able to defend himself in situations like that."

"You're crazy."

By the time we finished our drinks and I had eaten at least half of the snack-worthy contents of their fridge, we walked into the living room.

Standing in the middle of the room was Michelle's favorite luggage set. I didn't say anything to Billie, just walked forward, lifted the two plastic purple suitcases, and carried them to Billie's bedroom. When Billie followed me, staring at the suitcases like they were rattlesnakes about to bite her, I told her firmly, "Start packing your stuff before she changes her mind."

"I should check with her and make sure this is what she wants. Maybe she was just cleaning out the attic."

"The day before you leave, she decides to clean out the attic and the only things she saves are her favorite suitcases?"

"It's possible."

"B, if you're looking for a reason to stay, go and speak with her. But she's done this for you, and you're just wasting time fighting this. If she were really cleaning out the attic, our matching rhinestone outfits she made for us for our fifth-grade talent competition would have also been in the living room."

Billie laughed, but her eyes still showed me how conflicted she was. "I hate the idea of leaving and not having spoken to her in days, Zach."

"Then write a note, B. Tell her you love her and that you're coming back."

"There were 'I love yous' in my father's last words before he left for a better life that didn't include teenage fatherhood. He told her he might come back in his note."

"Then don't write a note. Just start packing. We all know you wouldn't leave me behind anyway. I'm too good-looking."

Billie smiled before staring at the door.

Before she had a chance to walk through it, I lifted the suitcase onto her bed, unzipped it, and threw in a random pair of shoes.

"I don't want those," she muttered before pushing me out of the way and packing the things she really wanted to take with her.

The morning I picked Billie up to drive her to the bus station that would take her to the airport, I lightly knocked and then poked my head into Michelle's room. "Miss B, I'm about to take Billie to the station."

She was curled up in the exact same way Billie did when she was upset, and tearstains were dry on her cheeks. She tried smiling and just nodded.

"She's coming back," I told her firmly.

"For your sake, Zach, I hope she does."

CHAPTER
FIVE

An act

Jax

The Nevada sun didn't disappoint, even late in the afternoon. The moment I stepped off the chartered plane, it welcomed me back to my favorite desert city with a warm embrace.

"Hey, Jax, over here," Sam cheerfully called from his spot against the limo. When I got near enough, we did our usual handshake. My closest friend and driver then grabbed my suitcase, put it in the back of his limousine, and started to fill me in on all that I had missed since my last visit. "Dude, too bad you couldn't get out here earlier. The party last week was hella crazy. That stripper Wendy—the one with your lyrics on her ass who turned into a total stalker in your VIP booth last time—tried stealing the diamond chain off the DJ's wife. Man, it reminded me of why I moved from LA to be here. The crystal was flying, and beautiful women with their fake tits bouncing everywhere were wrestling on the floor covered in Grey Goose vodka. You could have written another hit song for sure."

"Or gotten hit." I laughed. "I'm sorry I missed it. Nothing is more inspiring than sparkling diamonds and women wrestling on the floor. You offer to drive one of them home?" I chuckled, knowing Sam's usual MO.

"Of course. The lady's dress was ripped. Offering to take her home and let her get changed was the least I could do."

"I hope for your sake the DJ never finds out."

"Who said it was the DJ's wife?" Sam smirked. "Sometimes a little crazy is fun in the bedroom. You want me to call the club for tonight and let them know you're in town? I know Vaughn would love to see you and have bottles chilling for sure. You could probably get a taste of the DJ's wife."

"Wish I could." I smiled, thinking of our past nights on the town, but then it turned into a grimace and I confessed, "I've got to be on my best behavior this time. I can't be losing my new reality television acting career. Boss's instruction."

"I thought you were the boss. No way you're telling me Jax Bone has come to Las Vegas, having written an album about being young, breaking all the rules, and living for those too afraid to try something dangerous—that just went f*cking platinum, mind you—and is on his best behavior."

I took a long look at the strip as the limousine began its entry into the land of billboards, buildings, and booze, and let Sam know, "Donny warned me that with the number of camera crews surrounding me, following my every move for this show, I wouldn't get away with going to my usual places without articles about underage drinking ending up in all the headlines. The label execs have already sent photos of babysitter applications should I end up in any more news articles. Doris is their current leading lady at sixty years old with sterner eyebrows than Oscar the Grouch. I can't imagine she would be willing to wrestle on the ground for me. I'm on hotel arrest, buddy, if I'm going to avoid having that old lady holding my hand."

As we pulled up to the grand hotel *Superstardom* had booked for all its judges, contestants, and crew to crash at, with chandeliers in every direction and the time of day lost in a sea of evening gowns, T-shirts, shorts, and painted ceilings, I hoped this trip went quickly.

"You know my number if you change your mind. I'm pretty sure I could sneak you out of this place and back in without anyone noticing if you need me." Sam told me seriously.

"I'll remember it," I replied. "Thanks for the ride, bro. Catch up soon."

I climbed out of the car and barely had a chance to grab my bag before Cindy, one of the production assistants, was in my face. "Mr. Bone, welcome to Las Vegas. I just wanted to let you know you're in the penthouse. Your agent called ahead and insisted it be stocked with a couple of adequate disguises, bottled water, and your favorite writing material." She handed me my room key and an envelope containing the show's upcoming filming schedule. *I guess penthouse arrest isn't too bad. And I might even be allowed to leave my room.* "I've been asked to remind you that we need you in the lobby to film the contestants arriving in three hours. I could send a bellman up with your luggage or find someone to accompany you?"

I shook my head, grabbed my bag, thanked her, and waved at Russell and Claudia, who were also being given room keys, no doubt pissed that I was given the penthouse. Then I headed to the elevators. The doors were just about to close when I saw a hand slip through the middle.

The sensors had the doors opening wide, revealing Connor Graves standing before me. He was dressed in a pin-striped purple suit with matching purple loafers.

Of course, like every day of filming, the costume department would no doubt make him change into a pair of jeans and a loose button-down shirt before they filmed him meeting the contestants. He would be normalized for the viewers. Unfortunately, we would all have to listen to his complaints about how sick he was of wearing clothes that any fool could wear and didn't reflect his personal style. The only joy I felt at seeing him standing before me was the grimace that appeared across his mouth when he realized he would need to spend the next few minutes in my company.

"Bone," he murmured as he stepped inside and looked to press the button to his hotel floor. I could feel the tension radiate off his body when he noticed the show had given me the penthouse. He pressed the number 20 and stood in the corner sulking silently.

Donny had told me Connor received a notice from the show about his comments during our Charleston auditions. He then informed me that all the judges would be receiving a nice bonus and the footage of my hand around Connor's throat would be deleted as compensation for having to deal with him on a regular basis until the end of the show.

"I don't suppose I need to remind you of my warning in Charleston," I murmured when the elevator doors opened to the twentieth floor.

"I wouldn't dream of touching your girl, Jax," Connor gritted out. "I got the message. The blonde is off-limits." He stepped out of the elevator with his hands in his pockets, whistling as he walked toward his room.

"I wasn't just talking about the blonde," I growled before the doors closed.

I headed to my room thinking about what I would do if that a**hole tried something on the women in this competition. I doubted the label execs would just send Doris to hold my hand; I would probably lose my shot at a new contract entirely.

Then I thought about the way Connor walked around the set with his smarmy smile and decided it would be worth the risk.

Three hours later, all the contestants were repetitively filmed getting out of cabs. They were staring at the chandeliers in wonder and laughing in pairs and groups as they made their way inside the hotel holding their bags and star-shaped tickets. The youngest performers with their parents and kid brothers and sisters in tow were captured staring at their mothers and fathers as if they were looking for reassurance that this was truly happening.

Linda could be heard shouting from the edge of the lobby that she wanted everyone to appear like they had already won the competition. I thought it was a pretty good idea considering more than half these people would be gone in less than a week. If all they won was a week away in a fancy hotel, it was nice to have that documented.

For some, their surprised faces filled with wonder were clearly part of an act. They had likely been to Las Vegas before and weren't as impressed with the over-the-top decorations and flashing billboards as they wanted you to believe. However, after noticing a few people standing around with unshed tears in their eyes and shaking hands and legs, it was clear not everyone was acting. I wondered if a few were overwhelmed at finally making it to a position where, after years of trying to sing professionally, they finally would be in the room with people who could truly change their lives.

I bet a few of them thought I was one of the lucky ones. Discovered at sixteen by my idol while singing in a dive bar in downtown LA. The bar was owned by my father's best friend, who let me perform my angst-filled songs in a bid to keep me out of trouble and my anger in check. I never had to work another job to support my singing career or feel like crying when the big break I had been praying for looked like it had finally arrived. Although, if delaying my success meant I could have been one of the contestants with my father in tow, I would swap positions with them in a heartbeat.

From the corner of my eye, I watched Billie being filmed walking through the entrance of the hotel for the second time. Her gold curls were pulled away from her face in a messy bun, exposing her eyes and emotions to everyone watching. Sitting six feet away in my judge's chair beside Russell and Claudia, I could tell that the marvel in her eyes wasn't a pretense. I watched as her gaze drifted between the ornate ceiling decorations and the contestants checking into their rooms. Her hands had a slight tremor. When her eyes moved from the hotel to the production crew and the few of us sitting on the side of the action, our eyes met.

I saw the wonder disappear, her mouth dropping open a little, and felt my own chest tighten. I considered getting out of my chair, walking toward her, and telling her to breathe. Since she'd stepped onto the sparkling marble floors of the lobby, it appeared as if she were holding her breath. Yet I remained seated, remembering that Linda had already warned us that she didn't want to see any acts of favoritism or visible signs of friendships developing before they had a chance to sing or do their individual interviews.

"Billliieeeee," squealed a curvy girl with thick-rimmed glasses struggling to carry her guitar case and luggage from the other side of the hotel. I watched as both girls laughed, then discussed something and posed for a selfie.

The camera operator close to them captured the entire exchange and nodded to Linda, who must have decided that little reunion was the cherry on top of their afternoon filming. She gave the signal to the crew to gather all the contestants together in the middle of the lobby.

When they all stood huddled like schoolchildren on a tour of a history museum, they were filmed being welcomed by a freshly made over Connor and encouraged to scream the show's favorite saying. Claudia, Russell, and I were then cued to walk over, wave, and let everyone know they were the best we had ever seen in this competition and how selecting ten to go onto the live performances would be the hardest decision we've ever had to make.

I thought the script was a little over the top. A little too dramatic considering everyone at home watching would have seen the auditions. It wasn't too hard to determine who would go through to the live shows. Hell, we already had the shortlist of people who had the best auditions and would make great television. Unless they bombed their next audition or plain forgot to show up, the list was unlikely to change. This week wasn't really about making a final decision. It was about introducing the contestants to their rivals and getting a lot of individual interview sessions recorded before their schedules were filled with rehearsals and promotional appearances.

Once the cameras stopped rolling, they were all informed that they would be watching each other's auditions during this round. Unless they were here with their families, they had been assigned a roommate for the duration of the competition. They were also given a schedule with their audition time and individual interviews. They were warned that if they missed their allotted time slot due to experiencing all that Vegas had to offer until the early hours of the morning, there would be no second chance.

I took a look at the other contestants' mixed reactions to the news that they would be performing for an audience. I noticed Billie's nervous shaking and saw her friend grasp her hand and squeeze. I was just about to ask someone if we were done filming for the day when my phone started buzzing in my pocket. I held up my phone to Linda and gestured toward the elevator with my head. She gave me a thumbs-up, and I quickly made my way back to my room.

When I accepted the phone call, I didn't even wait for him to start talking. "Donny, I've been here for less than twenty-four hours." Rolling my eyes, I went on. "Don't put Doris on an airplane yet. Sam dropped me off, and I've been playing PlayStation in the damn penthouse until they called me downstairs for filming."

"Jax, I'm not sending Doris to you. I'm sending you a song the label wants you to think about recording."

"I only record my own stuff."

"I know that's what you've done in the past, but they just signed this new kid, and they figured if you sing one of his songs, it might help him out. I've heard him play. He's good."

"I only record my own stuff."

"You do this favor for them—"

"Then they'll want me to do another one. I'm young, Donny, not stupid. I get that you wanted me to do this show to fix my image by helping young kids like me get noticed. I'm happy to sit in a chair and tell them they sound good, but I'm not about to turn into some bleeding heart. I won't stop making music the way I want to make it."

"All right, Jax. I'm going to send it anyway. You listen to it, repeat that exact statement to me in a week's time, and we're all good. You need anything else while you're in Vegas?"

"Donny, sometimes when I talk to you, it's like I'm talking to a brick wall. You're unmovable, man. And I'm good. I'll probably hit the buffet for dinner and then keep playing video games."

"I can get the buffet to send what you want to the room. Save you some time."

"Dude, I've got to be allowed to leave the damn penthouse. You got me those disguises; I figured you'd actually let me use them. Plus, the suite's impressive, but it'll still feel like a jail if I can't leave it," I groaned.

"Jax, chill. I'm just trying to help," Donny explained. "Call me if you got problems."

"Will do," I replied dismissively before I hung up and walked into the penthouse. Before I could change my mind and give Sam a call, especially seeing as that conversation had me feeling the pressure from the label and wanting to let off some steam, I headed into my hotel room and began the process of disguising myself for dinner.

I changed into the ugliest gray sweatpants with holes in the bottom and at the knees I had ever seen, dark shades, a black T-shirt, and a LA Angels baseball cap. I didn't bother with one of the wigs I was provided, because thanks to the costume department constantly dressing me like my last album cover, the tabloids only had images of me walking around in white shirts and leather pants. It was what the paparazzi and fangirls were looking for in every town they heard we were filming in, so I could get away with a laid-back style and still escape prying eyes.

I grabbed my wallet and room key and headed back downstairs as a different guy. No longer Jax Bone, the celebrity everyone wanted to scrutinize. Instead I was just Jason, baseball enthusiast and an everyday hungry guy looking for a good meal.

I walked straight past a few girls loitering in the casino, wearing T-shirts with my face on them and trying to hide the signs with the words "Give a Girl a Bone" on them from security. I smiled when they didn't take a second glance at the guy who looked like a hungover LA drifter.

When I walked into the entrance of the buffet, I slipped a few bills to the head waiter to keep my presence a secret. I headed to the table that was filled with endless amounts of country fried chicken and grits, piled up a plate, and retreated to a booth at the back of the restaurant.

At least if I had to be trapped in a hotel, the show was smart enough to give us one with the best food options. I could hide in plain sight and eat until I passed out in a food coma.

Not my usual MO in Sin City, but as I took another bite of fried chicken, I was wondering why it wasn't how I spent my time during other trips.

This is freaking delicious.

CHAPTER
SIX

Old friends

Billie

"Th-This is our room?" I stuttered as Faith let out a squeal, dropped her bags, climbed up on the nearest bed, and started jumping. Her laughter and excitement were like background music as I walked in a daze to the window.

Everything was too beautiful.

I pressed my forehead against the cold glass and examined the tiny ant people walking along the Vegas strip. I tried to memorize all the billboard signs and hotel lights. Staring at the changing and twirling colors that made each hotel and attraction like an enticing lollipop, I understood why so many celebrities would choose to spend their time here. It was a man-made wonderland.

Faith let out another whooping noise, so I turned and examined the room we would be sharing for the week. There were two queen beds, a small writing desk, a lounge chair that faced the window, and what appeared to be a large bathroom.

"We've made it!" Faith giggled and flopped down until she was spread like a starfish across the bed. "We are in the top fifty of *Superstardom*. We're on our way to becoming *superstars!*"

I laughed and got my phone out to take a photograph of Faith's dramatics, the room, and our view to send to Zach. The moment it was delivered, he replied with a photograph of his room and a mocking text message.

Sure, your place looks all right, but I put up another poster of the King.

How many posters of LeBron James do you need?

At least two more. I had one on the floor, but Rocket thought it looked tasty.

Well, enjoy finding the next two while I spend a whole week in this place, eating free food and hanging with Faith.

Smiling at my phone as I sent my last message, I heard Faith cough and saw her eyeing me. "Stop texting your boyfriend and let's go eat. I'm starving," she whined, moving to the edge of her bed and pouting.

I rolled my eyes. "He's not my boyfriend, and you just want to use the free vouchers they gave us."

"We have fourteen vouchers to use in this hotel. I don't want to drink or gamble." Faith laughed, dropping her sulking act. "So I want to eat as much as Vegas has to offer, in case they kick me off the show before the end of the week and I have to go home to my dad's cooking. Please don't tell me you're one of those girls who's going to starve herself to get votes. Because if so, I'm requesting a new roommate."

"Hell no. I just didn't think they could send us home that quickly. They can do that? I thought we all had to be here until the very end so they can film our reactions to the top-ten announcement." My brow furrowed and I wondered how quickly this could all be over.

"Yeah, but this is television. I don't believe everything they tell us, and I know they could probably edit together some old footage of our faces." Faith grabbed her handbag and headed to the door. "So, you going to join me?"

"Yeah," I mumbled and grabbed my purse.

As we walked down the hallway, I observed some of the other contestants I'd seen filming earlier entering and exiting their rooms. I could hear the squeals behind closed doors and some even practicing their future song auditions already.

One guy wearing a cowboy hat and worn-out Levi jeans was leaning against the door that looked like it belonged to the cute brunette contestant opposite him. They both appeared to be the same age as Faith and me. Although he didn't seem too worried about getting food, practicing his song, or examining his room. He touched her shoulder, whispered something into her ear, and she started giggling. When she opened her door wider and he walked inside, I nearly tripped over my own feet.

"Did you see the cowboy go into that girl's room?" I whispered to Faith, even though there was now no one else in the hallway with us.

"I did. I'm also not surprised. I heard rumors during my last audition that Las Vegas week was filled with contestants hooking up with other contestants. I was warned that it can be fun, but usually the tryst will end with someone saying nasty things during their one-on-one interviews about the other person. As far as I'm concerned, I'm going to eat, sing, and stay out of trouble." She pressed the button for the casino floor.

"Me too." I agreed, adjusting my handbag over my shoulder.

"Oh please, you ain't got a chance in hell of staying out of trouble," Faith muttered as the doors opened and we made our way through the casino floor toward to buffet.

"I wasn't the one jumping on the bed," I reminded her, trying to think about what it could be that she thought I might get up to. I was wearing my skinny blue jeans, a loose white tank, and my hair was pulled back in a messy bun. Compared to the girls walking around the hotel casino in sequined miniskirts and bright red lipstick, I looked like a preacher's daughter.

"Give it time and you'll be jumping up and down on a bed." Faith giggled. "I saw the way Jax Bone was staring at you during filming today." She smirked. "It was how I found you. I saw the judges and then followed his attention to you. I do believe you were staring right back at him with your mouth hanging open until I screamed your name and broke y'all's sexy eye contact thing. I didn't even know you had a boy back home when I saw this all go down."

"I don't have a boy back home," I groaned. "And Jax just looked at me because I made a fool of myself during my audition."

"Girl, everyone makes a fool out of themselves during that first audition or they don't end up on television. I didn't see Jax trying to make smoldering eye contact with me after I accidentally dropped my guitar when they gave me my star ticket." She smiled at the head waiter and showed him our vouchers. When we sat down in a booth near the back of the restaurant, she continued. "I actually can't believe I'm already jealous of my roommate. Is it bad that I hope you suck when you audition?"

I burst out laughing. "Is it bad that I hope you don't really know how to play that guitar and just carry it around to look cool?"

"Does it make me look cool?"

"Yes."

"Then that's all that matters," Faith replied, giggling.

When she left to fill her plate with food, I wondered if I should be concerned that she thought I was some vixen. I panicked at the idea that others might have caught the moment Jax and I shared when I entered the hotel, but those fears quickly faded from my mind when Faith returned with food.

"I can't move," Faith moaned an hour later.

"You can't move? I ate two pieces of pie. Why did I think I could handle two pieces of pie?" I groaned while the brick sitting inside my stomach shifted to an even more uncomfortable position.

"I blame you for telling me about the fried chicken," she said as she examined her empty plate with regret.

"You were the one who pointed out the onion rings," I complained as I looked for a napkin to keep wiping away the food I was afraid still covered my mouth and hands.

"I think I'm going to need to go for a walk," Faith gritted out, then stood up like an eighty-year-old woman who needed a cane. "Hopefully if I walk around the block, I'll forget everything that happened here."

"I thought you couldn't move."

"If I don't move, I might never make it to my audition tomorrow. You know, when they said people missed their time slots because they experience Vegas until all hours of the morning, I thought they were just talking about the drinks, sex, and gambling. I never thought it could be the *food*."

"A rookie mistake we won't make again," I solemnly replied. "I'm so glad I don't have to sing tomorrow. I get three days to try and digest this food before I have to sing to a group of strangers."

"You walking with me anyway?"

"No, I need to sit for a spell. It's not a good idea for me to walk with you right now. I wouldn't want you to have to watch all the food I just pushed down my throat fight it's way back up," I explained.

"That certainly would not be pleasant to see. Okay, you stay here and pull yourself together. I'll meet you back in the room when you're ready." Faith stood up, waited until I nodded, and then shuffled to the exit.

I exhaled and thought about how comfortable the booth might be if I needed to sleep here all evening. I imagined I would be capable of returning to our room in a few minutes, but it never hurt to have a backup plan.

When a guy in a red LA Angels' baseball cap and sunglasses suddenly climbed into my booth and sat beside me, I nearly screamed.

He quickly put his hand over my mouth and removed his shades. "It'd be great if you didn't draw attention to us," Jax murmured before he noticed me staring at his hand covering my mouth. "Also, if you could avoid puking on me, it'd be much appreciated."

I snorted. When he let go, I stared at him in his baggy sweats. He looked like a normal guy, so far removed from the rock star he was during filming.

When I didn't say anything, he seemed to get nervous and mumbled, "I was sitting in the booth behind you. Heard you girls talking about your auditions and interviews, but when I heard you talking about puking, I figured it was you." He chuckled.

"That's who I am to you? The puking girl," I asked, totally mortified.

He smiled. "It's better than the fangirl, or the girl who keeps saying suggestive things about my butt when I walk by, or the girl who covers all my songs for every audition."

"I don't know, I might start singing all your songs to get rid of the puking girl label," I joked, then softly sang the first lyrics of his song "Strong Enough Alone."

"I thought you weren't a fan?" His eyebrows rose in surprise.

"You don't need to be a fan to know the lyrics of Jax Bone's latest hit. You just need to listen to the radio," I teased.

"Yeah, they're playing it a lot lately." He almost seemed embarrassed, his eyes shifting and his hands strumming on the table.

"It's good," I murmured. "It's actually one of my favorites."

"Thanks. I know it's a bit angst filled, but I wrote it after—" Before he could finish his sentence, a group of contestants walked into the restaurant. They were loud and laughing and had clearly had a few drinks to celebrate their first night in the hotel. I noticed the cowboy was with them, though his arm was draped over the shoulders of a blonde and not the brunette whose room he'd entered earlier.

He's going to make good television.

"I probably should get out of here before everyone notices me and I get a slap on the wrist from the producers for fraternizing with the contestants," Jax informed me as he slid his shades back on and pulled his baseball cap lower.

"Is that not allowed?" I asked, biting my lip. "You don't need to worry about my telling anyone we spoke, then. I wouldn't want you to get in trouble."

"Look, it won't get me fired. They just strongly encourage us judges to keep our distance because they don't want us to give anyone false hope that they'll make it through to the end of the competition." He started sliding out of my booth, and the brick I felt in my stomach disappeared into the pit that had been dug with his words.

We had just met, and I knew I shouldn't feel hurt or surprised that a huge celebrity wasn't allowed to be my friend during the competition. Yet I sat there staring at him hiding his face and body from the other contestants and pictured him doing that when I'd walked into the restaurant as well.

"You want to go for a walk?" Jax whispered.

"I thought you just said you'll get a slap on the wrist for befriending the contestants?" I asked, confused.

"You listened to my songs, right?"

"Yeah."

"Any of them about following the rules?" he asked with a twinkle in his eye.

I chucked. "Not that I know of."

"Exactly. And there's a loophole with us."

"Is that so?" I laughed.

"They told me to hang out with my old friends and avoid drinking with the contestants in Vegas. Now, we became friends in Charleston and aren't drinking, so what do you say, *old* friend? Want to get out of here?"

His diabolical grin would have had me agreeing to anything. I thanked Jesus that all he was asking me was to go for a walk; otherwise, I would have been like the girls opening doors and hanging off the cowboy contestant. Foolishly forgetting why I came to Las Vegas.

We exited the hotel like strangers. Jax kept his head down and walked a few feet in front of me. I tried not to giggle when his shoulder brushed against a girl wearing a T-shirt with his face on it, chatting with her girlfriends about locating him. They didn't even notice they were in his presence.

The smirk he sent my way when we finally escaped from the crowds turned my legs to jelly. "Have you seen the Bellagio fountain yet?" he asked curiously. When I shook my head, he led the way to stand before the immense body of water that looked more like a lake than a fountain. "It's one of the must-see attractions here. If you do nothing but stand and watch this each night, it's not a bad trip."

I grinned at him and stared at the still water with curiosity. I wondered, resting my elbows on the elaborate trellis, if standing so close would have us sprayed with water.

"You ready for all this?" Jax softly inquired, his elbow brushing against mine as he too leaned on the fence.

"The fountain?" I gestured to the water show.

"Not the fountain." Jax chuckled, nudging me with his shoulder. "The show, the attention, your rivals."

"Is there anything that could really ever prepare you for *Superstardom?*" I asked, nudging him back. "Even if I grew up with celebrity parents, sang every night, or performed for the queen, I imagine this show is another beast entirely."

"You aren't wrong there." He looked at me then, and I knew he was quietly dissecting everything about me. "I think you should say that during your interview."

"Call the show a beast I can't handle?" I chuckled. "While everyone else talks about their passion and their experience, I'm going to tell the camera guy and everyone in the interview room that I have no idea what I am getting myself into?"

"It would be a breath of fresh air. Fear isn't bad. Being afraid to do something and then showing people you're doing it anyway is inspirational. And everyone is looking for inspiration."

When he finished talking, our faces were extremely close together.

"Jax Bone, you wouldn't be trying to give me an unfair advantage, would you?" I teased, trying to shake the anticipation and chills that just ran over my body.

"Hey, I'm on this roller-coaster ride with you. I don't know what the hell I'm doing either. I'm just strapping in and hoping for the best." He winked. "Plus, we're basically the same age. I just got a little bit of a head start on this music business."

I thought about us being similar and decided he had to be joking. I was about to tell him just that when the music started to seep from the Bellagio fountain speakers and Jax stood up to take in the show. Watching him rise up had me ignoring the first few seconds of the show and completing my own examination of Jax. He looked damn comfortable in his baseball hat and sweatpants. It almost didn't seem like the disguise anymore; suddenly I felt like the leather-clad, slicked-back hair, and expensive cologne version was the disguise.

People started to crowd around us to watch the show. I was grateful for the jostling because we stopped talking, stopped touching, and I stopped thinking about things I knew I shouldn't about my new *old friend*.

CHAPTER
SEVEN

Your job

Jax

We spent all night walking up and down the strip, visiting every cliché amusement Las Vegas had to offer and losing ourselves amongst the tourists who filled the sidewalk. I kept expecting her to complain about how tired her feet were or how she needed to go back inside to get her beauty sleep. But she never did.

We rode the roller-coaster in New York, went to the top of the Eiffel Tower in Paris, and sat in the forum shops watching a very drunk couple stumble around announcing they just got married at Graceland. We were like kids in an adult playground, and watching Billie's eyes widen in surprise and listening to the sound of her laughter over places I took for granted had inspiration grabbing me by the throat and squeezing. My hand was itching to find a pen and paper. I could barely look at her reaction to the tigers lounging behind thick sheets of glass in the middle of the hotel lobby. When she noticed my twitching leg, she quietly suggested we head back to the hotel, and I nodded in agreement. There were so many more places I wanted to show her, but I needed to write down the words that kept bouncing around in my head, desperate to escape.

When we walked back into the hotel, music was thumping in my ears. I barely managed a quick goodbye when she stepped off the eleva-tor on the twenty-first floor. I was consumed by the sound of a chorus filled with seconds of soft laughter. As I swiped my room key, I didn't even contemplate going to bed or sleeping, just moved directly to the baby piano the hotel no doubt had in the penthouse merely for decora-tion and got to work.

After four hours, it wasn't even close to perfect. I needed to send it to Donny, get the boys in the studio to have a look and tweak it, until it was less of a torch song and more rock and roll. I thought about the possibility of getting an hour of sleep before I needed to start filming but quickly forgot about the possibility when my phone started buzzing.

"One day," I answered as I raked a hand through my hair and turned to look out the window to the sky that finally seemed to have fin-ished changing from dark to light. "I would like to make it through one day without you calling me. Isn't this what I pay you for? Shouldn't you be calling radio stations or sponsors or someone who might want to talk to you *about* me rather than talking to me at all hours of the day? I speak with you more than I talk to my mother."

"I know, I spoke to her yesterday," Donny replied with a hint of su-periority. "She told me you need to call her and organize flights for her birthday. Also, Missy passed away."

"Sh*t. Is there a 'sorry your cat died' card I should send?" I muttered.

"You sent your mother a pretty bouquet of pink roses to cheer her up."

"Great. Do you happen to know if my mother wants me to visit her or if she wants to visit me on the set in LA?"

"This is when you need to call your mother yourself," Donny ex-claimed. "Although, if I know Bambi, she probably wants to visit the set. She is a big fan of the show, after all."

"I do happen to know that already. Is that why you called today?" I chuckled. "Yesterday it was about recording a new song, and today it's about lecturing me on how often I call my mother?"

"Actually no, the lecture was a bonus. This phone call is about the pre-air premiere of *Superstardom*."

"What the f*ck is a pre-air premiere?" I muttered as I turned my attention back to the piano, wondering if Donny would even notice if I put the phone on mute so I could play through the song one more time.

"The show wants to do something different this season, so they're airing some of the best auditions from the past few seasons with a couple of the best auditions from this season before the show premieres in a couple of weeks. They'll play it in a few days and then again on Friday. I think it's a great idea. They already sent me a copy of the episode, and Jax, you look great. Your outfit promotes the last album, and your kindness to the nervous contestants makes you much more likeable. Hell, I like you more now, and I occasionally liked you before."

"Great, man," I muttered dismissively as I replaced a word in the chorus and began humming the melody.

"Do you want me to send you a copy?"

"Dude, as long as this show is doing what you wanted it to do for my rep, I'd rather not have to watch myself on television. Hell, if you're just calling me to give me updates about the sh*t that's out there making me look good, don't bother. You care more than I do. Don't waste my time if we're not talking about the music."

"All right, then." I could hear him already shifting papers in the background. "I'll just buzz you when the label wants to start talking contracts or new songs. Good luck on set today. And Jax—"

"Yeah, I know. Keep being *nice*."

It was tiresome watching people sing and sing and sing, desperation leaking from every pore. Too many of them were focused on technique rather than emotion. I tried to be grateful that at least all of the songs in this round were different.

I just wished that a few of them stopped treating music like cooking, as if there was a performance recipe that resulted in automatic success. It was as if every kid under the age of sixteen had gotten together and decided they were all going to pay tribute to Etta James and Nat King Cole. I figured their parents or vocal coaches thought making them sing classic love songs would have them appearing older than their years. It didn't. The young ones also tried walking back and forth across the stage like soldiers, hoping it would make them seem comfortable and ready to handle an audience. It *really* didn't. Their voices were often too quiet to be heard properly when they moved, and the tears suggested they were struggling to handle the power of the stage lights. The youngest might be ready to be on television, but they weren't ready for the stage.

I still told them, "You're way better than I was at your age," and "Wow, I can't believe that voice comes out of someone so young," making Donny proud. I didn't utter the words I really thought, leaving that chore to Russell and Claudia, who also seemed to cringe every time a kid started pretending they only loved songs from the 1950s.

The older kids were a little better. They sang songs written in the last decade and focused all their energy into projecting their voices to the judges' table in the middle of the arena. However, they all seemed to be pretending to be some past contestant or celebrity they admired, their runs and tone almost perfectly mimicking some current singer. I was tempted to start asking them if they knew their own names.

I still managed to give the country guy in a cowboy hat and overalls, who I knew was making it to the live shows, a standing ovation when he made a few of the girls in the audience cry with his imitation of Keith Urban's "Only You Can Love Me This Way." Claudia and Russell followed my lead and also showered the best imitators with cheers and praise.

With only two more auditions to go before we could finish for the day, I decided I was done with standing up or praising the contestants. I planned to do as little as possible without actually falling asleep at the judging table or being accused of not fulfilling my contract. Based on my clearly sleepless appearance, I knew the makeup girls and other judges thought I'd spent the night partying and would try and cover for what they believed to be a bad hangover.

When I slouched in my chair, I forced myself to keep staring at the stage. I believed that Billie had to have been sitting behind me for some of the auditions, with at least one camera trained on her to ensure they captured some of her reactions to the others auditioning. I didn't think our being friends was wrong, but I also didn't want to bring even more attention to her should I turn around and make eye contact with her under the watchful gaze of every camera operator in the room. If I even smiled at her while someone else was singing, I could only imagine what plotline the show would invent.

When Billie's roommate, Faith something, walked on stage, I straightened a little in my chair. Billie had explained during our time together how she and Faith met during the audition process. She told me how happy she was to discover that they would be roommates and could enjoy dinner and the highs and lows of the competition together. I knew she was good and remembered her first audition—a sweet acoustic rendition of Alessia Cara's "Scars to Your Beautiful." I didn't mention to Billie that I knew Faith wasn't as good as her or that the producers already thought Faith would be good for the live shows due to the young songwriters watching at home dreaming of performing with their guitars. She also had one of those multiple audition stories that encouraged past unsuccessful singers to keep trying in future seasons. The show loved the publicity.

I should feel relieved that Billie would have another friend during the competition, someone she could talk with about the demands of the show and the pressure of appearing on television for the first time. I knew how scary that sh*t could be.

But I didn't. She annoyed me.

My face turned into a scowl and I stared daggers at the girl. I thought about insulting her performance, good or bad. I was ready to act like a jerk and wasn't caring even a little as to the reasons why I felt that way.

Until she started singing "Secret" by The Pierces.

I swallowed the lump that seemed to get caught in my throat.

*F*ck.*

As she crooned about people's inability to keep secrets, I wondered if Billie had told her new roommate about our evening together. Faith would have questioned Billie about getting in late last night. Billie had told me she wouldn't tell people about us. However, that was before I told her I was okay with breaking the rules. She might not have thought about what could happen if her roommate was voted off and Billie wasn't. I knew some girls could be vengeful, jealous, and petty. I had no doubt that she'd spin the time Billie and I spent together to the press for her own personal gain. Billie and I were friends—we didn't hold hands or even kiss last night—but I knew what a bad story in the press could accomplish. The crew would think that I had something to do with her sticking around, especially after that crap Connor had said at the end of her audition.

Billie deserved for people to know she made it through this competition on her own.

When Faith finished playing her song, I decided to take the lead, the jerk inside of me having grown bigger than before. "Interesting song choice," I stated firmly. "Not exactly the same caliber as the original."

Her eyes widened at the sneer I couldn't keep off my face.

"I-It's from my favorite television show. I chose it because I always thought an acoustic cover made the song reflect the type of music I would like to record. It's a little mysterious, dark and emotional." Her words were strong and confident, but her nerves were revealed in her shaking legs.

"I couldn't agree more, girl." Claudia applauded. "It was definitely emotional and even a little sexy. I loved it."

"Me too, darling," Russell agreed. "Although I don't know how our producers will like hearing that *Superstardom* isn't your favorite television show." Laughter could be heard from the audience, and the girl began recovering from my scrutiny; her legs stopped shaking and she smiled at everyone. I felt glares from the crew around me.

Donny wasn't going to be happy.

When she was escorted off the stage, I reclined in my chair, acting as if I wasn't bothered by the whole ordeal. Inside, I contemplated remaining detached from Billie for the rest of the season so I didn't intimidate any more random girls on stage who I feared may hurt her or our relationship. Hanging out with Sam for the rest of the week might result in some bad headlines the following day, but getting recorded being an ass to a contestant would lead to some serious headlines for *weeks*.

I then thought about the song I'd written in my room and the songs I knew would come if Billie and I spent more time together. I thought about her honesty and naivety. Her horror at me finding her puking out front of the auditions. I thought about how I felt standing beside her as her eyes filled with shock and awe.

I decided as long as I told her not to talk to her roommate about our friendship, there was no reason why we couldn't keep hanging out.

We would prove the girl and that damn song wrong.

We could keep a secret.

And neither our relationship nor our careers would have to die.

Hell, she was good for my music, and really, music was the most important thing in my life.

It took me hours after filming wrapped before I saw Billie lined up at the front of the hotel's Starbucks. She was in tight black jeans and a loose yellow blouse. There were showgirls and waitresses walking around in what appeared to be sequined swimsuits, yet it was Billie in her yellow top that took my breath away. I quickly glanced around, saw there were no cameras and other contestants, and made my approach.

"If you order a hazelnut mocha coconut milk macchiato with five sugars or something equally disgusting, our friendship might be over," I whispered in her ear.

I watched as she jumped, recovered, and then stared daggers at me before returning her attention to the menu. No words.

I tried engaging her again by asking, "How was your first day filming in Vegas? Did you do your one-on-one interviews? Follow my instructions?"

She kept ignoring me.

When the lady behind the counter called, "Next," Billie moved forward and without hesitation asked for a "Tall hazelnut mocha coconut milk macchiato. Thank you."

"Any sugar?"

I felt Billie hesitate. "No, thank you."

"Ahh, see, you don't want our friendship over, not really. Otherwise you would have committed to the five sugars." I laughed.

"Sir, did you want anything?" the smiling girl asked, unaware she was talking to the very musician whose tour badge she was wearing on her front pocket as I hid behind my sunglasses and navy blue Cubs baseball cap.

"No, I'm all good, thank you. Just here to educate everyone about their poor drink choices," I gruffly replied, trying to disguise my voice.

The girl laughed while Billie stomped away to collect her coffee and sit at a small table with only one chair. Her eyes narrowed when she watched me grab a spare chair from a nearby table and drag it to hers.

"I asked how your first day went, but clearly you've got something else on your mind," I said before sitting directly opposite her. "So, let's hear it. Otherwise you're going to need glasses from giving me too much stink eye."

"You were mean to Faith today," Billie gritted out. "She was crying all afternoon in our hotel room, worried that you made her look stupid. If it weren't for the other judges, I don't know if she would still be here. You don't realize how important your words are to people like us. I don't think we can be friends if you're going to be mean to contestants just trying to give this show biz career a shot."

"Trust me, I can promise you I have no intention of giving

contestants a hard time. Hell, I'm on this damn show because my agent thinks I need to improve my image before signing my next contract. Apparently, I need to be *nice.*" I noticed her flinch. "That's not why I'm here with you," I clarified. "If anything, our friendship makes me forget to put on a show. Hell, I thought your roommate was singing her song to tease me about us," I told her bluntly. "And I stopped pretending and just got *pissed.*"

"She doesn't know anything," Billie replied, clearly shocked. "I didn't run up to my room and tell her what we did. Firstly, because she was already sleeping and secondly, there isn't anything to tell. We saw fountains and roller coasters, not the inside of a dirty hotel room."

"I know that, but I've also had some experience with jealous girls who want to be famous. And I spent all night after we came back writing a song. Then my agent called me to remind me yet again, after no sleep, that I needed to make a good impression on everyone, and then your roommate sang that song. I jumped to conclusions and got pissed. I get that people look at us like us judges are superhuman, but we're not. We screw up, and our words aren't always motivating, and it might have nothing to do with that person."

Billie exhaled, took a sip of her coffee, grimaced, and put it down again. "Okay, I can see how someone tired might misconstrue Faith's song, especially seeing as we never did talk about what we wanted to say to others about our time together."

"It could all be taken out of context because of the competition, and I know the show would love that gossip circulating. I hate saying it, because I don't want you to feel like I'm hiding you, but it's best we keep everything we do just between us. I don't want people thinking you're only on the show because of me, and I don't need any more headlines in magazines. And I'm not sure if you've noticed, but I don't only have to hide you, I have to hide myself every day." I gestured to the latest disguise I was sporting.

"I totally agree," she softly murmured. "And I've noticed your costume changes." She laughed.

"You laugh, but everyone who goes on the show is now dressed by the costume department from the very start. Once Michael gets his clothes on you before your first performance, everyone will be disappointed if they see you and you aren't dressed in *Superstardom* character clothes. You'll be begging to borrow my baseball caps afterward because it means you can hide from not only your celebrity status but the celebrity clothing.

But enough about the clothes. I need you to know that if you wanted to tell someone at home about our time together, someone who isn't in the business and might be able to keep their mouth shut—" I offered.

"Jax, I don't need to brag about hanging out with you." Billie laughed. "I'm cool with us not telling people about how we spend our free time. I'm not blind. The girls in the lobby—hell, the coffee girl—it's like everyone is waiting around for a piece of you. I don't need more than you're able to give. I'm just happy to have more than one friend around here who gets how crazy this show is for as long as you think you'll be able to manage it."

"Thanks," I muttered, staring into her blue eyes and pushing aside the urge to pull her face close and kiss her.

When she broke our eye contact to sip from her cup, her nose scrunched up in disgust. "This really is awful," she told me, glaring at the drink in her hand.

"See, I knew we were meant to be friends. Now tell me how your interviews went before I drag you to some of the things we missed last night."

"We're going to walk the strip again? Haven't you seen everything there is to see here already?"

"Billie, weren't you listening? My agent tells me I've got to keep out of trouble."

"And I guess that's my job as your friend?"

"That is definitely your job."

"Well, in that case, I'll just quickly summarize and tell you I did exactly what you told me to do during the interviews and admitted on camera that I have no idea what I'm doing in this competition. And now I'll admit to you that I have no idea how to keep you out of trouble Jax Bone."

I just laughed before telling her, "Not going to lie, figuring out the former will likely be easier than the latter."

CHAPTER
EIGHT

You look like a star

Billie

"**A** leather dress? Are you serious?" I asked, contemplating the sanity of the tall skinny man with a neat man bun atop his carefully shaved head standing in the small costume department behind the stage.

"Billie, you have to trust me," Michael encouraged, holding up the dress that had sleeves and pockets but clearly wouldn't make it even halfway down my thighs. "If this is the start of a long and beautiful friendship, which I hope it is, you need to believe that I am the best stylist in the world and you never have to doubt my choices."

"Michael, I've seen the amazing outfits everyone has worn during their performances so far in Vegas, but you have to admit you've been putting most people in tight jeans and stylish T-shirts. This dress is in a different category entirely. Think about the camera. Do we really want the nation to see each crease and crevice on my body? Because that's what that leather dress is going to show" I adamantly stated.

"You're delusional. I've been dressing contestants for the last three seasons, and you haven't got a single crevice on your damn body that you need to worry the camera will find. Plus, this will hit your hips and then hang loosely. It's short enough that you won't have a problem moving around the stage, but its long sleeves ensure you won't look nasty, and the open back will keep you cool. Hell, there are pockets at the front. Who doesn't love pockets?" Michael's pleading expression had me smiling, even though fear still coursed through my veins.

"If wearing this makes me look like a fool, I'm telling everyone in my one-on-one interviews that it was your fault." I grabbed the dress and headed toward the curtain they'd erected for contestants to change behind.

"You wouldn't dare," he called out, holding his hand over his heart dramatically and looking stricken. I laughed and closed the curtain. "Although you'll likely still talk about me in all your future interviews, it won't be because I made you look like a fool. It'll be because I know exactly which of your shoes will complement that dress and how that dress will look to people at home."

"At least it fits," I admitted from behind the curtain, realizing it didn't cling to the areas I'd worried it would grip unforgivingly.

"Of course it does. We're a fantastic department. We know exactly what size our contestants need, when we want them to shock and wow the audience, and when we need to send you out there looking demure and sweet. You're right that this is different than what the other contestants have worn thus far, but baby girl, do you really want to be forgotten?"

When I stepped out from behind the curtain, I knew from the way it stretched over my chest and clung to my shoulders that this dress would raise eyebrows. Discussed over talk shows and in blogs online? Definitely. Forgotten amongst the many? Never.

"I don't even look like me," I muttered when I stood in front of the full-length mirror and examined my reflection.

"You look like a star," Michael gleefully stated as he held up my own black ankle boots.

I took a deep breath and hoped that would make a difference.

Walking onto the stage holding the microphone Connor gave me, I took it all in. This was the first time I had ever sung in a theater of this magnitude, and the fact that it made the hall where we held our school's annual talent show look like a country shed made me question my ability to perform.

What am I doing?

When the heels of my boots clicked along the surface, I felt every pair of eyes in the audience follow me. I hoped that once I started singing, all the contestants watching would turn to the person sitting beside them, like so many did yesterday and the day before that, and chat about what songs they'd sing if they make it to the live tapings in Los Angeles. I needed them to remain uninterested in anyone's performance or journey on this show other than their own if I was going to make it through this round.

"Hey, Billie Bishop," Russell welcomed me when I eventually stood in front of them all. "You ready to show us what you've got?"

My nerves were caught in my throat, and I couldn't remember what I'd planned to say. I was pretty sure I told myself I was going to be charming and relaxed, but I suddenly didn't know what words would make me seem anything other than frightened and panicked.

"Of course she is," Claudia covered for me. "Look at that outfit. I'm jealous. I need that dress for the next time I'm in Vegas and have a hot date. Although, I doubt I would look that good in it."

I smiled at her kind words and tried not to pull at the hem, like Michael instructed.

"We finally going to hear you sing country?" Jax asked, smiling. His real smile, not his camera-persona one. "You going to show us your best Miranda Lambert impersonation?"

It was like we were back sitting in that small dive bar we found last night just off the strip. Just us, away from cameras and contestants, teasing each other about our music taste and talking about our past like old friends. It was exactly what I needed to hear, and how I needed to feel.

I couldn't stop the real laugh that followed or talking to him like I always did in private, rolling my eyes and telling him, "Not going to make myself look like a fool trying to do that. I know better. Today, I'm going to sing Demi Lovato's 'Stone Cold.'"

"Ex-boyfriend got you feeling bad?" he asked with an edge to his voice that I hadn't heard before.

"This song never makes me think about some boy," I replied softly. "I heard it shortly after I found out my father had a new family. Saw photos of his new baby daughter. The one he planned. I guess I figured a few people can relate, and that's who I want to be as a musician. Someone people can relate to."

The crowd cheered, and a few stood and hollered at me.

Jax smiled at me, his cocky, reassuring smirk calming my nerves yet again. "Well then, let's hear it. Try not to be terrible, okay?"

I laughed once more before I heard the piano begin to play.

It took only seconds before it felt like I was transported back in time. I didn't notice that there was complete silence in the auditorium. I no longer worried about what the contestants were doing because I was lost in the song and the first moment I'd ever heard it.

I pictured the Facebook images of my father and his new family Zach had stumbled upon. I heard my voice begin to sing the first few notes softly, like tears building behind my eyes. They were powerful, re-petitive, and fell to the floor like sharp shards of glass. As the emotions of the day rushed back to me, I rasped out my pain and gripped the mi-crophone with all my strength. I looked at Jax as I told him my story through the lyrics of the song. I didn't stop unveiling my past heartache when it overwhelmed me; I just kept singing, getting louder and louder. I closed my eyes until I felt the song and my past rip me open and soar to the ceiling. When I reached the final lyrics, I barely had enough energy to whisper them to the audience and let the song end in silence.

The moment I opened my eyes and looked out into the faces of the other contestants, some of whom had tears streaming down their faces, they all stood and began cheering.

When I looked back at Jax, he merely smiled, shook his head, and then finally joined his fellow judges, who were already giving me a stand-ing ovation.

The noise was so loud that I didn't hear the praise or feedback

Claudia and Russell tried to give me because there were just too many people calling things out to me. I was overwhelmed by the support.

People finally stopped clapping, and I managed to hear Jax state between chuckles, "Well, that definitely wasn't terrible."

Before I could smile at him, Connor Graves walked on stage cheering and pretending to wipe away tears. "Billie, I know you just sang on your first Las Vegas stage, but I don't think I'm the only one who will say this certainly won't be your last. And how grateful we all are to be here for free, knowing one day you'll be charging us hundreds of dollars to sit and watch you sing. I wish I could keep you on stage, but unfortunately some poor fool has to get up here now and try to follow your song with one of his own."

His words should have made me want to smile, but his tone and the nasty glint in his eyes had me moving as quickly as possible to join Faith in the audience and attempting to fade back into insignificance.

Four hours later, I was lying on my bed in the hotel room staring at the ceiling. My body was on strike, exhausted and unwilling to follow any more commands after the day it had. I didn't know if it was the performance or the endless one-on-one interviews the show insisted I film that nailed the coffin closed on the possibility of my doing anything this evening other than groaning and taking a very long and very hot shower.

If I never again had to talk to Connor Graves about my father's new family, my nonexistent love life, and my desire to sing songs that connect people, it would still be too soon.

"I didn't know you could sing like that," Faith prattled from the bathroom still energized from her day watching auditions. "Like sure, I figured you had to be good because you're here with me on the show. And Jax did give you that look at the beginning of filming, but I thought that was because he found you hot. Now I get it, he knew you were going to *win* this thing."

I wanted to object to her declaration but didn't have the energy to respond.

Not that Faith seemed to mind; she just continued talking while applying her makeup and doing her hair. "I thought you were sneaking off each night to talk dirty to your boyfriend on the phone, but you've been practicing, haven't you? Did you rehearse how your voice broke? And your story... I was crying in the audience like a banshee amongst a whole bunch of people who don't even know you. And everyone else, well, they were ugly crying right along with me. Girl, I hope your dad watches you on the show and feels like a d*ck. I'm so proud of you for talking about your past like that. Sure, there are always contestants who have a sad story and try to use it for some more time on screen, but it was clear that wasn't what you were doing. You were being relatable and singing for all the girls who have deadbeat—"

With a knock at the door, Faith seemed to finally take a breath and pause from her never-ending monologue. When she didn't start up again after she closed the door, I lifted my head to see what had broken her focus on my performance. She was holding a basket with a big blue ribbon on top.

"What is that?"

"A gift for you," she muttered.

"You're not going to give it to me?" I laughed.

She turned and poked her tongue out.

"I wanted to see who it was from because it is *weird*."

"What is it?"

"A basket of baseball caps."

Knowing exactly who those were from, I couldn't help the grin that appeared on my face. I tried to look out the window so she didn't see my smile and start asking questions.

"Maybe someone will call soon and explain, because the card just says your name," Faith said while rummaging through the basket. "No sender. No note. Nothing. I bet it was that country boy Ryne. I've heard rumors he's slept with six different contestants already. Now that he's seen you perform, I bet he wants to be like some weird power couple, and he wears that cowboy hat, so maybe he's giving you options. If he calls you after I'm gone, you have to fill me in with his smoothest line. I bet it includes the word 'peaches.' He's so gross." I wanted to laugh but didn't want her to start coming up with other possibilities. "You still going out?" I asked.

"We only have two more nights in this city," Faith replied while spinning around in her flowing red dress. "I've put contacts in and lipstick on, which means I am ready to convince someone I'm twenty-one, have them buy me drinks, and hopefully be married by Elvis this evening."

"Big night for you, then." I chuckled. "Don't forget to take wedding pictures to show your boring roommate."

"Will do. You're sure I can't convince you to get out of bed in case I need a maid of honor?"

"After the day I've had, there is absolutely no possibility of my leaving this room. I'm sorry."

"All good. Just don't wait up," she replied before winking, grabbing her purse, and heading for the door.

Silence settled in the room the moment the door closed. I exhaled and shut my eyes. Maybe I wouldn't even have a shower tonight. Maybe I would just fall asleep right here and now.

A bang on the door had me opening them again. Knowing Faith probably forgot her room key, I groaned and got up to let her in. Damn that girl. At least the carpet was soft and fluffy beneath my feet. "If you're already married, I'm going to warn you that I won't be giving up our room so you can consummate your vows."

Jax's raised eyebrow and pursed lips greeted me when I opened the door. "Not married, and rest assured, if I was going to consummate anything, it wouldn't be in your room."

My mouth dropped open.

He was still wearing his celebrity judging suit from earlier: tight leather pants molded to his thighs and a loose black shirt stretched over his broad shoulders falling loosely over his narrow hips. His dark eyes were no longer hidden behind a baseball cap but focused on mine with an intensity I didn't know what to do with. I felt my body shiver and my brain shut down.

"Y-You're dressed like a celebrity," I stuttered, trying to get my neurons firing again.

"I just came from a small party with the director and crew. You need me to go get into sweatpants and come back? Will that help you close your mouth?" He grinned. "Come on, just let me in. I promise not to act like a celebrity and break anything. I'll pretend I'm wearing pajamas with sheep on them too."

His teasing comment broke the trance I was in and made me look down at my outfit. Yep, flannel pajamas with flying sheep. *Well, sh*t.*

"Michael didn't let you keep the dress?" Jax asked when he walked in and sat down on the edge of my bed. It was like it was completely natural to him, hanging out in my hotel room and chatting with me about my clothes. If it was so easy for him, why was it freaking me out?

"God, no, I wouldn't want to." I shivered and moved to the edge of Faith's bed to sit opposite him.

"Leather looked good on you. You should change your mind," he muttered while turning his head to look around our hotel room.

"You look good in leather, yet I don't see you rocking this look unless you have work."

"You think leather looks good on me?" Jax smirked.

"Oh don't look at me like that. You know it does. But we both know that, just like me, you prefer clothes that breathe. And baseball caps."

"Speaking of baseball caps, you get my present?" he nervously asked, his eyes searching the room.

"Yeah, my roommate thinks they're from the cowboy contestant who's been 'romancing' all the girls," I told him, chuckling. "She put them on the chair in the corner."

"After they air your performance today, you're going to need a disguise," he said softly, stopping his perusal of the basket to stare directly at me.

"You think my flannel pajamas won't be enough to trick people?" I joked.

"I like what you're wearing." He leaned until our bodies were inches apart. "But if the aim is for you not to be noticed, your pajamas won't work."

"But they're comfy," I tried joking again, only to have my breath stagger out as his hand reached out and ran along the bottom edge of my pajamas shirt.

"I was thinking upstairs, surrounded by all the crew and big entertainment people," he slowly began, "about how exhausted you would likely be after today's performance."

"You knew that?"

"Yep. Been there before, babe. I've sung about family to a group of strangers. I know it leaves a different impact. And I started getting pissed that their self-promotion and preening at me would prevent me from getting a chance to see you tonight. Tell you how amazing you were today."

"Is that why you're here, in my room, for the first time?"

"Partly."

"Wha-What was the other part?" I timidly stuttered.

He leaned in closer, his hands moving from the hem of my pajamas to my chin and angling my head to his. "This." He kissed me, soft and sweet, but with an edge that had me tumbling into a fog that concealed everything but how good it felt to have his lips pressed against mine.

He leaned back and then just held his lips still against mine again for a second, two seconds, until what felt like an eternity passed and he finally slipped his tongue in my mouth and took another taste of me. It put me on my toes, reaching toward his hard body, desperate to be closer and feel what it would be like to be against him without clothes getting in the way. I could feel the heat radiating off his body, knew instinctively that he wanted to push this into something more, but his hands stayed still on my face.

Lost in the fog, I nearly slipped off the bed when he moved his lips away and rested his forehead against mine. "I want you to come back to LA with me when this is over. Stay at my place before you have to film the live shows. I've got a spare bedroom. I'm not expecting anything. I just want to spend time with you like we have here. This is going to sound really lame, but you inspire me."

"Mmmm," I hummed until his words pierced through the haze. "Huh? What? Why? Is this because I wore leather and for, like, a few minutes we matched. And you can't tell me I'm going to be in the live shows." He chuckled. I kept rambling. "I thought you wanted to be my friend so I kept you out of trouble. I'm thinking us hanging out in LA for a couple of weeks before we start filming, with me a contestant while you're a judge, is totally not trouble free."

"Definitely not," he murmured, staring into my eyes.

"So then we both agree that it would be a huge mistake, and we're going to pretend you never asked and you didn't just kiss me, right?"

He smirked at me. I could tell he didn't care in the slightest about the trouble this might cause. He stood up and walked to the door. I remained frozen on the edge of Faith's bed, trying to process everything that just happened as I stared out the window to the flashing lights of the Las Vegas strip.

"I don't think I want to go a day without seeing you," Jax said, forcing me to turn at look at him standing by the door. "If I'm being honest, I've been thinking about you since the moment you told me you'd just puked in a trash can. So, I guess if you don't feel the same, that's sweet. I'll go back to LA and we'll see each other on set. Otherwise, I'll leave details for the plane with the concierge. Oh, and act surprised when they announce you're in the top ten. Keep me out of trouble while you can."

And then he was gone.

CHAPTER
NINE

He's a player

Zach

It was like explaining the rules of basketball to a foreign exchange student who didn't speak English. "The show doesn't air for another week. There is no reason why y'all had to come pushing your way into the room and take the remote. Go back to drinking your wine and gossiping about the neighbors on the front porch and let me finish watching my movie. You don't just turn off Bruce Willis."

"Zachary, don't sass your mother with that tone," my momma, Cora Montgomery, replied with her eyebrows raised. "You've seen that movie at least a dozen times, and there was an ad for *Superstardom* yesterday. They're doing a special segment on it tonight, like a sneak preview."

"Zach's right, Cora. I looked up when the show starts, and it isn't this week," Michelle quietly stated, patting Rocket as he leaned against her hip. "If she makes it through the Las Vegas rounds, Billie's meant to come home for a couple of weeks. When she leaves for Los Angeles to rehearse, they start airing the auditions and snippets from their time in Las Vegas. As soon as they finish their rehearsals, the live performances start. We should see her before we see the show on the television."

"I know that's what y'all keep telling me, but there was an ad for the show, and I swear on my grandmother's pearls I saw Billie's face," my momma repeated. She channel surfed until she saw Connor Grave's smile fill the screen and the theme music for *Superstardom*. "See, I told y'all."

"They're just playing old footage of past winners. You've seen every season," I complained from my spot on the couch when the winner from last season appeared on the screen. I had a bowl of popcorn in my lap and wasn't exactly excited about my movie being turned off, but I returned to stuffing my mouth and scowling.

"Boy, I am sick to death of your brooding," Momma announced as she picked up a cushion and threw it at me.

I protected the popcorn, swatted the cushion away, and muttered, "I'm not brooding."

"Cora told me that unless you're at practice or school, you sit here all day eating and watching movies," Michelle stated. "You don't hang with your teammates after games, and even when you have a movie on, you spend most of your time staring at your phone, hoping my daughter will call or text you. Basically, you're worse than me."

I had no reply, because she wasn't wrong. Rocket, sensing my unease, came over and curled up at my feet. I began patting him, hoping to avoid spending any more time talking about my feelings.

"Look! Look!" Momma started jumping up and down, and when we all turned to the screen, we watched Billie walking nervously into the judging room.

"Holy sh*t," I muttered, staring at Billie's tumbling blonde curls and big blue eyes as she looked at the judges and cameras like a deer caught in headlights. She was unbelievably beautiful in a naive innocent way that I knew everyone watching at home would be drawn to.

When she told the judges her name and age, and Russell Conway told Billie her name was cool, I heard Michelle's gasp. The reality of Billie being on television became real. When she teased Jax Bone about not considering him as her favorite musician, knocking his ego back a peg, I couldn't help but grin. "That's my girl," I mumbled under my breath.

When she began softly singing Jewel's "Foolish Games," her hands resting on her stomach, Michelle, my mom, and I all held our breaths. We knew how good she was, but every time listening to Billie was like the first time.

Our chests ached at the beauty she revealed. Watching her sing always reminded me of the wild horses I once saw grazing and galloping on my grandparents' ranch. They were quiet and easily spooked, avoided everyone unless enticed by the right brand of carrot. But given the opportunity, they showed the world a form of beauty when they galloped that left everyone speechless. I'd been in love with Billie since the first time I saw her sing. She was no longer my goofy best friend; she was the sun and stars in a world of obscurity. It was like she had a fire inside her that burst and burned and then just as quickly settled back into a timid shell.

I didn't need to look at Michelle and my momma to know they were crying; I could hear their sniffles from my spot on the couch. But when Claudia asked Billie to sing something a little more upbeat, I swore I heard Michelle growl.

When Billie began singing Lady Antebellum's "Downtown," laughing between lyrics and flicking her hips, I wasn't seeing her on the television. I was back in her bedroom when she first heard that song, watching her dance around her bedroom while trying to convince me that it was the best song on the radio.

The memory was broken when Russell led the judges into a standing ovation and my mother started clapping in the living room like a dork.

When Jax Bone asked Billie who was with her at the audition supporting her, Cora and Michelle abruptly stopped clapping and the tension in the room became intense.

When she began discussing her mother's disapproval of her singing and the fact that she was able to convince me to stay behind, Jax Bone's reaction transformed my face into a scowl. When he stood up to give her the star ticket, I was pissed. Acting like she was alone and needed him to hold her hand. Acting like there was something there between them and they didn't just meet two f*cking seconds ago.

Dude, she told you I was the reason she was at the damn audition.

When he encouraged her to grab hold of her dreams and not let go, I wanted to shout at her that she could do that and it didn't mean she had to let *us* go.

The episode ended with Connor Graves reminding people to tune in next week to watch the entire season. I had no idea how the episode affected Michelle, but I knew that after watching all that transpired, I wasn't sure things would be the same.

The phone rang and rang.

"Hey," Billie answered, sounding as if she were just waking up. "I'm sorry. I know I've been a terrible best friend and haven't been texting you a ton lately. They're keeping us pretty busy with filming interviews and our reactions to each other's performances. I basically passed out tonight after the day I had. Wait, have you called me six times tonight? Do I need to jump on the plane? Are you okay? Are the moms okay?"

"We saw your audition tonight," I told her bluntly, raking a hand through my hair.

"What? How? The show doesn't air for another week. I was meant to come home first," Billie muttered, sounding confused. I heard rustling on the other end of the phone. It sounded like she was climbing out of bed. I pictured her long blonde hair piled on top of her head and the goofy pajamas she always wore, and the tension I felt since watching on television opposite Jax Bone lifted a little.

"They aired your audition early. They kept calling it a pre-air premiere to promote the new season. They replayed old auditions of past winners with a couple of new auditions. There was your friend with the glasses and some cowboy's audition as well. Although, they were shown just singing. They aired your audition start to finish. B, you sounded amazing."

"Oh, well, I guess that's a relief. But, um, did my mom—"

"Hear that she doesn't support you? Yeah, B. It didn't look like they edited anything out."

"I should call her," Billie said, sounding panicked. "I've spoken about how amazing she's been my whole life in interviews ever since, but if they only showed my audition—"

"Look, you didn't say anything she didn't already know. Thankfully, it was before you guys had that argument in the kitchen. I would give her a day to calm down."

"Do you think she's angry with me?"

"I think she's angry at herself." I sighed. "Once the show ended, she left our house and didn't even say goodbye to my mom. I think she needs to beat herself up a little before she'll be able to talk to you."

"How you feeling?" Billie asked tentatively. I imagined her twirling a single curl around her finger like she usually did when she was nervous.

"Guilty."

"Zach, you don't need to feel guilty," Billie said softly.

"I dared you to go there and let you convince me not to join you. I knew it was going to be a big moment in your life. I should have just ignored your complaining. I should have been there when you got that ticket."

"Zach, if you think for a moment that I didn't know how much you cared about me and my winning that ticket, then you're crazy. I wouldn't be here if it weren't for you, and I never forget that. There was a reason I didn't tell you the questions they asked me. I never wanted you to feel bad."

"Look, once you're back next week, maybe we should go down to the lake and talk about everything. There are things I haven't told you either. I also wouldn't mind talking about how we might make this work in the future."

"Make what work?"

"Your singing career and my college plans."

"Zach, you don't need to change your life to fit into mine. We'll never stop being friends and supporting each other. Distance doesn't change that."

"Maybe I want to. Look, we don't need to talk about it now. When you get back—"

"About that." Billie paused, and the silence caused the hair on my body to stand on end. "I've been thinking about not coming home for the weeks before the live shows if I make it. I've been asked to go to Los Angeles early. If Momma is already upset, I don't think my coming home will be the best idea. It was so hard to leave the first time. If I thought she was hurting, I don't think I could come back. And being here, Zach, it feels too important to walk away from."

"Was it Jax Bone?" I growled. "The one who asked for you to go to LA?"

"What does it matter?" Billie replied defensively.

"I saw your audition, B. That guy, he made you feel alone—"

"Zach, I *was* alone."

"Don't let him convince you that you need him to win the competition," I begged. "Don't let him make you believe that to hold on to your dreams, you need to hold on to him. I've read the articles, seen him in the papers. He's a player. I don't want you to become a groupie instead of a performer. He's also a user. More than a few people in interviews have said he used his dad's death to get famous."

I heard her sharp intake of breath, heard her begin to pace up and down her bedroom.

"That was a sh*t thing to say to me," Billie hissed. "And a sh*t thing to say about a person you haven't even met. Jax isn't like that, and if he was, I'm certainly smart enough not to trust someone like that. People can be jealous when you're on top."

"I know the competition must be stressful," I tried explaining. "I just don't want you to make a decision you'll regret."

"Zach, you don't know anything about what the competition is like, and I don't need you helping me make decisions right now—"

"The reason I don't know about the competition is because you've been too busy to tell me. Besides that first day, you barely text. You don't send me photos, and you don't vent any of your concerns to me. You used to tell me everything," I interrupted heatedly.

She didn't say anything. I could hear the sniffling and suddenly felt like a jerk. I felt guilty, and now I'd called her and made her feel guilty as well.

I didn't know what I expected this conversation to be like, but this wasn't it. We rarely ever fought. We usually always had the same opinion on people, and I didn't remember there ever being a time in our lives when we couldn't tell each other exactly what we were thinking.

Unless it was me, hiding how I felt about her to protect our friendship.

Now it didn't feel like we were just on the phone, separated by distance. It felt like we were separated by thousands of pages of unknown dialogue. We were on different pages of entirely different books. And I hated it.

"Look, I know you've been busy. I know you're meeting people I don't know anything about other than what I see online," I tried conceding. "I just don't want to lose you."

Billie sniffled once more before whispering, "I don't want to lose you either."

"You should go to LA," I encouraged. "Get settled in before the live shows if you feel like that will be the best for you."

"I don't really know—"

"You do. Otherwise you wouldn't have mentioned it to me."

"I guess I do," she confessed. "But, Zach, you should know, I don't want to lose you either. I miss hanging out with you."

"It's all good. We'll be hanging out again before you know it."

"Yeah, we will." Billie sighed. "I should probably get back to sleep. After the last few auditions tomorrow, they announce who's making it to the live shows. It's going to be a massive day of filming."

After we said goodnight and hung up the phone, I jumped online to look at credit card applications and flights to Los Angeles.

I knew Billie was making it to the live shows after Vegas.

I knew she wouldn't be coming home.

And I knew I wasn't letting her go through the next part of this competition without someone cheering her on. Not again, and not for all the money in the world.

CHAPTER
TEN

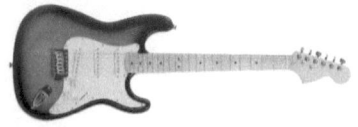

Mega-rich teen idol

Billie

The sun rose, dusty gold, over the green hills and lavish homes of California's rich and famous. From the guest room of Jax's house, I thought the modern white cubes and green swirls tumbling down from the Hollywood sign looked like expensive confetti celebrating a life of luxury and excess.

Downtown Los Angeles, on the other hand, resembled fierce little Lego blocks from a distance, threatening pain on anyone who dared to step foot amongst the most powerful businessmen and women. Since Jax showed me this room and this view less than twenty-four hours ago, I took what was likely my hundredth glance at the glass and glittering steel and pondered how I wound up there.

I still couldn't decide if I needed to pinch or kick myself.

The choices I was making terrified me. And the secrets, they were only getting more and more ridiculous as days passed. First, it was just my friendship with Jax. Then it was hearing I made it into the live shows of *Superstardom* before everyone else. Pretending to be surprised when they gathered us together in those final days in Las Vegas. Laughing along with Faith as we received our new star tickets to Los Angeles. Now it was sneaking onto a private jet and hiding out in a Hollywood Hills mansion, waiting for Jax to return from meetings with his agent and the television executives to spend our first day exploring LA together. It felt wrong. I needed Zach to tell me again that what I was doing was okay.

"Billie," Jax called from somewhere inside this massive house, and my heart raced.

Kick, definitely kick myself. What have I gotten myself into?

I left the sprawling room, heading down the stairs and toward Jax's voice.

I saw him standing near the front door and inexplicably I started to relax. I wondered how it was possible that staring at him calmed me down and didn't freak me out. Why his chocolate eyes and smirk made me want to throw caution to the wind and believe our hanging out was completely right.

"Hey," I said casually.

I could tell by the way his back got straighter and he raked his fingers through his hair before adjusting his Dodgers baseball cap that ever since he kissed me, Jax was less sure of himself around me. He smiled and teased me but appeared more nervous. I didn't really understand why he wanted me here or what made him want to kiss me the night after my performance. He certainly hadn't made a move to do it again since.

Jax turned and opened the door behind him. "You ready to visit Santa Monica Pier?"

"I'm ready to go anywhere," I replied honestly. "This entire place seems so different than home."

"We'll start with the pier. There's also this crab shack nearby. The owners are discreet, so we'll be able to have lunch without fear of being interrupted."

"That sounds great. Although, won't people recognize your car?" I asked, staring at the fancy white convertible.

"Maybe, but this thing goes pretty fast." Jax smirked. "It'll be hard for the paparazzi to keep up. Just you wait. You'll enjoy watching them try."

"Jax Bone, are you trying to corrupt me?" I laughed.

"Billie Bishop, are you corruptible?"

"I'm here, aren't I?" I replied, feeling the heat creep into my cheeks.

The day was perfect. The water. The rides. The food.

I would never regret breaking the rules to spend time with Jax.

We didn't talk about the competition. I didn't feel like he was a judge and I was a contestant. Instead we were two teenagers spending time together discussing our favorite foods. We argued over what the best movies and television shows of all time were and admitted to our guilty-pleasure Netflix shows. I confessed to him that it was musicians from the nineties who had me first falling in love with music, and he told me about the latest jazz musicians that kept his love alive. I told him about the first time I sang and played my secondhand keyboard in public, the nerves and the joy when no one laughed or pointed. He talked about his dad teaching him how to play guitar on the beach and his disappointment that his dad never saw him play to a giant crowd.

It was like this time together had nothing to do with those times I had, and would have, to stand on stage in front of him, waiting for him to judge me. The sun disappeared with the tide, and I barely noticed the few girls who walked past us and saw Jax's disguise for what it was and giggled. I didn't notice the squeals that came from the roller coaster above us or the excited chatter of tourists. The world faded away.

He reached for my hand, and it felt right to hold on. It didn't feel like he was some mega-rich teen rock idol who could charter his own plane and afford to buy us lobster from the most expensive restaurant on the pier while calling it a crab shack. It felt like he was only this incredibly cool high school guy who listened when I told him that I wished I knew my father and laughed when I said Lindsey Lohan's *Parent Trap* was my favorite movie.

The wind made me to shiver, and Jax unzipped his jacket and put it over my shoulders.

"You ready to head back to the house?" he asked softly.

"Sure," I whispered, pulling his jacket tighter and smelling Jax's musky, delicious scent.

The easygoing chatter between us died, and we became almost too quiet as we approached his car hidden amongst the trees. I started over-thinking what going back to the house might mean. For the first time since I'd asked the concierge to provide me with the details Jax left behind, I panicked that he was lying when he told me he didn't expect anything from me. Only today did I realize it was like an electric wire existed between us and vibrations traveled down my body each time Jax moved or looked at me.

I wasn't totally sure that if Jax made a move to kiss me, I would have the self-control to say no. Actually, I wasn't sure that if he kissed me, I wouldn't be the one who steered us into that unfamiliar territory.

I wondered if he could tell that I had limited sexual experience. If he could take one look at me and see the naïve country girl who lurked below, or if he assumed that everyone was like the girls in his music videos: confident, liberated, eager to climb all over him, and wise about where to touch.

I dreaded the prospect that if he tried to kiss me tonight, with no one in the house to interrupt us, I would likely have to tell him all about my past love life or lack thereof. I wouldn't be able to pretend like I knew what I was doing.

I figured that the way he was looking at me now, like I was a mystery that he couldn't wait to solve, would be gone. He would know.

I was just a shy girl who could sing love songs.

But I had no clue how to actually make love.

Jax parked the white convertible in his underground garage beside three other expensive-looking cars. I knew nothing about car brands or models, but I had never seen anything like them back home. With their strange windows, winged doors, and chrome finish, I doubted I would again. They looked like they came straight off a Hollywood set.

When I stepped out of the car, I felt my knees shake a little. Jax held out his hand and I grasped it eagerly. The last thing I wanted to do was fall over walking into his house. I was already feeling like a nervous child.

Yet instead of leading me up the stairs into the main house, Jax nodded toward a door I hadn't seen before in the corner of his garage.

"I thought I would show you the recording studio," he said. "I told you in Vegas you inspired me. And I thought if I did the same for you, you should know where you can come to write songs, sing with great acoustics, or lay down some tracks."

"You think you inspire me?" I quipped, trying to pretend that he hadn't just transformed from the cool teenager back into the mega-rich rock god.

He opened the door to reveal thick black stairs that appeared to descend and twist into a pitch-black room. "With my good looks and sense of humor, I believe *Rolling Stone* wrote that I would inspire many love songs for those in my generation." He grinned. "But if you would like to pretend you aren't inspired by awesomeness, go right ahead."

"They really wrote that, didn't they?" I laughed. "But I doubt any of those reporters made this journey into the dark with you. If this is actually a basement and you're trying to kill me, I'm telling you now, this is the first place the cops will look."

"Thanks for the advice. If I decide to kill you, I'll be sure to move the body," Jax replied as he turned on the light, which had me blinking quickly.

"Smart choice," I choked out while staring at the state-of-the-art home studio. It was hard to take it all in. The computer, the piano, the keyboard connected to cables, the guitars on the wall, the control system, the mic booth, and the plush lounge were more intimidating than the entire house made of glass. This was the reminder that I was a girl who might be able to sing and Jax was a musician. "I don't think I should be allowed to touch anything in here," I quietly confessed as if standing amongst church pews. "I haven't ever tried recording my own songs and would more than likely break something if I did."

"I can teach you the basics," Jax replied. "We can start with the computer software that links with your cell phone. We both know if you win this competition, people will likely offer to write your songs for you, and there will be a whole bunch of people who can help produce and engineer your music to sound amazing. They already have the best in the business writing songs for each of the top ten contestants to launch their career if they win. But I like knowing how everything works and understanding what they're doing behind the scenes and what they're talking about during meetings. I thought if you didn't already, you might like to learn."

"I think you're right," I said, "but I might really suck at this."

"I think you're doubting my skills as a teacher," he teased. "I can do more than just judge people."

We spent the rest of my time at his house in the studio. He would suggest we take a break, offer to drive me to the best sites of LA, to explore beaches and shopping malls. And I would encourage him to order another pizza and show me again how to turn the keyboard into a base guitar and stack my vocal recordings.

I wanted to know how everything worked. We weren't creating anything of substance—I was mostly playing with sounds and instruments—but I knew with enough practice, the songs I had inside my head would play through the speakers. Thicker and richer than I could ever have managed on my little secondhand keyboard at home.

I could see that some nights it drove him crazy; he rolled his eyes and threw cushions at me to break my focus from the computer. He moaned about wanting me to get out of the studio and breathe fresh air. I dreamed that he was really complaining about not having another opportunity to hold my hand and stare into my eyes. But then other days he couldn't keep the grin or excitement off his face as I got closer to being able to produce my first song, and there would be no further discussions about us running around town. And I would go back to thinking that maybe he thought our kiss in Las Vegas was a mistake. He had gone back to wanting us to just be friends.

I didn't admit out loud that it wasn't only creating music that kept me content with staying in the home studio. I loved watching Jax teach me how to make music. There was something about his patience when he showed me something he loved doing that made my toes curl. His face transformed when I selected the right instrument to layer or appreciated the sound of an acoustic guitar or base.

It was almost sexual.

When we would sing together, I closed my eyes and imagined what our voices molding together to create a new sound would look like. The image in my mind always wound up in a California king bed with white sheets and pillows everywhere. I would open my eyes and immediately look away, hoping Jax didn't see the desire that lurked within them.

His voice was better than mine, of course, more rehearsed and a tool he knew exactly how to wield at the right moment. I was a novice. He told me my voice was better than some of the most seasoned professionals, but I knew he was just being nice. Compared to Jax Bone, I was inexperienced in all things and couldn't quite live up to everything he offered a girl.

I wasn't ready to leave tomorrow. But I also knew I couldn't stay.

The contestants were all staying at a hotel right near the set where they would be filming all the live shows. And there would be no way Jax and I could share a house and remain a secret.

I had spent the week learning new things, but some things couldn't be taught, and some things neither of us was ready to share.

"You need to get to the hotel tomorrow," Jax muttered while leaning back on the home studio couch.

"Yeah," I nervously replied while staring at the platinum albums displayed along the wall, avoiding making eye contact with Jax.

"My friend Sam is in town. He'll drive you from here. No one will suspect anything."

"Will we get to see each other a lot? Between live shows?" I asked, feeling the disappointment before I even heard his words. From his posture, the way his eyes didn't meet mine, I already knew the answer.

"It's unlikely. I've seen the schedules. It's grueling. They have you recording your song choices, making appearances on talk shows, and then there are the live show rehearsals."

"You'll be there? When they record the songs we're singing?"

"They bring in other guest musicians to help with your recordings. It boosts their ratings. They like to keep us judges away during the recording sessions so when you wow us on stage, we have more genuine reactions. Although, they do make us come to set pretty regularly to film us giving you pep talks before rehearsals."

I already knew that. I had seen the celebrity guest stars helping contestants in past seasons. I didn't know why I asked. I think I wanted things to be different. I wanted more time. I didn't just want dance rehearsal pep talks. I wanted other opportunities to hold his hand and listen to him sing in a recording studio, just the two of us. I was annoyed at myself for desperately wishing for more. Then I reminded myself that this was Jax Bone. If he had really wanted me, he surely would have made a move by now. There had been lots of girls in the magazines snuggled up to him, so he clearly knew how to make a move on a girl. He probably just didn't want to make one on me.

"It's only about three months. We should be grateful that it's shorter than any other reality programs on television. Then we won't have to hide our friendship," Jax told me. "People won't think I'm forcing you to hang out with me due to my celebrity judge status."

"Who would be stupid enough to think that Jax Bone needed to force a girl to be friends with him?" I muttered. "But if you think people will think differently of us both, then it'll be something to look forward to once my part of the competition ends. And if I get kicked off the show next week, it'll be like we never had to," I teased, sounding more like myself and not a sulking lovesick fan.

"You really don't know how good you are." Jax chuckled. "It's going to be interesting to see how long that lasts."

Jax had a driver drop me off at the hotel without a word spoken between us. I figured he had probably done this before. This was likely the guy Jax called to transport all the girls who spent the night so they didn't have to perform the walk of shame. I wondered if Jax explained our situation. If he told this guy he just wanted to be friends with me. If he knew I wasn't like the other girls. I didn't have the courage to ask. I also didn't really want the answer. Instead I decided to text Zach.

Besides the short messages from him to make sure I landed safely in LA and his updates that my mom had returned to her usual self, we hadn't had any conversations. I figured we both were dealing with our guilt since we spoke after they watched my audition. I went to text him a couple of times about Jax and the recording studio, but something always made me stop. Now that I was on my own again, I didn't feel this brick wall preventing me from reaching out.

Done playing in LA like a tourist. Just arrived at the new Superstardom hotel. Do you think the room will be as good as the one in Vegas?

Better. Top 10, B. They'll start treating you like royalty soon. You practiced your princess wave yet? Got your diva demands ready?

His reply made me smile and sigh in relief. I could always rely on Zach. I could trust that my mistakes would never ruin our friendship. He would always be there with a wiseass comment and a smile.

Just found out I got my own room this time. No sharing.

Faith will be relieved she doesn't have to listen to you snoring then.

I don't snore.

Summer. Camp.

I was twelve and sick. My nose was blocked! Those girls telling everyone I snored was just to bully me.

I still have the video recording they sent to everyone.

Those b*tches.

Hey, when you make it big, I'm going to make a lot of money off this video. I might need to send them a fruit basket, or do you think they would prefer a pie?

You show anyone that video, Zachary, and people will see the video of you practicing your victory dances.

I don't know why you think that's a threat. I was nine, and my victory dances are still awesome.

I chuckled, then unlocked the door to my new hotel room, contemplating the best way to ask Zach if I should call my momma. Then I saw the note sitting in the middle of my bed. A small cream-colored piece of paper with blue pen roughly scrawled across the page.

It's almost the end.

I wondered how Jax managed to have his friend put the note in my room without me noticing.

I picked it up and carefully slipped it into my purse, thinking about how strange it would be to finally have our friendship out in the public. I wondered how Faith would react.

I decided I really needed to give Jax my cell phone number. His handwriting wasn't that messy, but if we were going to be friends, well, friends texted. They didn't leave random messages on beds. I chuckled thinking about it.

Although, it didn't stop me from worrying about what everyone was thinking, because Jax wasn't wrong. This would be all over in a matter of months. The auditions aired this week. Rehearsals were about to start. The live shows were days away. I hoped things would end well and not in tears.

CHAPTER ELEVEN

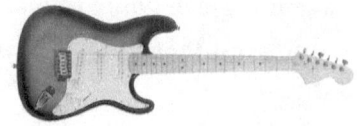

Sweet on each other

Jax

"Five spotlights? Is that necessary?" I heard Billie ask Carey Leigh, the guest musician helping the top ten with their first live show. After a week of rehearsals and interviews on talk shows about their auditions that had been airing with unprecedented ratings, it was finally the night where the public could see Billie perform live. And from the tapping of her feet and the high-pitched tone with which she asked her questions, I guessed she might have wished the week of rehearsals had gone a little slower.

"You mean fifteen spotlights, right?" I teased, leaning against the open door to Billie's dressing room.

With her curls intricately styled on top of her head and wearing a floor-length black gown that sparkled as she turned, Billie looked at me with fear filling her eyes.

"There are fifteen?" she gasped. "I won't be able to see the keys. I won't be able to see the audience. This is ridiculous. Why did I think I should play the piano during the first live show? Connor keeps repeating that you can't screw up during a live show. I'm not ready. I'm not ready."

"Don't stress about the lights," Carey replied, staring daggers at me.

"You'll barely notice them. We've rehearsed this. You'll be sitting at the piano anyway. There will be five spotlights above you shining down, but there will be ten on the ground. You'll look like a star. This dress Michael picked out will sparkle, and people will be so mesmerized that they won't believe you're a girl who should go back to high school. You could and will sing with twenty lights on you at some point, and they'll be like trees in a background. And Connor's an idiot. Live television isn't too different from normal."

"What if I forget the lyrics?" she whispered.

"You won't," Carey reassured her. "Every rehearsal, you've killed it. And I've seen your audition and your performance in Vegas. You are more than ready."

"And if you do forget a word, make some up," I stated offhandedly. "Sure, people will give you a hard time about it during judging, but those watching at home won't know the difference. And they're the ones you need to impress."

Carey glared at me again, clearly unimpressed by my advice. She then took a long look between Billie and me before she asked me curiously, "Jax Bone, what exactly are you doing in here? The camera crew is with Cowboy Ryne right now."

"Us judges thought it would be a good idea to go around and wish all the contestants good luck off camera. It's more sincere this way," I informed her, grinning. I didn't mention that it was my idea, or that in the entire history of the show judges had never seen the contestants before they performed.

"Well, that's sweet," Carey said, rolling her eyes. Her title as the latest pop princess meant she and I had seen and performed with each other a lot at different musical events. And I knew she cared less about this show than anyone on the planet. Yet, she also had to improve her current unflattering image in the press after she made headlines over her latest stint in rehab, so here she was. "I don't suppose you could tell the other judges to keep out of my way as I try and keep Billie calm, check that Faith's guitar is tuned, see that Katie knows her kids are in the audience, ensure

Ryne doesn't have Whitney in his dressing room, and handle the other five contestants who all have their own issues and need my help tonight?"

Billie chuckled.

I laughed before replying, "I'll tell them to wait to wish them good luck until after you've left each contestant's dressing room. That help?"

"I knew I agreed to work with you again for a reason." Carey smiled.

I winked at Billie, whispering, "Good luck," before stealthily making my exit and heading to my seat at the judges' table.

I managed to hail Cindy down to pass on Carey's instructions to not let the judges bother her with helping each of the contestants before they went out on stage. Then I settled into my judge's seat and imagined what Billie planned to do after the show. I thought about revisiting her dressing room afterward and suggesting we take a drive.

My phone buzzed in my pocket.

"We start filming in ten minutes," I told Donny dismissively.

"You think I don't know that? I organize your schedule, for Christ's sake."

"Then why are you calling?" I sighed.

"I got an email from the record label, and I figured that while I talk to you about their latest deal on the table, I'd encourage you to talk to the curly blonde girl as long as you want on stage tonight."

I felt tingles at the back of my neck. "Why would you want me to do that?"

"You told me you didn't want me to tell you if it wasn't about the music. Let's talk about the label's deal first—"

"Donny."

"Okay, the pre-air premiere was a massive success. People loved your connection with the country girl—"

"My connection?" I interrupted.

"You guys looked sweet on each other. A reality teenage love story. You put the star in her hand, told her to hold on to her dreams. It was a cute moment, and the public have been calling it a *connection*. Anyway, when some kids snapped photos of you together, the record label loved it."

"What photos?"

"Of you guys at the pier. It looked romantic. You were holding hands, taking in the sights. You looked like real boyfriend material, Jax. It caught me a little off guard."

"F*ck."

"Don't worry. This is great. People are loving it. The execs for the show think it's wonderful publicity, you guys being so close in age and all, and now that we're at the point in the competition where the public votes, we haven't got any liability. Plus, everyone loves a love story. Of course, they don't want you breaking up with her any time soon or having photos of you guys doing more than holding hands out in public. But it's creating buzz."

"It isn't like that," I explained to Donny, groaning. "We're friends. There's nothing to break up."

"Pretty country girl. Young rock star. She'll be half in love already. And boy, if you're trying to convince yourself you aren't interested, you need to take another look. She's gorgeous. I'm actually surprised you haven't seen the photos already. I figured you knew about them and didn't care. They've been circulating online all week."

"I've been busy."

"With the girl?"

"Don't sound so eager."

"The label wants to sit down and have us all sign your new contract now. There's a huge bonus on the table if we release an album with a couple of love songs. They think with this hype around the girl, the show, we put out some love songs and the public would eat it up. Every girl at home will think if they audition for *Superstardom*, they might be your future girlfriend."

"Donny, this isn't just my life—"

"Don't worry, the girl will benefit from this as well. The label has already agreed that if she doesn't win, with her parents' permission, they'll sign her anyway. You think she'll be willing to meet with me this weekend? I might give her a few days with her family before I reach out."

I groaned. "Donny, her mother is in South Carolina."

"Boy, the show has flown out her family and friends to watch her perform for the first time. They're right behind you somewhere in that audience. Apparently the best friend was already organizing his way to visit, trying to put flights and tickets to the show on a credit card, but after the reception of the audition and the public response to her being alone, the show intervened. They've got them all in that same hotel she's in. They've been keeping them separate though. Once she sings, the show will bring them on stage. It's a good PR move. They can film their relationship growing as her success does."

"Did you suggest the PR move?" I asked skeptically as I looked at the audience, trying to locate Billie's family amongst the rows of people. The idea that her mother was in the audience also made me want to check my hair and adjust my clothes. But there were too many people to work out which were there to cheer on my girl.

F*ck, why am I thinking of her as my girl?

"Look, it won't hurt you to talk to the girl. She's either going to be in the business or go back to living in her small town once her fifteen minutes are over. Give her a thrill and show everyone in the world that she's worth Jax Bone's time."

"She should know this is happening around her."

"Jax, I'm going to honest with you. She signed up to a damn reality television show, and she might have gone after you because she knew the public would invade her life and it would boost her ratings. It's the unspoken rule of television shows. Don't get so upstanding on me now. It's not like I'm asking you to marry the girl."

"Just go back to work and let me deal with the show."

"It's amazing to see you evolve in each performance. There's a control and power in your voice that is astounding for someone so young, but watching you play the piano in that dress, singing that enormous ballad? If anyone was doubting that you'd be able to sell out a stadium tour or handle thousands of people watching you, after tonight's performance that is no longer an issue. You were born to perform," Claudia praised.

"Vote. Everyone has to vote to keep her on our stage," Russell yelled, climbing on his chair and making the audience laugh. "I don't want to stop watching her. Three contestants go home tomorrow night, people, and she can't be one of them. You have to save this teenage singing sensation."

Billie stood there, her mouth gaping open and her gaze shifting back and forth from Russell's antics to a six-foot-tall guy with blond hair who stood in the audience, whistling and clapping enthusiastically.

She seemed bewildered.

I waited until she looked at me and smiled, visibly calming on stage before I told her what I thought of her first performance on live television.

The hush that filled the room when the audience realized I was about to speak to her even had the giant blond guy sitting back in his seat and observing our interaction. "People will remember you and watch that performance over and over again," I told her. "They won't only relate. They'll replay you singing that song when they're happy, when they're sad, and when they have nothing better to do, because what you created on that stage was pure magic. You might have joined a singing competition to see if you were good enough, or you might have joined this competition to start your career, but you'll leave having put a mark on this world that will never be erased."

Tears shone in her eyes, as she whispered, "Thank you." Then, as if she'd just remembered there were other judges at the table, she looked at Claudia and Russell and added, "All of you."

I almost cringed when Connor Graves walked on stage and wrapped his arm around her shoulders. He smiled at Billie like they were best friends before smiling at the audience and announcing, "Now I know we have the creative and unique Faith Randall up next, and we can't wait to see what she has in store for us. But before we do that, we have a small surprise for Billie here from the *Superstardom* team. And from how loud they were cheering at the end of the last number, she might already know what it is."

Billie looked back at the tall blond guy and the woman with straight brown hair who stood beside him. "You brought out my family," she said softly, smiling and letting that first tear fall.

"Well, we knew you were alone at your first audition, but we couldn't let you be alone out here in LA."

Her family were then invited on stage. The blond Adonis hugged Billie until her feet were dangling off the ground, causing her tears to dry up and her laughter to bounce around the auditorium. I tried to keep the smile on my face, knowing the camera would be trained on my reaction. Once Billie was back on her feet, her mother wiped away her tears and repeated, "You were phenomenal," before hugging her. Cindy then helped escort them back to their seats.

"Thank you so much for this," Billie shared with everyone. "I truly appreciate it, but I want to let people know I'm not alone out here."

The entire audience went "Aww," and Billie's eyebrows drew together.

"I just wanted to say that the cast and crew have been so welcoming. I've already made lifelong friends in this competition. Faith, who is up next; Michael, who selected this phenomenal gown; and the judges—" The crowd sighed again, making Billie's brows furrow. "It's like I have two families."

As the crowd began cheering, Connor turned to the camera and told everyone watching at home, "Well, you heard it here first, folks. You join this competition and you might start making a new family."

He knew how those words would be twisted in the media. I had no choice, texting Donny immediately. I didn't care what the cameras captured on my face.

Making a new family.

Those damn words.

They would start a whole new hysteria when accompanied with the photos that were already out in the public.

Connor Graves was a d*ck.

CHAPTER
TWELVE

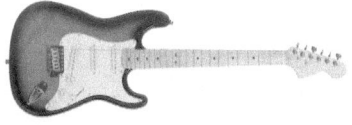

You won't be by yourself

Billie

"I can't believe you're really here," I told Zach and my mom in my small dressing room.

There was makeup haphazardly covering the table. My jeans and white shirt, inside out, hung over my chair. One of the personal assistants grabbed us two extra chairs so we could squeeze into the small space together. If it weren't for Faith's voice singing Lewis Capaldi's "Bruises" being broadcast through the speakers in every room, I would almost think we were back in my bedroom at home.

"I'm so glad we are," my momma murmured before reaching out and squeezing my hand. "I never imagined it could be like this. You even have your own dressing room. It's all so amazing. I'm so sorry I tried to convince you not to come. It was as if you were born to be on that stage. Ever since I saw your audition, I wanted to tell you how proud I am of you. How embarrassed I am over the things—"

"Momma, you don't need to say anything. You've spent your life trying to protect me. I knew you were just worried about me," I reassured her. Her words weren't something I needed to hear, not after feeling the joy of singing on stage. There was no reason why she should feel guilty for not understanding that feeling from the beginning.

But knowing she thought I belonged on that stage made me feel confident, powerful, *purposeful.*

"How long do you get to stay?" I asked. Momma had work and Zach had basketball, so I knew they wouldn't be able to be in the audience for every performance.

"I need to go back tomorrow morning. I'm so sorry I'll miss the first elimination night, but Cora's letting Zach stay for the next two weeks. She wishes she could have been here, but her boss wouldn't give her the time," my mom answered.

"But what about practice?" I asked Zach, confused.

"The season doesn't start for another month," Zach declared. "Coach understands, and Craig made captain, so it's not like I need to be at every practice."

"Zach, Craig made captain? I'm sorry—"

"B, I still get to play. I haven't been benched. And if it's between practicing and watching you crush the competition on television, I know where I would rather be. It was a good call. I've been distracted with you gone."

He had this look in his eye that practically screamed "Don't even try it."

There was a knock on my dressing room door. Cindy, the personal assistant who seemed to be everywhere these days, a blonde with a pixie haircut who I saw running around the set constantly, greeted me when I opened the door.

"I was sent to let you know that if you guys would like to get dinner together tonight, we no longer need Billie this evening."

I raised an eyebrow. "I thought I had to film the last segment when they remind everyone to vote for us."

"Connor is going to remind viewers about your family visiting. And because Russell already told the audience to vote for you, Linda doesn't want the other contestants to feel disadvantaged," Cindy stated apologetically, then brightened. "The show has offered to pay for your dinner."

"Sounds great," Zach replied. "We never turn down a free meal."

The waitress was acting strange, making this face when I asked for a refill or when Zach would lean in close to ask me a question. It was as if she smelled rotten eggs.

I decided to ignore her angry tone and the way she somehow managed to splash me with water every time she refilled Zach's and my momma's glasses. Maybe that was just how waitresses acted to out-of-towners in fancy Italian restaurants in LA.

I focused on enjoying this rare opportunity where my mother was sitting at the dinner table and not sending fancy leftovers out to Zach and me from the kitchen. I told her about Las Vegas and the lights that never stopped sparkling. I wanted her to feel like she was there at the pier at Santa Monica that blended the sea with the surreal. I even began talking about all the things I was learning about performing and the industry.

It took her only an hour before she was visiting the chef to praise him on his homemade pasta and ask for any recipes he'd be willing to share with a fan. You could take the chef out of the kitchen, but like Hansel and Gretel, she couldn't help but follow food wherever it may lead.

The moment she left, I turned to Zach and said, "I dare you to go home and make it in time for practice."

"Billie, don't do that," Zach replied, shaking his head at me. His green eyes stared into mine with disappointment.

"Two dares, Zachary. Every year. That's what we promised each other. I haven't used one this year, and we always agreed to follow through," I reminded him. "Even if we hate the dare."

"To help each other, B, not to keep each other away." He groaned, raking his fingers through his hair and reaching out to squeeze my hand. "Take it back."

"Zach, two weeks of missing practice and you're telling me Coach isn't going to bench you for the season? I don't believe it," I stated firmly. "You forget that I've been at nearly all your practices and games for the last three years. I've heard the warnings he's shouted to the team and to anyone who arrived late. No one is allowed to miss practice. Not freshmen, sophomores, juniors, and definitely not seniors."

"That's exactly why I need to be here. Billie, you've been to all of my games. You never missed the biggest moments of my life. Don't force me to miss out on yours. Once I'm back, he'll let me play. I'm sure of it. I'm talented, and I'm going to make it to the NBA. He won't risk the season because I missed a few practices. But even if he does, it'll be worth it. I won't try to get a scholarship to Duke at the expense of you." He seemed so determined.

"It won't be. I'm not going anywhere," I told him softly. "I'll be okay by myself."

"But you won't be by yourself. You're going to lean on Jax Bone when you need someone," Zach stated bluntly, then looked at me like I had never seen him look at me. It was as if I were hurting him.

I swallowed the feelings his pain provoked.

"I don't know what I'll do when you leave," I admitted. "I'll likely be too busy filming and rehearsing to see anyone."

"Too busy? Like you were too busy in Vegas? You'll lean on him, like you leaned on him when you were in Las Vegas and when you arrived in LA," Zach remarked loudly.

"H-How did you know about that?" I hissed, looking around the restaurant to determine if anyone overheard him.

"If it's meant to be a secret, you should know, B, you suck at keeping secrets. It's all over the internet," Zach told me. He pulled out his phone and showed me the photos of Jax and me walking along the pier holding hands. The photos were innocent but easily interpreted as something more. With the way I leaned in to Jax and the way he smiled down at me, if I didn't know we had spent an entire week together without even a casual touch between us, I too would think the couple in the photo were dating.

"I think the waitress is trying not to stab you with a fork due to jealousy," he mumbled.

"How long?" I tried asking, still staring at the photo of Jax smiling at me.

"How long what?"

"How long have people been sharing these photos?"

"Just this week. They came out shortly after the show aired," Zach answered. He reached for my hand and squeezed. "Let me stay. Let me be the person you lean on during this thing."

"We're just friends. It looks like it's more than it is in those photos, but none of this matters. My appearance on some television show or online isn't worth risking your future for mine," I replied, squeezing his hand in return.

Zach leaned over and lightly brushed his lips against mine. I froze. I barely breathed. "I've been meaning to tell you for a long time exactly how much you matter to me," Zach stated.

"What—" I had no idea what to say. We didn't kiss. Never. Not once in eighteen years. We weren't some Joey-loves-Dawson complicated friendship.

"I've also been meaning to kiss you," Zach told me.

Okay, maybe we are like some Joey-loves-Dawson complicated friendship. Holy sh*t.

My silence had him continuing. "But I actually wanted it to be near the lake or somewhere that if I started to kiss you, I wouldn't have to stop. And ideally, your mother wouldn't be so close by, and waitresses wouldn't be staring daggers at you because they think you're dating their dream man. I never wanted anyone else to be in the equation when I brought up the possibility of *us*, of being more than friends. I sort of hoped you would bring it up one day. Didn't you ever wonder why I never dated any of the girls at school?"

"Zach, I've never thought that—"

"I know. I know you. I never once thought you were scrawling 'Billie Montgomery' on your notebooks when I wasn't looking. But now I'm asking you to think about it. I was waiting for the right time, but I won't waste any more time, B. Not without saying that, to me, you're worth a hell of a lot more than a damn game." He squeezed my hand again. "Let me stay.

Let me cheer you on from the sidelines. I'm not asking for you to want to be with me yet, but let me stick around until you know what you do want. After you've thought about how good we would be together and how nothing in this world would be more important to me than the future we would make together. A lifetime of daring each other to be better people. That's my dream, Billie."

I could see it. The future we would have together. Zach supporting me through every aspect of my life. His reliability never faltering. His self-sacrificing nature keeping him from the dreams he didn't think were possible.

I took a deep breath and said, "Zach, I dare you to go home."

"You won't even think about it." He sighed, letting go of my hand and leaning back in his chair.

"I will," I corrected. "But not now. Not at the expense of the possibility of you making it to the NBA. As soon as I get home, we'll talk this through, how you feel and if it's worth pursuing."

"You just don't want to admit that you're picking Jax Bone over me."

"I'm not. I'm picking you over *me*."

Before I could continue explaining to Zach all the reasons why his hanging around wasn't in his best interest, my mom returned to the table gushing about the chef and recipes she'd collected.

Zach kept looking at me like I had stolen one of his kidneys, and I kept glaring back at him when Momma discussed going home.

I knew deep down that Zach would go home, no matter how much he argued against it. Because no matter how confused I was about him liking me, how unsure I was about myself when it came to singing or dating or what the future held, I knew Zach.

And he never backed down from a dare.

A representative from the show organized a car to take them to the airport the next morning. My mother fussed over me, hugging me and wishing me luck in my next live show. Repeating how disappointed she was that she wasn't able to stay for that evening's taping so she could be there when they called my name for the top seven contestants.

I shook my head. Nothing was set in stone.

"I might be seeing you tomorrow afternoon at home," I muttered.

She just laughed, kissed my cheek, and climbed into the car.

Zach and I stood awkwardly outside the hotel, trying to hide from my mother the conversation we'd had last night. I had no idea how she or Cora would react to the notion that Zach wanted to date me, but I knew this wasn't the time to find out. He gave me one long look before climbing into the black sedan, and I knew I wouldn't be getting text messages from him until I sent him one asking him to come back.

It hurt my heart.

We had never been at odds like this. If it wasn't for his own good, I would have backed down.

Faith stood beside me as reinforcement. I called her room last night knowing she would have seen the photos of Jax and me, and I wanted to fill her in on Zach's proclamation at dinner. As the car faded into the distance, she made jokes about the first world problems I was dealing with, choosing between a blond athletic hunk or a sex-on-a-stick rock idol.

It felt good to laugh, when a part of me was desperate to cry.

I crumpled the note I held in my hand that I figured Zach must have convinced a maid to leave on my dressing table this morning.

You will regret the things you've done.

I just wish he understood.

CHAPTER
THIRTEEN

It's just television

Jax

There were now new pictures circulating online. Billie's lips pressed against her best friend's in a glamorous Italian restaurant. It was taken and tweeted by some girl in one of my fan groups. #Jaxisstillsingle was now circulating amongst the press.

It shouldn't bother me. It should have been a relief.

It fixed the problem of Connor pathetically trying to have people believe I had impregnated Billie with our love child. It ensured the rumors around the photos of us holding hands were now being questioned.

No one was sure of anything anymore.

Donny was pissed. He spent hours ranting on the phone to me about how he didn't want headings about my return to the single life. He didn't want to read articles about a small-town country girl returning to her good-looking small-town boyfriend. He wanted everyone thinking that Billie and I were the next Hollywood sweethearts. He wanted to sell the fantasy of a rock star falling in love.

If I wasn't a little pissed thinking about Billie leaving the competition to go back with her small-town boyfriend, I would have laughed at his hysteria.

We were three weeks from signing the contract that included the additional love songs. He was on crisis management mode. I couldn't care less about recording love songs. Sure, I had a couple I had written since Las Vegas, but they didn't need to be recorded.

I kept telling myself those songs meant nothing to me.

I tried to remind Donny that this could be a good thing. I figured some of the contestants might want to sue me if they felt that I showed preferential treatment to Billie over them. He just reminded me that any lawsuit would be ludicrous, because it was the public that voted the winners through and not the judges, and talked about ways to convince the audience there was still something romantic between us. I eventually gave in to the idea of trying to promote a romance. I told myself it was because Billie needed to see what a rock star life could be like before she threw it all away for some small-town boy.

She was too talented.

She needed to know exactly what she was giving up.

I suggested that Donny float the idea that, after the elimination that evening, the top seven contestants have an opportunity to sing with the judges. Some of the other singing competitions I'd seen on television occasionally did it to promote the judges' latest album. And although *Superstardom* tended to solely focus on the contestants' talents, I knew Donny could convince Linda and the executive producers to mix it up this season.

The fact that Billie and I would be required to attend additional rehearsals together if we needed to perform a duet wasn't lost on Donny. Multiple opportunities for cameras and record labels to observe our interactions was just a part of the business.

And that was all this was.

Business.

I grabbed my guitar and car keys from my bedroom and was making my way toward the stairs when I heard my front door unlocking. There was only one other person who had keys to my house, and hearing them in the door had me pausing in the hallway and shaking my head. I forgot I had organized this, too distracted by staring at those damn photos each night.

Maybe I should hide.

"Jax!" my mother screeched from the entrance of my house. I heard the bags hit the floor and didn't need to see them to know they would be covering the entire entryway. She never traveled light. Only in the city for a few days to watch the taping of our next show and celebrate her birthday, yet she would have brought enough to live here for a few months.

I stared at her from the top of my staircase, wondering how I was going to manage her coming to the rehearsal and seeing Billie and me perform. And there would be no way I could convince her to stay here until I returned. Bambi Bone waited for no one.

She was a boisterous woman. Big hair, sequined tops, tight leather pants, and red lipstick. She was a total diva, even at fifty-five. An old-school LA groupie who refused to age gracefully, like she refused everything else expected of a woman her age. The widow of a starving musician, the mother to an overnight teenage success, she lived life unapologetically. If I asked her to tone it down for a red-carpet event or award ceremony, she would just give me a glare and, in the closest thing she had to a mother-like tone, lecture me that "Life is too short to not be yourself."

I walked down the stairs and straight into her arms. I was trained to not linger in a room without hugging her or else I'd be subjected to hours of outspoken chastising. Even if it meant my body reeked of her perfume for hours afterward.

"Hey, Mom, we should have rescheduled. I'm on my way to the set to rehearse right now," I told her when she finally finished hugging me. I hoped if I left fast enough, I might have a small chance of leaving alone.

"I know. Donny let me know I could go with you," she gushed. "He told me you're singing duets with three of the contestants. I don't think I've ever seen you sing a duet in person. I can't wait." The glint in her eyes revealed her hidden agenda.

"Of course he did." *After you hounding him because you had seen the photos circulating and wanted your own close-up look at the girl.*

The woman devoured gossip magazines like a dehydrated person drinking bottled water.

"The television people even sent me the paperwork so they can record me there. Isn't that exciting?"

I sighed. I knew what Donny wanted—video footage of Billie meeting my mother. Good or bad, he knew it would make good television.

"I don't suppose I could argue that this isn't 'bring your mom to work' day?"

"Well, seeing as you don't seem to get the memo when it's 'call your mom' day or 'visit your mother in Manhattan' day, I'm sure you'll recall later that this is definitely 'bring your mom to work' day."

"All right, let's get this over with." I chuckled. "I didn't really want to be a judge in the next season anyway."

"I promise, you'll barely notice I'm there," she tried to convince me as she grabbed her handbag and followed me to my car.

I gave her a pointed look.

"Okay, you'll probably notice, but I won't interrupt the singing."

I gave her another look of skepticism.

"Once, I promise I'll only interrupt once."

I grinned. "It certainly won't be the first time you've stolen the show."

"You know, that's exactly what your father used to say to me every time I went on stage with him," she replied wistfully.

The wound those words created stung, but I knew she sometimes forgot how I didn't talk about Dad casually. Only she liked to talk like he was just on an extended vacation.

"And just like him, you'll deal. Musicians always know how to regain the attention of the audience."

I didn't correct her. I didn't tell her that Dad never knew how to capture an audience's attention. If he did, I wouldn't be driving us to rehearsal. I would be in college, and he would be here with her. He wouldn't have been performing at dive bars where people got high, smashed into your car, and drove off, not realizing they left you unconscious and bleeding to death.

I just sighed and drove her to set, wondering how long it would take her to interrogate Billie.

It was going to be long day.

It was as if my mother stepped on set and transformed into a different woman. She didn't ask Billie any questions, just took one look at her, politely introduced herself, and then whispered to me that she was going to sit in the audience seats and watch.

I almost turned to the paramedics who were on set as a precaution to protect the contestants and asked them to examine her. Billie looked nervously where my mother watched silently before she quietly asked if we should get started.

I nodded, walking over to the stage manager. "Hey, Steve, do you have microphones we can use now?"

He looked surprised.

"Faith said that you played the piano first and decided who would sing each verse of the song before using the microphones," Billie informed me.

I turned to stare at her. She looked sweet. She was wearing light blue jeans and a light pink off-the-shoulder cardigan. I desperately wanted to bend over and kiss the part of her collarbone that was exposed.

Instead I was curt. "I don't rehearse all songs the same way. Tomorrow, I'll probably make Ryne practice in the street." I grabbed the microphone Steve held out to me and walking to the center of the stage.

Billie hesitated before grabbing hers and following me. I wondered if it was the photos and the headlines about us, the fact that my mother was staring at us, or the song that was making her appear nervous around me.

We were singing "Location" by Khalid. The show made a big deal about the judges drawing contestants and songs out of a hat for the camera. As far as the audience was concerned, it was fate that had the two of us singing a love song together this week. A higher power that encouraged us to profess our feelings through sexually charged verses.

I didn't tell Billie that I had been given explicit instructions to reach for the pieces of paper that were the smallest. I didn't reveal that the higher power included the director of the show and Donny. They had all the songs, the contestants I would sing with and even the staging planned.

We would have three backup singers clicking their fingers and echoing some of our lyrics during the live performance while a video montage of cars traveling from South Carolina to Los Angeles played behind us. It would be a big production, but the lyrics were still so intimate that I knew the best way to sell the song would be how Billie and I interacted on stage.

"We have to stand close together," I informed her softly. "Duets need to appear real, as if we have a relationship that we're letting the world in on."

"Okay," she murmured, moving until our microphone cords were almost touching.

"Do you know the lyrics to the song?" I asked curiously.

"All of them."

"Great. Rather than us divvy up the verses and choruses evenly, I thought it might be best if you start singing, and then I'll jump in when it feels natural. We go from there. You stop singing when you feel like it or jump back in when you do."

Billie nodded. She began the first verse smoothly, her eyes closed, her pitch perfect.

"You need to look at him!" my mother yelled from the stands. The band stopped playing. "Can't see what you're feeling with your eyes closed."

"Mom," I groaned from the stage.

"You know I'm right," she huffed.

Billie opened her eyes and laughed at me. Her shoulders dropped and she visibly relaxed for the first time since I'd walked on set. It was as if I was finally standing opposite the girl who spent a week alone with me hanging out in my home studio.

"You're right. I can do that," Billie called back to her from the stage.

I grinned at the shock on my mother's face.

Then Billie started the verse over again, this time looking into my eyes.

When I suggested we sing a duet, I thought it would be like when we sang a few songs together in the studio. Enough tension and sexuality to satisfy Donny, but not powerful enough to bring me to my knees in front of an audience.

I was wrong.

She was killing me, her big blue eyes and clear voice telling me that she needed only me. The lyrics, her tone, and her body so close to mine, it was like nothing I had ever experienced before. Carey Leigh and I performed one of my songs at the Grammys not two months ago, and nothing. Carey crooning at me was always a good show—there was a reason she was the princess of pop—but I never felt *this*.

I decided to start singing, coming in on the second verse. It was as if I was begging her not to lead me on.

I saw the understanding in her eyes. I watched her chest rise and fall dramatically. I wondered if she was having the same reaction to my singing as I had to hers. She stood frozen on stage, her mouth slightly parted, allowing me to sing the chorus to her without interruption.

When she began the third verse, it felt as if we were no longer singing the lyrics written by a stranger. We were discussing her best friend. I moved in time with the music, getting closer to Billie, and we started singing in unison. Our bodies swayed back and forth like we were on the cusp of performing a sexy tango. I watched her flinch each time I would sing the lyrics about wanting only her. During the last notes, she rocked into me, and I didn't move backward. She pressed against me, and I fin-ished the last line of the song holding on to her hip.

I was ready to rip her clothes off. Her lips parted. My head dipped down.

Steve yelled out, "You're moving too far stage right during the chorus."

It was as if the bubble we had erected around us shattered and we remembered we weren't alone. I let go of her, and her eyes widened as if she had seen too much.

My mom started cheering from the stands, and Billie blushed. We weren't singing without anyone watching, we were singing in front of my mother. And this would be nothing compared to Friday night's live performance.

I regretted the decision to suggest we sing a duet on national televi-sion. This could only get me into trouble.

I wasn't sure I wanted everyone to think I was in love with someone I still had to spend weeks judging.

And for some reason, it bothered me that I wasn't exactly sure what Billie wanted either. If she felt some sort of pressure about me.

My mother joined us on stage after we sang it through twice more. I had hoped that after we sang it over and over again, the feelings I felt when I heard her sing those words to me the first time would fade. But it was as if they got stronger as we went on. She sang them with more con-fidence each time, which made each lyric sound more real. More personal.

"That was amazing. I think I even got hot and bothered. Voters are going to love it," Mom said as she stood before us both.

"Mom—"

"Oh, don't be embarrassed. Sexual tension isn't something to be ashamed of, especially with a pretty girl."

"Uh, thank you, Bambi," Billie mumbled.

"Ignore her." I sighed. "It was just music, and my mother has a weird fetish for music."

"You're not wrong," my mom replied. "Although, after you perform

119

that song for everyone, they'll probably have a fetish too. Unless your poor lovesick fans don't want to imagine you with anyone else."

Billie's face went blank. I pretended I didn't notice.

"My fans will be fine. Everyone knows it's just television," I muttered before leaving my mother and Billie standing together while I went to speak with Steve about lighting.

Five hours later, I was done. We had everything the show had requested. We filmed our discussions by the piano and us chatting on the stage. The camera guys had at least two rehearsals of the songs from different angles to create a behind-the-scenes clip. I was leaving before they asked for anything else.

I couldn't sing that damn song one more time without giving in to the overwhelming urge to rip Billie's clothes off. I needed to leave before I turned this family-friendly show into something that should only air at 3:00 a.m. I needed at least two damn cold showers.

Luckily, Billie was swept up into another one-on-one interview and we didn't need to have an awkward goodbye. I grabbed my guitar, waved to the production crew, and made my escape.

I had forgotten my mother was even there until she came up beside me. "I like her," she said softly.

I snorted. "Everyone does."

"No. For you. I have a feeling she's a Gemini. She's got two different personalities: the lost small-town girl and the powerful rock star. You need both. And a Gemini matching with an Aries is perfect."

"Mom, please don't start with the star-sign bull. I'm tired. She's sweet and nice and a contestant. Don't make it into something more."

"My little boy, always the fire sign burning his own path and leading the way. You can call it bull, but she's going to follow you, my love."

"I'm her mentor. She's supposed to take my lead."

"She's also going to take your heart." My mother chuckled. "Now let's go get me some birthday cake."

I frowned as I followed my mother out of the studio and thought about the idea of Billie taking my heart.

It was crazy.

No one took anything from me.

Unless I decided to give it.

I was standing in my dressing room, getting ready for the live show. The costume department decided they wanted me to be dressed like myself for a change, so I was given jeans and a white shirt, and they insisted on the damn baseball cap. I figured it probably had something to do with the photos that were released of Billie and me on the pier. They wanted my disguise exposed to the world. It wouldn't surprise me if they put a pier on the screen behind us when we sang. Someone wanted to recreate that moment for the audience.

I was shocked that I missed the leathers.

A knock sounded on the door, and I called out, "Come in."

"That's good. You look great," Donny said when he waltzed in and lounged in the only chair in the room. I shook my head, not surprised in the least that Donny walked in and started acting like the star.

"What are you doing here? Why aren't you just calling me like usual?" I asked carefully.

"Your mother asked that I attend tonight," he informed me, staring at himself in the mirror and adjusting the pale blue tie he had carefully matched to his very expensive suit. "I never turn down a good-looking woman."

I inspected his receding hairline and his bulging belly that tried to escape the white button-up shirt he wore. "Not sure if you noticed over the years, Don, but my mother's got a type. And it isn't someone who can't sing and could be considered management material."

He laughed and stood up. "Jax, I'd never date a client's mother. I'm merely here to keep her company. Hold her hand if she needs it as her son performs on live television and judges contestant performances."

"And to be sure she doesn't storm the stage." I chuckled, remembering the last time I performed on live television with my mother in the audience.

"An added bonus." Donny shrugged before grinning at me. He then dropped the smile and, with a serious expression, asked, "Is tonight going to impress the label?"

"Donny, what are you really trying to ask?" I replied bluntly. "Or rather demand. Are you just in my dressing room to tell me to kiss the girl on camera? Grind my hips into her on national television?"

"Whatever works, Jax. The label needs to believe the public thinks it's real or there's a real chance we lose the deal on the table. If they don't, we've got to start thinking about how we go bigger."

"What's bigger than a duet? You want me to do a home visit with her next? Change this damn show from a singing competition into one of those dating shows where I propose at the end?" I smirked.

"That's not a bad idea," Donny murmured, his eyes lighting up. "The record label would likely double their bonus."

Sh*t.

"No, Donny. Just no."

"Think about it, Jax. We end the season with an engagement ring like those dating shows and it'll give us a platform to discuss three new albums. There's a reason those shows have higher ratings than this one," he replied excitedly.

There was a knock on the door. "Sorry to interrupt, but they're ready for you on stage," Cindy told us before looking down at her clipboard and heading to the next dressing room.

I closed the door and turned to Donny. "I was kidding," I stated slowly. "You told me all I had to do was be nice, and I'm being nice."

"And now the label wants to have a love story. Nice won't cut it. So, let's give them a silly love story. Just for the duration of the show. This is for your future, Jax, for the music. Don't forget that while worrying about some country girl's fifteen minutes of fame and hurt feelings."

"Proposing is going too far, Don. I won't do it. Not for a record deal."

"Then you better make this performance look *real* good."

"It *will* look good, and then I don't want to have this conversation again."

I got mic'd and made my way to the side of the stage. Billie was waiting for me dressed in black leather pants and a white tank top. Her lips were painted red, and her heels were covered in black spikes.

The costume department had turned her into a rock chick ready to seduce a rock star. I missed the pink cardigan they made her wear for the last elimination episode.

"You stealing my pants?" I teased when she looked my way.

"I—" Billie began before pausing and inspecting my ensemble. Her eyes landed on the Yankees baseball cap and then widened in distress. "You should change. I don't think you'd fit in my pants, but we could try...." She reached for her zipper, and I grabbed her hand.

"You look great. Keep your pants on." I winked trying to lighten the mood.

"They're stealing your disguise," she whispered furiously.

"It won't matter what I'm wearing tonight. They'll all be looking at you."

"Us. They'll be watching us for sure." She chewed her lip nervously. "I should have said something earlier, but there are photos—"

"I know," I said, rolling my eyes. "I should have figured the paparazzi would see through my disguise eventually."

"But, Jax, our rehearsals...." She took a deep breath. "They've been *intimate*. People will think the photos are something more."

I gazed into her eyes and replied honestly, "Singing usually shows what you're trying to hide. Can't be in the business and not risk your emotions for the world to see."

I watched her process my words, her blue eyes blinking slowly. She whispered, "We could try and tell people we rehearsed our facial expressions?"

I couldn't help but laugh. "No one will believe that. After this evening is over they'll have watched me sing with Faith and Ryne and noticed the difference."

Her brows furrowed. "I don't want you to risk your fangirls for me."

Her words leveled me. She wasn't worried about her performance or her chances at winning. She was concerned for me. My fans. My future.

I squeezed her hand. "They'll get over it. We don't tell them anything." I told her, smirking, "and they'll make up excuses in their heads to keep me their fantasy boyfriend."

"They do that?"

"Girls do. Guys won't. Which is good considering the guys who are after you will realize they have some competition."

She blushed and looked away. I stopped talking.

She slowly looked back at me. "Competition?"

"After this performance, I want the next photos of us to not leave any doubts in anyone's mind."

Her eyes widened. "You want people to take photos of us?"

"If it's what you want. If it means we'll see each other more. If it means I'll get a chance to kiss you again."

She didn't have time to verbalize her thoughts on the idea before Steve was telling us to get on stage and that the sound crew were turning our mics on in three minutes.

When the song started, Billie sang each lyric to me with more sex appeal than any of our rehearsals. She casually ran her hands over my body, and it took all my control not to kiss her in front of the audience. My lips had lingered very close to hers one too many times more than was necessary or rehearsed, but I couldn't control myself.

I completely forgot about the show Donny wanted.

All I could think about was whether or not she was ready for us to explore whatever *this* was. I was ready to lead us into something else.

And I could admit, whatever it was had nothing to do with the music.

Nothing to do with business.

It was all personal.

CHAPTER
FOURTEEN

A walking cliché

Billie

The dressing room door only partially muffled the sound of the producers, production crew and cast celebrating an amazing show. Word traveled fast that it had broken all the rating records. Tonight had been the most watched episode in all of *Superstardom* history. It was also clear from the bottles of alcohol floating around and looks of utter exhaustion on every crew member's face that the contestants weren't the only ones who had been stressed in the lead-up to the judges singing this week.

I contemplated going around and thanking everyone who helped me this evening. Most of them managed to say something supportive to me before I stepped on stage, even with all the added drama of the duets. However, I could hear Connor Graves boasting about how the duets had been his idea and how grateful he was for everyone making *his* dream a reality.

I didn't want to deal with that right now.

Instead, I spent longer than necessary removing my stage makeup and blocked out the world.

I also felt that I needed to get Jax out of my head first before I spoke to anyone else. I worried that if anyone asked me about my night, all I would do was talk about Jax Bone.

"If you want this, come to dinner with me and my mom. Sneak off with me after the show and everyone's gone home," he whispered when we left the stage. I barely had a chance to squeeze his hand and nod before his agent was there hugging him and pulling him into a whispered discussion about his next duet.

Now I wasn't sure if I was meant to meet him at my hotel, wait for him here, or get an Uber to his house. I was confused and apprehensive. *What does sneak off even mean?* My brows were drawn, and staring in the mirror, I noticed my blue eyes had turned stormy with distress. *What am I getting myself into?*

When a knock sounded at my dressing room door, I swallowed my fear. "Come in. I'm just taking my makeup off," I choked out.

"Cowboy Ryne and I decided to bring tequila and celebrate our duets," Faith squealed before perching herself on the makeup table and dramatically putting the bottle in front of me. "Sure, we could celebrate with the other contestants, but we're the lucky three who got to sing with the infamous Jax Bone. Let's have a little celebration with just us."

"Hope you don't mind," Ryne crooned, tilting his cowboy hat and reminding me of every Southern gentleman advertisement. No wonder half the female contestants had climbed into his bed already. I even heard some of the production crew were desperate to see how polite he could be. I watched him carefully as he put shot glasses in a row on my table. "And it's just Ryne. Only Faith here insists on adding the cowboy bit."

"That's what you think." Faith laughed before inspecting herself in my mirror and fixing her glasses.

"Is this a good idea?" I challenged while keeping one eye on the door. I had no clue what I would do if Jax suddenly burst in the room. "We're all underage and could get thrown off the show."

"We won't tell anyone if you don't," Ryne replied, flashing his dimples and reclining in the only empty seat in the room.

"Come on, Billie, a little tequila shot won't hurt you." Faith groaned and flopped across my table dramatically.

"My vocal cords and everyone in the world who has had tequila before might protest that fact." When Faith pouted, I relented. "Go on and pour the poison. Let's get this celebration done so I don't have to watch you pouting."

Faith laughed and Ryne grinned.

After we clinked our glasses together, I closed my eyes and swallowed the clear liquid as quickly as possible. I'd tasted tequila at a house party after last year's homecoming game, but it certainly wasn't my idea of a fun time. It burned.

"I meant to tell you that your Vegas audition was phenomenal," Ryne drawled as if he'd just sipped water. "I should have told you earlier, but we haven't really had a chance to speak."

"Been a little preoccupied with Whitney? Or is it Katie today?" I joked before I could stop myself. It was mortifying how quickly alcohol loosened my lips.

Thankfully he chuckled and shrugged. "What can I say? I'm attracted to talent."

"Well, don't waste your time getting attracted to this one. I believe she's already spoken for." Faith laughed.

"It was just a duet. It doesn't mean anything," I defensively replied.

"I was talking about your town-boy who you were caught kissing a few weeks ago, but I'm glad you're finally confessing that Jax is definitely on your lineup as well."

"Sounds like you're a little preoccupied yourself," Ryne teased.

I had no idea what I was going to say when they realized just how preoccupied.

When a knock sounded at my door, I flinched. Cindy, the personal assistant who seemed to be everyone's saving grace, popped her head in the door. "Hey, guys, noticed you brought the party in here and thought you might want to take it back to your rooms before the security guys come by in ten."

"Thanks, sweetie. We're done here anyway. Billie, we'll do coffee tomorrow," Faith replied, winking at me before making her exit.

"Thanks, Cin," Ryne drawled, kissing Cindy on the cheek and turning her olive complexion bright red before he nodded at me. "I better go too and congratulate *Katie* on her song tonight before Wade beats me to it."

It had me laughing, until I remembered what my plans were meant to be this evening.

As I made my exit an hour later, having not heard anything from Jax, I tried to think about what I might eat for dinner. I thought if I focused on food, I wouldn't feel the crushing disappointment.

I only made it two steps before I heard "Hey, Billie."

I turned my head to the right, and there was Jax waiting for me. He was standing next to a black Harley Davidson with a spare pink helmet under his arm and a small smile tugging at his lips.

Beautiful, dangerous, and every girl's fantasy come to life.

My nerves made my hands shake as I approached him. "You always have a spare pink helmet handy for when you leave set?"

"Why do you think it took me so long to get here? I had to go drive around until I found a place that sold one small enough for your head. I started to worry that you might have left without me."

"You're a walking cliché right now," I told him, stuffing my hands in my pockets when I finally stood within touching distance.

"The rock star on a motorcycle waiting at the curb for a pretty girl? That's a cliché I can deal with." He smirked. "Plus, as long as I'm all about safety, I'm sure you'll survive me riding my favorite toy."

My heart skipped a beat. *He better be talking about his bike.*

"I thought we were having dinner with your mother?"

"We are. She has her own motorcycle. She just left a moment a go so she could take the scenic route."

"She has her own motorcycle?"

"Donny always organizes one in LA for her to use."

"Your life confuses me, Jax Bone."

"As long as I'm not boring you." He chuckled before placing the helmet on my head and adjusting the chin strap for me.

"I can't imagine you would bore anyone," I murmured, staring into his eyes. Those dark chocolate eyes that reminded me of my sugar cravings. His eyes briefly drifted to my lips then back to my eyes and winked.

"You'd be surprised. Climb on and we'll see if we can catch up with Mom. Then I'll tell you all about how boring I can be."

I stared timidly at the motorcycle. "I'm not sure I agreed to get on this death trap."

"I promise I'll drive really slowly."

I took a deep breath and imagined Zach standing beside me, daring me to get on. Before I could chicken out, I adjusted my handbag to go across my body and reached for Jax's hand to help me straddle his favorite toy.

"You're lucky I'm wearing jeans."

"So no drugs? No broken hotel rooms? And you haven't been banned for life from Planet Hollywood?"

"Nope. Not me," Jax replied as he tried to steal some of my tortilla chips. He was lucky I wanted to hear more and didn't stab him with a fork. I was equally enthralled with dipping my chips in guacamole and the revelation that Jax's life wasn't the dangerous rock life the tabloids had made it out to be.

"They were all lies," his mother inserted while eating her burrito with gusto. "Now if they were reporting on my twenties, well, that would be another story."

Jax rolled his eyes.

"Even the stories of your Vegas exploits are lies?" I asked skeptically. "There were photos of you coming out of clubs."

"Okay, *most* of the stories were lies," Jax muttered sheepishly. "Sam's my best friend, and he takes it upon himself to use my stardom to get us into the best clubs in Vegas."

"But that didn't stop your roadies from calling you boring?" I replied, shocked.

"They never said it to my face, but no, not even my shenanigans in Vegas stopped them from saying it behind my back. Some of my guys toured with the Stones. It's hard to compete with rock legends."

"Why not fire the ones who complained?"

"And have them run to *TMZ* and inform all my fans that I'm a buzzkill and not the party man my songs suggest?"

"I see your point. Although, you'd probably have fewer problems with Platinum Music Group if everyone knew the truth," I said softly.

"How do you know I have problems with my record label?" Jax asked.

"Was it meant to be a secret? Everyone on and off the show gossips about it. Surely you knew there would be talk when Jax Bone, the face on the cover of every high-profile magazine and writer of the top ten songs on the Billboard charts, decided to give his time to a talent show?"

"Okay, yeah, maybe a little. I just hoped they thought it was because of the goodness in my heart," he muttered, rolling his eyes. I couldn't help but chuckle. "But unfortunately, the record label picks and chooses what gossip they listen to, so long as they can hold it over my head and try to control my latest album."

"And there will be more gossip tomorrow morning," Jax's mother stated, nodding toward an elderly woman who was sneakily taking photos of Jax and me using her cell phone above her menu. "It might not just be the record label that will want to control you both tomorrow. The show might put their two cents in as well."

"We don't care," Jax declared.

"We don't?" I whispered while glaring daggers at the woman and encouraging her to put her cell phone back in her purse. She continued to snap pictures clearly unfazed about being caught.

Jax leaned into me, making me forget about the woman in the corner as well as my first name.

He hooked his finger under my chin and kissed me. Holding it, he dared me to close my eyes and sink into him.

But lightning bolts zapped behind the skin where our lips met, and I couldn't close my eyes even if I had wanted to. They were locked on his.

"We don't," Jax repeated firmly when he moved his mouth an inch away from mine.

"Okay, then," I managed while trying not to swallow my tongue. He still didn't let go of my chin, and suddenly I was touching my lips with the tip of my tongue, preparing for another taste of Jax Bone.

"There is always some nosey old lady when we go out," Jax's mom muttered. "Jax here can't go anywhere without some paparazzo following him."

"It's part of the business I signed up for." Jax shrugged. "I can't really complain when half of their pictures help sell my albums or attract new fans."

"I'm not sure I'm ready for it," I reflected out loud. "Although, I might not make it much further in the competition, and then no one will care about me anymore. And in past years, the paparazzi have really only followed the super good-looking winners of the show. They might not even want to follow me and take my photo."

"She's kidding, right?" Bambi asked Jax as if I wasn't sitting at the same table.

He turned to her and, as I stared at him in shock, replied, "Sometimes she is super country, meaning she's ready to break my balls at a moment's notice with an imaginary loaded rifle. And sometimes she's so country she's naïve and innocent like a new lamb brought in for slaughter. It's part of her charm."

I raised a brow. "What are you guys talking about? If you're referring to me, you should know I'm no lamb. I wouldn't break your balls with a rifle when a hammer will do just fine."

Both Jax and his mother burst out laughing, and I wasn't sure if I should laugh with them or keep scowling.

"Little girl, you're the prettiest contestant *Superstardom* has ever had. If you think the flies with cameras aren't going to start buzzing around you, you better think again," Bambi told me softly. "But don't you fret. I think you'll take to this life like a duck to water. Speaking from experience, it's usually family and friends who have the harder time of it. We're not born for the spotlight like our talented kids."

"You think your friend is going to have problems if these and other new photos come out?" Jax asked me somewhat urgently.

I felt like his question was asking something else, so I decided to lay it all out there.

"Zach's going to have a problem with everything. And he's going to be hurt about photos of me with you. He left me a note before he returned home. I don't think anything I'm doing in LA is something he's going to be proud of now, but I hope in time he'll understand."

"What did the note say?" he growled, loud enough for even the snooping lady to hear. "He pissed because you wouldn't leave your chance in the music industry to follow him back to some small town?"

"No, not at all. He wanted to stay. He wanted to support me and be with me. But he has his own dreams, and I made him promise to put those dreams first. His note just said 'You'll regret the things you've done.' Look, I'm sure he was just being dramatic because his feelings were hurt. He probably wrote it straight after I asked him to leave. He was probably hoping it would change my mind and I'd say I need him."

"You won't regret anything." Jax looked directly into my eyes. "And you won't need anybody to make it in this music industry. If he thinks you're spending time with me because you need my help or I believe you can't do this on your own, he's wrong. He also clearly doesn't understand your talent. You're not like the contestants who keep needing us to tell them how to manage the stage and their pitch. You stand on that stage and everyone in the audience is under your spell."

My heart leaped at Jax's words, but I felt the need to defend my best friend's opinion of my talent. "He really does think I'm good enough to make it in the industry. I wouldn't be here if it weren't for his confidence. He also didn't say anything about you helping me through the competition when it should be him. Hell, he wrote the note with a red lipstick. I think he was just upset and reacting after our dinner."

His face went from enraged to confused in seconds.

"It was written in lipstick," he repeated, his brows furrowed.

"Yep, that doesn't say to me that he thought out what he was going to write and really believed it. Although, it doesn't mean it didn't hurt my feelings," I confessed.

"Does he usually write notes in red lipstick?" Jax asked slowly. He appeared lost in his own thoughts.

"No, but my mother was wearing red lipstick that night, so I figured he probably grabbed it from her purse after dinner." I shrugged. I thought it was time for a new topic. Jax's face had gotten hard, and I wanted us to go back to the moment when he was smiling at me and thinking of me as a lamb. "I'm thinking I could go for some ice cream after dinner. Is there a—"

"Did he sign it with his name?" Jax interrupted.

"No, but it's not like I upset people every night." I laughed nervously, feeling the tension Jax began to radiate.

"Billie, you're on a show thousands of people auditioned for, and that's enough to upset some people. And you've been photographed with me, and I've received a few notes in red lipstick since I became a popular musician. They were never from friends or family."

"You've also never told your best friend since birth that you don't want them to spend time with you after they've kissed you for the first time," I replied, rolling my eyes. "I doubt you've had to deal with that issue."

"You're sure he sent you that note?" Jax asked firmly. "After he begged to stay and support you? You truly believe it was him and no one else?"

"Well, there's a small chance someone else could have written it, but I really do everything in my power not to piss people off."

"Have you gotten any other notes?" Jax asked, his voice going eerily quiet. "Usually when a crazy fan leaves one note and gets away with it, they tend to leave another."

"The only other notes I've received since arriving in L.A are the ones from you." I smiled.

"What do you mean, the ones from me?" He gripped the table tightly.

"The notes you left me in the hotel room," I said hesitantly. "After our week together when I got to LA."

Jax looked to his mom, who watched us both with fear in her eyes. He exhaled slowly. "Billie, I haven't sent you any notes. And in this business, you don't need to do anything specific to have some crazy fan after you. Hell, this might be one of *my* crazy fans. We need to call Donny. Now."

The hairs on my arms stood on end.

"Precious, like it or not, you're a celebrity now," Bambi began while squeezing my hand. "And Jax is right, there are plenty of people in this world who like to come after those who look like they have everything they ever wanted. It's best to leave it to the professionals like Donny to work out how to handle them."

"Will I need to hire him? I don't have any money, Jax. I know that's not something we've really spoken about before, but I couldn't afford to hire him. And if I need security, I can't afford that either." My hands shook. I couldn't handle this. This was never a part of my daydreams.

"Billie, I pay Donny enough that if I asked him to build you a house free of charge, he would do it, and the security can be charged to the show if we need it. You don't need to worry about the cost. We just need to keep you safe."

CHAPTER
FIFTEEN

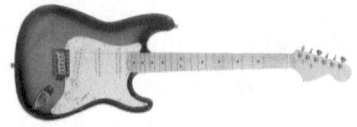

She can't be kept in the basement

Jax

'd planned on taking Billie to my favorite lookout after dinner. I wanted
to show her the way the traffic lights of downtown Los Angeles shined.
I intended to convince her to slow dance with me before kissing her
deeply. I was going to pretend to be a huge romantic idiot, hoping it
would lead us back to my place. We would spend the rest of the night sitting on the couch together with our legs tangled, my hands in her thick
curls, and really great music playing softly in the background. The competition and her hometown best friend would be mere memories.

I never imagined that Billie and I would end up back at my house
with Donny, two executive producers from the show, one record label
representative, three security guards, and my mother handing out coffee
and snacks. The lights of downtown Los Angeles were completely forgotten. The executives and security who were scattered around holding cups
of coffee and paperwork kept making me want to fidget and run for the
hills. All I had to do was force myself to keep looking at the scene everyone created in my living room and let the frustration and anger I had for
the person who ruined my plans keep me from my flight impulses.

I tried to ignore the hushed argument between the producers, the record label guy, and Donny about who was liable for trying to make my relationship with Billie public. I didn't let myself think about the amount of time the hired guards spent inspecting my security system and every bedroom window. When I heard discussions about identifying the differences between stalkers, fanatics of the show, and my superfans, I ensured my face appeared relaxed when my insides felt as if they were boiling and about to explode.

"Should we call the police?" Billie asked me when I stood in front of her. She was chewing on her lips and hugging her arms tightly against her body. She had curled up on the couch when I first opened my doors to all the people currently standing in the room, and she hadn't moved since.

I sat down beside her. "If that would make you feel safer, we can."

"No need to involve the cops," Donny told us as he sipped from the cold coffee cup my mother handed him hours earlier. He turned into his best car salesman's persona, unaware that sweat marks on his shirt revealed how he really felt about this situation. "They would just waste our time with warnings. Brian and Corey are the best in the business."

"The police would just make this much more difficult. Plus, more people would just mean greater chances of leaked information," one of the producers said before excusing himself to take a phone call.

"She shouldn't stay in the rooms upstairs. Too many windows and access points for intruders," Brian, the larger of the two security guards, said after he rejoined us in the living room.

"All of Jax's rooms have floor-to-ceiling windows," my mother stated. "Even the ones downstairs."

"The studio doesn't have windows," Donny countered.

"She can't be kept in the basement," I groaned.

"I can go back to the hotel. There aren't that many windows, and with the guards watching me—" Billie started.

"You aren't going back to the hotel," I stated matter-of-factly. "We already know the a**hole can get inside your room. For all we know they're still f*cking in it." When her face turned white, I wanted to hit myself.

"Maybe I should just go home to my momma," she whispered softly.

"No, my dear, you definitely don't need to do that," the remaining producer told Billie calmly. "You will be perfectly safe in your room." He turned to face me. "The show would never put her at risk. Linda has re-assured me that we can change things up, keep her around some of the other contestants."

"If she goes back to the hotel, I'll stop doing the show," I declared, then turned and looked directly into Donny's eyes. I knew he understood that I was completely serious about the threat, contract or any lawsuit that followed be damned. "She stays here or she goes home. My master bedroom's windows are bulletproof to protect me from stalkers. She'll sleep there."

One of the producers cleared his throat and adjusted his tie. "No need to make threats. We're all on the same side here. If the girl feels safe here, there's no need to have her return to the contestant accommodation."

I almost laughed. I knew the ratings were too important for them to let her leave or put an end to our chemistry on screen.

"We keep Corey and Brian with her at all times," Donny informed everyone. "She can stay here with Jax in the master, and they'll set up in this room as their base of operations until the person doing this is caught."

"If I get another note—" Billie began, sounding frightened and confused.

"You won't be getting another note," I cut in adamantly. "That sh*t stops now."

Everyone slowly made their way to the exit as the soft light of day dawned. They kissed Billie's cheek, wished her well, and pressed their cell phones to their ears as they walked through the front door. The producers were still chatting with Linda and making plans for additional security during rehearsals as they made their farewells. And Donny walked out drinking his fifth cup of coffee while ensuring all mail for contestants was now re-directed through his office and every room was swept prior to our arrival.

My mom decided to get a hotel room to give us some space but let me know in no uncertain terms that until she knew her only son was safe, she would be remaining in town. I hugged her, then reminded her that no one had threatened me, but if she felt she needed to stay, I would cover the costs. Her eyes shifted to Billie stock-still on the couch and she hugged me tighter. "Take care of her," she whispered, and I nodded.

I watched Billie's eyes follow my mom's exit and then return to Donny's ex-Marine Brian setting up a makeshift office in my living room. She appeared frozen, flinching only when he laid out a new weapon on the coffee table like they were books and a nightlight.

When I approached her, she began fidgeting with her necklace, and I thought about the rope I wished I could wrap around the neck of the person who made her look so lost.

"Let's go upstairs. Get some sleep before you need to get to rehearsal," I encouraged quietly while squeezing her hand. She kept staring at Brian. "Babe, come with me. I got you."

That time she squeezed my hand back, reached for her purse, and gradually got to her feet.

"I'm not sure I want to be in your room by myself," she told me shyly as we began walking up the stairs. She didn't look at me, just continued staring at her feet.

I paused us on the staircase and squeezed her hand until she looked me in the eyes.

"I wasn't taking you to my room to leave you there by yourself," I replied. "I don't want you out of my sight. We're going to my room. We'll both stay dressed. This isn't me making a move—"

Before I could finish my sentence, she rose on her toes and brushed her lips against mine. "I wouldn't mind the distraction," she murmured. "I think I'm ready."

I figured from the slight tremor of her hand that she wasn't telling me she was ready for bed. "Billie, I want you to know there isn't a moment with you that I don't want to press my body against yours and kiss you until you can't catch your breath. Every rehearsal, every performance, every smile—it takes every ounce of my self-control not to reach for you. Tonight though, I'm exhausted, and even though you say you want a distraction, I won't have us being together be something else you need to worry about tomorrow morning. Hell, I'm starting to think I might not be ready until this whole show is over and I know you really want to be with me. So tonight we're just cuddling."

"Cuddling?"

"Yep."

"Jax Bone cuddles?"

"Even better than I write songs."

She laughed and the anger I'd been holding on to disappeared. I also remembered why I needed all my self-control around her. "Don't get me wrong, there will be a time when I want us to do more than cuddle. We will share a bed, I'll make a move, and nothing else will be on your mind except how it feels when I run my hands over your body," I told her, letting her see the heat I had inside me before I locked it down.

"Okay," she murmured, her breath hitching. After a minute passed with us both just standing still staring at each other, she squeezed my hand. When we moved, she led me up the stairs.

I noticed Billie was the first woman I had ever invited into my bedroom who didn't gush about the view or the size of the room. She ignored the famous artwork, the marble fireplace, and all the expensive features the interior decorator insisted would get my place in *Architectural Digest*. She simply walked directly to the two plush green chairs Donny had given me as a housewarming gift, hanging her jacket over the back of one before placing her purse on the other. I watched her slip off her shoes and walk to my bed without so much as a hiccup.

"Did you want one of my T-shirts?" I offered. "It might be more comfortable to sleep in than your jeans."

She nodded, and I pulled off the shirt I was wearing and threw it at her. She laughed and rolled her eyes at me. "I thought you said we were both going to be dressed. If I'm wearing your shirt, what are you wearing to bed?"

"My boxers, which is me dressing for bed. Should I have mentioned that earlier?"

She rolled her eyes again and simply turned her back to me to undress. I decided to give her privacy and turned my back while stripping off my pants.

When I turned back around, I saw she had climbed into my California king bed, her blonde curls spread out across my white sheets. I couldn't move fast enough. The moment I lifted the blankets over my body, Billie turned to her side and pressed her body against mine.

"Where do you think Brian and Corey will sleep tonight?" she asked when I wrapped my arms around her. "Will they fit on the couch?"

"As long as it's not at our door, I don't care," I said, pulling her closer and smelling her hair.

"Do you think they'll try and check on me during the night?" She shuddered.

"I doubt they'll feel compelled to do that knowing you're with me."

"Jax Bone, my protector. I never would have imagined." She chuckled before closing her eyes.

It took an hour, but I finally felt her body go limp with sleep while I replayed her words again and again in my head. I never would have thought of myself as a protector either. Yet feeling the weight of her body pressing against mine, the utter faith she had in me to keep her safe, I knew it would be a cold day in Hell before I let something happen to her.

The alarm on my phone beeped incessantly, and I felt her stir in my arms. I tried to turn the damn thing off without jostling her or letting her go.

Unfortunately, her eyes began to flutter open. I nearly looked away.

I didn't want to seem messed up watching her sleep. I also didn't want to remind her of the night before with the circles under my eyes first thing in the morning. But the temptation to see those big beautiful eyes opening was too hard to ignore and I couldn't look away. A small smile graced her lips, and I just wanted to savor it.

"I'd ask how you slept, but considering we only went to bed three hours ago, it probably goes without saying," I stated softly.

"Actually, I'm surprised how deeply I slept. I wasn't scared at all," she told me, sleep still coating her words. "I probably look like crap though."

"You don't, but I'm sure everyone would understand if you wanted to take the day off." I brushed my lips across her forehead. "I can call the producers or Donny and tell them you changed your mind. No rehearsals or interviews."

"And have Connor tell all the other contestants how the only work I put into winning *Superstardom* is on my back again? I think not."

"He say that crap to you before?" I growled.

"Not to me, but Faith told me she'd heard him saying things to the crew and to some of the other male contestants. I've also seen him treat everyone like they're all here to promote him or be his personal slave. I'm lucky really, he basically keeps three feet away from me whenever I walk into a room. But the distance doesn't mean I haven't noticed that he's kind of a jerk."

"There's nothing 'kind of' about him. He's a total jerk," I muttered.

"You don't think he's the one sending me notes, do you?" she asked seriously, her eyebrows furrowing.

"I'm not going to lie and say he's harmless. But there is an intelligence in getting in and out of someone's room without anyone noticing them, which I'm pretty certain he lacks." I sighed.

"Is that a second alarm?" Billie asked when she heard louder, more annoying beeping noises start from my phone.

"Yep, in case I sleep through the first." I shrugged.

"How often does that happen?" Her lips twitched with a smile.

"Enough for me to need two more alarms after this one."

142

Billie laughed. "We should probably get up, then."

Before she could climb out of bed, I pulled her in tight to my body. She smelled so good, the perfect mix of jasmine and something so uniquely Billie. "Just two more minutes," I whispered into her hair. "I like you in my bed."

I felt Billie's body melt into mine. When she turned her face to me, tempting me with a knowing smile, I couldn't help but lean forward and softly brush my lips across hers. I heard her breath catch and waited for her to say something. Her eyes widened, and I could have sworn there was an invitation in them. I wasn't sure I could be the better person now that we were warm and tangled together in my bed.

I pressed my body tighter to hers. She leaned forward until we could feel every inch of each other.

My third alarm erupted from my phone, making us both flinch.

"I think we need to get up," Billie groaned. "That's the third alarm."

"All right," I grumbled. "But I need you to get out first and give me a couple of minutes."

She giggled and winked at me before climbing out of bed.

CHAPTER
SIXTEEN

Sluts from the South

Billie

It was clear that Jax hadn't slept at all. He was moving sluggishly, and when he thought I wasn't looking, he yawned. The only time he didn't appear like he was going to pass out where he stood was when his eyes would capture mine and then quickly drift to the Marine team to check they were standing guard. He was exhausted, but his fear kept him alert and on edge. I felt it too.

Since I heard the word "stalker," my body had shut down. The only time I felt my mind clear and function again was when Jax looked at me with emotions swirling in his eyes. When they left mine, I wasn't sure I could move. I felt myself yawn and my eyelids grow heavy, but then I would look out the window and would be jolted awake.

I stared out into the city, and it was as if I could feel eyes on me. Greasy, vile, disgusting eyes that made my body prickle in defense. Jax offered to make me breakfast, but I assured him I wasn't hungry. I worried that if I ate anything, it would come right back up again when I was forced to look out the window.

I just wanted to go to rehearsal, hide in my dressing room, practice the song I needed to sing at our next live recording, and then sleep again.

I suggested we catch a lift to get to the studio, but Brian insisted that transportation to the studio was his and Corey's responsibility.

I reminded Brian that I would need to go to my hotel room for a new set of clothes before we went to the studio, and I could feel Jax's body recoil beside me.

"You don't need to go back there," Jax reassured me. "We can just swing by the stores and grab you something. I'll buy it."

"Jax, I'm not Julia Roberts, and this isn't *Pretty Woman*. You can't take me to Rodeo Drive before rehearsal."

"If that's meant to be some movie reference thing, I haven't seen it. Not a lot of time to watch movies when you're touring around the world. And I was thinking more along the lines of Gap or Target than Rodeo Drive, but if it means we don't need to go back to that damn hotel, I don't care where we go."

"How could you have never seen *Pretty Woman*? It's a classic. Rich guy meets a prostitute and falls madly in love."

"Sounds like a chick flick." Jax chuckled as we climbed into the car.

"It is. The best chick flick of all time," I muttered, getting in beside him.

"Who did the soundtrack?" He looked interested.

"How would I know?"

"If it's a classic, it's probably someone good," Jax muttered to himself. "Maybe we'll watch it tonight."

"For the soundtrack?" I asked, shocked.

"Yeah."

"Jax Bone, I can't believe I had started to think of you as a normal nineteen-year-old."

"You're the one who wants to go to Rodeo Drive before rehearsal."

"Target will be fine," I returned, relieved to find the windows tinted in the Marine team's vehicle. "I just want to get to the studio."

I had barely climbed out of the black sedan when Faith came running up to me. "Did you hear? They're doing a mass elimination during the next live show."

"What?"

"We all got this message at the hotel this morning over breakfast that due to unforeseen circumstances, they need to speed up the production."

When she said those words, my eyes caught Jax's. I didn't need his shrug to confirm this was because of me.

Faith kept explaining as we walked from the parking lot to the studio. "Instead of two people being eliminated to determine the top five, they told us they'll be eliminating four people in the next episode. We'll start preparing for our two finale songs, but unless we're in the top three, we all might have done our last song for the show. These rehearsals are just in case we get chosen." Faith's eyes began filling with tears.

"It's okay. You were wonderful in your duet. And I think as nice as the others are, they haven't been crowd favorites. I can't even remember Wade's or Joshua's backstories, and I haven't seen anyone screaming their names or holding signs. I truly believe you'll be in the top three. Maybe the producers feel the same," I tried reassuring her. "Hopefully they think the ratings from the duets showed who people really want to watch, and if they build from that momentum, it'll result in more people voting for the finale, so they're moving it forward." I really did hope that maybe that was the reason and it wasn't all because of me and my safety.

"I just wanted to sing a little more in front of the larger audiences. I know I can't really compete with yours or Cowboy Ryne's star power, and they've never chosen a curvy girl as their star before. I'll likely end up singing at people's weddings and coffee shops, but I wanted this to last a little longer, you know?" Faith hiccupped.

"Faith, you're being crazy. You have as much star power as us. There is no way that after this is over, some big studio producer isn't going to want to sign you and help you make your first album. Your original songs are phenomenal," I stated as we walked through the front doors of *Superstardom's* current set.

"I know you girls probably don't want me in this conversation, but Billie is right, Faith. Studio executives will be contacting you as soon as this is over. Hell, the only reason they don't reach out during the show is they know the contract you signed to participate prevents you from signing a deal with them until after the finale," Jax told us, shrugging.

As if his voice was a beacon of light, suddenly three interns and assistants popped out of offices to give him notes on the day. The security team, who had been hanging back, stepped closer because of the new people.

Faith kept blinking at Jax as if she had never seen him before, unaware of my new protection. "Thank you," she replied before Jax tipped his head and turned to speak to all of the people demanding his attention. "Jax Bone just spoke to me like we're friends," she hissed under her breath as we started walking toward our dressing rooms. "He didn't even speak to me like that while we were rehearsing."

I whispered back, "He's actually a nice guy. If you want, maybe you can hang with us next time we go out. I think you might get along."

"I doubt Jax Bone will want me to intrude on your dates," Faith muttered. "We've all seen the latest photos. The boy is all about you."

"Those photos are already out?" I groaned. "That old lady is such a cow."

She raised her eyebrows. "Of course they're already online. I'm sure the photographer, cow or not, got quite the payday."

"How bad are they?" Maybe the angle or the lighting wasn't great and no one could really see anything.

"Your lips are touching in a romantic little Mexican restaurant, in front of Jax's mother. The headlines are all about how his mother approves of your relationship. You might as well be wearing white and a veil. His fans are going crazy. You look hot though. Your hair was a little messy, like you'd both just gotten out of bed together."

"That was motorcycle hair, not bed hair." I rolled my eyes. "So they've completely forgotten about the photos of Zach and me kissing, then?"

"Oh no. They just keep putting both kissing photos up side by side in their articles. I do believe they're trying to slut shame you, my friend."

"It's been a busy competition for me, then." I laughed, then realized I was both stalked and a slut in twenty-four hours. My smile vanished.

"And it's only going to get busier with mass eliminations, so if you're going to keep your love triangle up, you might want to start blocking out some alone time with your favorite rock star and best friend forever," Faith told me cheerfully, oblivious to the current emotions swirling inside of me.

"I think at this point in time, Jax is happier with me surrounding myself with friends," I replied, looking at Brian and Corey standing stoically behind me against the wall. Close enough to grab me, but far enough not to have anyone ask any questions. "And I'm ready to just lose myself in the music and rehearsal."

"Well, sorry to be the continual bearer of bad news, but we won't be rehearsing today. We're all trying on our potential getups for the pre-finale voting and grand finale show. Apparently due to the shorter schedule, all seven of us will be measured and consult with Michael in the same room. And as sad as I am about not having at least one more week before they decide on a top three, I am excited to check out the competition in their finale outfits before the live taping. I've hated how my last two live show outfits were practically identical to Whitney's except how my body is completely different, so I end up looking awful in comparison."

"People are comparing your songs, not your outfits."

"There you go again with your naivety. It actually makes me smile. How do you stay this sweet while hanging out with the rule-breaking Jax Bone?" Faith teased.

"Well, keep watching, because I'm not sure how sweet I'll be able to stay having to undress in a room full of people who know I'm kissing the judge."

"Oh, I didn't think of it that way. Maybe they'll have curtains separating us?" Faith suggested, linking her arm with mine.

I just took a deep breath and prayed for calm.

There were no curtains. Racks of clothes stood between each contestant as makeshift room dividers, but the rows of evening gowns and tuxedos wouldn't block anyone's prying eyes.

As I walked in the door, I felt the contempt pulsating from not only the other contestants but the seamstresses, production assistants, and interns who filled the room. Not even the expensive designer accessories were distracting anyone from my entrance. And from the grimaces, rolled eyes, and hard glares, I became very aware that the tabloids had everyone believing my desire to win this show had surpassed my morals and integrity.

When Michael approached me with a huge smile on his face, some of the tension I was feeling slipped away. "I've got the most fabulous ideas for your next few shows," he informed me. His man bun remained motionless even as his body moved in circles around me and took me in from head to toe. When he finally led me to my assigned podium and encouraged me to stand on it, I tried to pretend we were the only ones in the room.

"I'm interested to see what you think might work for the finale," I asked, ignoring the whispers.

"It looks like you've lost a little weight since the first few shows," Michael murmured, truly oblivious to our audience as he inspected my body closely.

"Stress," I explained.

"Yes, that usually happens every season. It won't matter. We'll measure you again and ensure your next few pieces are showstoppers that fit right." He started to pull dresses and shirts from the racks, passing them to random interns and assistants who seemed to pop up and then vanish at a moment's notice. "These will no longer do."

A blonde seamstress came over and, without saying a word, began measuring my shoulders and hips. I tried to focus on her movements and Michael, but the sound of Ryne laughing and Faith squealing over a jacket had me looking at the other contestants instead.

I could see Katie and Whitney both wearing short black dresses while blatantly staring at Ryne as he began removing his Levi jeans to try on a ridiculous white rhinestone tuxedo with a matching cowboy hat. He was almost down to just his Calvin Klein briefs when the interns started to hand the girls new dresses. They both reluctantly turned their heads away.

However, before they could become completely focused on their own looks, Whitney noticed my eyes on her and sneered. "Have a fun night?" she asked as she unzipped her dress and slipped it off her shoulders, knowing I could see her entire body, the black sheer lingerie she was wearing not really concealing anything. "You know, I'm used to being the most hated woman around. I'm not afraid to take what I want, be confident of my talent, and feel like I belong around other talented people. But, girl, maybe when you win this thing, you'll be able to teach me a thing or two, because it never even occurred to me to lie on my back to get into the finale. Don't get me wrong, I love to get laid, and if Jax Bone himself had shown interest, maybe I would have taken a bite. But I would have taken that bite *after* I won this thing. I guess I'm still learning."

"I thought I heard you tell Connor in your last interview that you've already learned everything there is to know about the music industry from your famous Grand Ole Opry-singing grandfather. Or was it your pop star mother?" Faith mocked as she came up beside me wearing a leather jacket with a white T-shirt dress underneath. "If only we all could have come out of musically gifted vaginas. Or sit on those fancy Opry seats."

"And I do believe I heard you tell him in an interview that you felt like none of our performances had any soul," I recalled. "I guess if we haven't seen it done since childbirth, the only way I could win is through sleeping to the top."

"Don't forget the last elimination when she told the audience her grandfather was suffering from cancer and she hoped he could see her make it in the industry on her own before it was too late," Ryne added, striding up to flank my other side. "For a man so ill, I was surprised to see him backstage after the duets taking shots and laughing with the producers."

As soon as Ryne stopped talking, Whitney's cheeks filled with color and she turned back to her rack of clothes as if we were dirt beneath her boots. Wade and Joshua were both busting a gut laughing, and I suddenly wished I had spoken to them more. I smiled at them before they both turned away with uncertainty in their eyes.

"Thanks," I whispered, looking at Faith and Ryne, wondering if this was when I should ask if either of them had lingering resentment toward me.

"We sluts from the South need to stick together," Ryne teased before I could say anything. He then winked at me and walked back to the interns holding a new pair of jeans.

"He seemed completely unfazed by the photographs," I stated, shocked.

"Don't even sweat it," Faith murmured as her intern tried to wave her back to her own pedestal. "Those of us smart enough to listen to one another's auditions know you don't need to sleep with anyone to win this thing. You good here without me?"

"I think I can handle them by myself now," I told her. "But the backup was sure appreciated."

When she returned to her own area, I noticed Michael staring at me. "You're going to survive this industry. I worried when I first met you, but if you can deal with this drama, you'll be able to deal with the rest."

"Don't get too excited. It might be my last show this week." I reminded him. "Then I'll just go back to being a nobody."

"Girl, you're not stupid. I'm not wasting any breath on discussing whether or not you'll be chosen to go on to the finale. We have better things to talk about, like chiffon, leather, and rhinestones." Michael laughed.

Before I could ask if that would be all on one dress, Connor Graves strutted into the room like he was ready for his close-up, whistling through his teeth. Michael draped a robe over my shoulders, and I sighed in relief.

"Mr. Graves, why do I have the pleasure of your presence at this time?" Michael asked with an eyebrow lifted. "I do believe the producers stated that you refuse to work with me and only employ your own stylist because you described my talents as 'mainstream mediocre'?"

"I'm here to interview the contestants, Michael. Let's not get our panties in a twist over our different roles here," Connor replied, rolling his eyes.

"You plan on filming the contestants in their undergarments?" Michael chuckled. "I highly doubt the studio plans to change their television time slot to make that appropriate viewing for families."

"I received an email, so here I am. Talk to the brass if you're uncomfortable with your artistic process being documented."

"And where are your cameramen, then? Surely you won't be doing this on your cell phone?" Michael asked, looking over Connor's shoulder.

"They aren't already here?" Connor looked up and down the fitting room in shock. "Well, undoubtedly they'll be here any minute."

"Feel free to wait to the side until they arrive, then, but I have work to do."

As soon as Michael turned his back and all the other assistants resumed their jobs, Connor huffed, tapped his foot, and stated, "This is ridiculous," then stormed out of the room.

Michael returned to me with a big smile on his face. "Now that the blond troll is gone, where were we?"

"You were about to tell me if you planned to put me in a version of Jax's leather pants again," I teased.

"You know, stealing Jax's ensemble for the duet wasn't my idea. That stroke of genius came from above, but I supported it because you looked phenomenal. But we're going back to basic b*tch for the elimination. Then my plan is to blow everyone away for your final song and then let the lights shine for your grand finale number," Michael told me with glee.

"Okay, then. Show me, what does a basic b*tch wear?"

I could hear the audience cheering and stomping for the next contestant to grace the stage and find out if they were going home. With each vibration from the crowd, the pink frills of my dress fluttered around me. I tried not to grind my teeth.

"You look like you belong on top of a cake," Faith told me, giggling as she stood behind me in a silver sequined jumpsuit and black leather jacket. "Or maybe attending your first prom."

"Michael told me it'll look good under the lights," I attempted to say without annoyance coating each word. "And at least I don't look like I'm about to break into disco dancing."

"You wish you could wear this." She laughed.

I didn't bother replying because she wasn't wrong. I decided once this competition was over, I needed to learn how to stand up to my fun, passionate stylists. Even if they were so excited about their vision and I felt bad over the things idiot hosts called their talent that I forgot that I was the one who had to wear their choices in front of strangers.

I was now stuck in a pink ruffled strapless cocktail dress monstrosity for the next four hours. It was also really itchy. I kept wanting to run my fingers over my skin everywhere the fabric rubbed against my body. I had been wearing the outfit for over two hours already, and it seemed to only be getting worse. At least they had slicked back my hair in a straight ponytail. I hoped that at least the dramatic hairstyle change would have everyone focusing on my hair rather than this crazy pink cloud.

When Connor Graves approached me in his designer blue suit to lead me to the stage with a camera crew closely following, I put on my biggest smile and acted like I was completely comfortable and ready to hear what the nation had decided for my future. Ryne remained on the side of the stage, having already been informed that he was moving on to the semifinal. But Wade, Katie, and Whitney had been told their journey was over. Only two spots remained, and there were three of us left.

"Now, Billie Bishop, are you ready to find out if you've made it into the final three of *Superstardom?*" Connor asked joyfully as he ran a hand through his hair and smiled at the camera. It was his signature pose and almost a cue to smile at the camera too.

"I'm ready," I replied, exhaling my fear.

He nodded and led me out from behind the curtain. I tried to forget how hopeful the eliminated contestants looked as they entered the stage and how quickly the tears welled up in their eyes when they were asked to leave. Connor then stared down the camera and, without wavering, said, "Whitney and Katie have both been very emotional finding out that the nation has chosen not to vote them into the semifinal. If you don't make it, do you think you'll be as upset?"

"I don't know," I replied honestly. With the extra security and the tension from my fellow contestants, I truly didn't know if the end of this competition would have me in tears or sighing in relief.

When we reached the center of the stage, I stared at the judges. Claudia was wearing a short violet wig that emphasized her green eyes. Russell had on a denim jacket and beanie, appearing completely at home in the studio. Jax was in his signature rock star outfit, struggling to stop watching the exits and looking through the audience for any possible danger. When he heard everyone screaming my name, he caught himself and looked directly at me with a smile on his face. It was an "I've seen you wearing my T-shirt" smile. F*ck. If people hadn't been paying attention to the news reports on our relationship, that smile gave us away. I also suddenly knew that I would be upset if this was the end.

He kept smiling at me, and I nervously shifted in my spot and felt my dress rub against my skin again. The shooting pain reminded me of how much I hated my outfit and how I needed to pray that this ended quickly. It was causing a throbbing in my ears.

I was concentrating so hard on not scratching that I missed Claudia's statement on my last performance and Russell's joke. I just nodded, smiled, and laughed, hoping I didn't look silly.

When Connor asked me a question and waited for my response, I knew nodding wouldn't be good enough.

"I'm so sorry, what was the question?" I nervously asked.

He repeated something, but it was as if he was standing in a long corridor. I took a guess that it was about my journey in the competition like he had asked all the other contestants. "I'm just so grateful to have made it this far, and if I make it through or go home, I know I've done my best."

It seemed to work, as the crowd cheered and Connor moved on to open the envelope that would announce whether I was staying or going home. I stood as motionless as possible, but it felt as if the itching had amplified under the lights and now everywhere the dress touched me was burning.

When the crowd exploded and the three judges stood and clapped, I knew I was in the semifinals. I grinned and with shaking limbs walked over to join Ryne.

The moment the cameras left me and went to seek out Faith and Joshua, I turned to Ryne. "I'm so sorry for this."

"Sorry for what?" he asked, still smiling for the cameras and giving me a sidelong glance.

And with that, I stopped trying to handle the pain and let go.

Everything went black.

CHAPTER
SEVENTEEN

I don't want to start ignoring you

Jax

"How did this happen?" I growled at the doctor. We were standing outside Billie's hospital room, and I was struggling not to punch somebody. The white walls, the smell of antiseptic, and the hushed whispers of nurses were driving me crazy. "I watched. Before she fainted into another contestant's arms, no one even touched her."

"It was poison ivy," the doctor informed us. "Traces of the oil were found all over the dress you brought her in."

"Why did she pass out?" Donny questioned. "Poison ivy usually just causes rashes, doesn't it? Wait, will there be scarring? It won't extend to her face, will it?"

"No, there will be no damage to her face," the doctor replied, clearly confused by Donny's onslaught of questions. "There were rashes where the dress touched her body. They'll take approximately three weeks to go down, but they shouldn't spread without further contamination. She had some swelling of her abdomen, which I believe is the reason behind her fainting."

"She needs to be on stage in a week. Will this be a problem?" Donny continued, obviously focused on the impact Billie being sick would have on the show.

"Shut up, Don," I groaned. "Just tell us what needs to be done to make her feel better."

"Movement might be difficult. I wouldn't recommend large dance numbers in her future. However, there are a few over-the-counter creams she can use, like calamine lotion, to alleviate the rashes, and there are oral antihistamines she can take to sleep better."

"We can do that, sure," Donny muttered. "Jax, you find out about the creams, and I'll call the studio executives to let them know she's fine."

"No doubt her trying to pretend everything was all right and she wasn't having an allergic reaction also increased the amount of pain she was in. However, no need to fear. She won't have any long-term side effects. The rashes will go down. It was likely it was contaminated when she first tried it on. Most reactions like hers are following a second exposure. She's lucky really that she didn't experience any swelling of her vocal cords," the doctor explained.

"Lucky," I repeated, rolling my eyes. "I'll let her know."

Before I went back inside Billie's room, I turned to Donny, who was already pressing his cell phone to his ear. "After you've called all the producers, I want you to check in with your Marine team and everyone who's been near that damn dress. First the notes and now this. Whoever is after Billie is escalating, and it's not looking good, Don. I want a list of who could have done this. And I wanted that list yesterday."

He nodded and turned back to his phone.

Billie was sitting up in her hospital bed when I walked back in, her arms crossed and her eyes shooting daggers at me.

"All y'all having a conversation about my health without me would be very aggravating if I couldn't hear you through the *damn* door," she snapped. "I'm not an invalid. I just fainted, and I might have liked to ask the doctor questions myself."

I winced. "I thought you might like some rest. If you want, I can go get him back to explain anything you didn't overhear."

"Lucky for you, I overheard everything. Poison ivy with rashes all over my body where that disgusting dress touched me. It's almost embarrassing. I can't believe they even told someone who isn't my family what's wrong with me. Isn't that illegal?"

"Donny can be very persuasive when he wants to be, and the doctor had seen our photos together."

"Oh, so patient confidentiality doesn't apply to superstars?" She rolled her eyes.

"Exactly." I grinned. "Plus, it was a miracle that we got out of the studio without the press hearing. You were a true professional, fainting off camera. The whole show just made it out like you went to the bathroom, and we were able to put you in Donny's car and rush you to the emergency room. If we called your mom and had to wait for her to arrive at the airport, the press would have been all over us. You want Donny and me to know you have poison ivy rashes or the whole world?"

Billie laughed. "I guess you've got a good point there. So what's the plan for the next few rehearsals and interviews if I can't dance?"

"You have the week off," I said sternly. "You rest and worry about the competition when you feel better."

"I can't have the whole week off, Jax. We have press interviews and rehearsals. The semifinal and finale have the most grueling schedule. I've seen it. I know they've sped up the production, but I can't imagine they're canceling those big talk show interviews. I'm in the top three of a nationally televised show. I won't be throwing that away over some poison ivy."

"Look, you're still in the competition. You'll perform and record a song for the semifinal, but the girls who were eliminated will take your place during the press tours and send you video of the rehearsals," I explained. "It'll give your body a chance to recover, and Linda and the production managers have already agreed. They've done similar things in the past when contestants have fallen ill."

"Jax, I really don't want special treatment. I want to go on the press tours. People are already questioning my position in the competition because of our relationship and the photos in the media. I don't want to give people extra responsibilities because I can't meet them and give them more fuel for their fire," Billie groaned.

"It isn't like Katie and Whitney won't be thrilled to do the interviews for you. It's additional publicity for them as well," I reminded her as I moved closer to her hospital bed and sat in the visitor's chair.

Billie stared at me with concern. "But they might talk about you negatively. They might blame you and our relationship for them not making it to the semifinal. They already said a few words to me during our costume fittings; who's to say they won't say it on nationally broadcast talk shows? Jax, this show was meant to make you look good for your record label. I don't want to be the reason you lose that."

"You won't. I'm ready for whatever they want to say about me, and Donny and my record label actually love the publicity about us. The more people want to talk about our relationship, the more money it'll make them in the long run."

"They like it? You dating a contestant?" Billie asked, shocked.

"Look, if we weren't basically the same age and if the public weren't the ones who keep selecting the winners, I think I would probably be in a lot of trouble. But my record label has given me a better deal thanks to the photos of us. They think the audition tape caught us falling in love and will mean great love songs in the future," I confessed, raking a hand through my hair.

"So if little old ladies take photos of us in public, you're going to make more money? I'm the only one risking her integrity and her career by spending time with you? Is that why you've wanted me around all along, because my audition tape made us look like we were in love?" she asked with hurt in her eyes.

"No, of course not. I wanted you around before I even knew they liked the tape. I care about you," I admitted as I reached for her hand in the hospital bed. "Billie Bishop, just watching you fall down on that stage scared the sh*t out of me. It also made me admit how much I don't want to be just your friend."

"Jax." Billie exhaled and squeezed my hand. "We haven't known each other for very long. This is ridiculous. You can't be telling me you think you might be in love with me after a handful of times together and also tell me you might make more money from being seen with me. I don't know how to deal with all that information. We haven't even made love yet. And in case you haven't figured it out, I've *never* made love with anyone. I could be bad. I could be really, really bad." Her voice rose with each declaration.

"I don't want to laugh at you right now," I told her, grinning. "You're in the hospital, and it's been a stressful twenty-four hours. But I am going to tell you that there is no way us sleeping together would be bad." I stared at her solemnly and kissed her on the forehead. "I'm also not going to lie that knowing I'll be your first, if you choose to sleep with me, makes the whole idea even better."

She laughed and rolled her eyes. "I can't believe you said that."

"I want to be honest. There's too much going on for us to be lying to each other as well. You needed to know that our spending time together won't damage my career. And, if you're regretting spending time with me because of everything that's going on, I want you to share that sh*t with me, because I'm starting to have feelings."

Billie stared at me and then stated, "I risked a lot coming on this show. My mom forgave me, but I still put our relationship in jeopardy to see if I could do this, and I won't let some stalker keep me from doing what I came to do." The soon-to-be rock star attitude shone through her piercing blue eyes and strong words.

"And knowing our relationship won't impact my career like it will yours?" I tested.

"Well, I need to have a career to impact before that's even an issue. But I don't want to stop that either. I don't know what the future holds, but I don't want to start ignoring you now. I might have a few feelings too," she said softly, not quite as fierce as before.

"Okay, then we'll work out a way for you to build that career, and I'll do everything I can to ensure some crazy stalker or my stupid career doesn't get in the way."

"Without interfering with the schedule I have?" she asked cautiously.

"Without interfering," I agreed before adding, "as long as you're safe."

"Deal."

Three days later, I was standing backstage of a local talk show as Billie, Ryne, and Faith were being interviewed in front of a live audience. They were promoting the upcoming semifinal, and everything was going smoothly. There were no questions about our relationship, no mention of the hospital visit; everyone was focused on their potential musical careers and the style of songs they planned to release on future albums.

Donny had given the TV producers strict instructions about not approaching me. I ignored everyone around me by watching videos on my cell phone. I knew that even with orders from above, if I made eye contact with anyone, they would try to persuade me to greet the audience. Donny did have me promise the producers of the talk show that if they kept my presence backstage out of the tabloids, Billie and I would sit on their stage together for an exclusive interview once the competition was over.

That didn't mean the production crew weren't giving me knowing looks. *Superstardom* celebrity judges never accompanied any of the contestants on their talk show rounds. We had our own schedule. I knew canceling my appearances to follow Billie around would have everyone talking about us, even if it didn't end up printed in a magazine. However, Billie and I agreed that we weren't going to stop seeing each other, and that meant there would be talk. We would just have to deal with it the best way we could, addressing it once the competition was over and ignoring it while it was still going on.

We also spoke about her damn schedule and commitments that she refused to stop even though the security team still hadn't determined a clear suspect. There had been too many people who visited the fitting rooms and too many with access to the contestants' hotel. I worried that the next event would be even more serious. Every time we were apart, I kept thinking about her collapsing on a different stage without anyone to get her to the hospital in time, so she reluctantly agreed that I could join her backstage during public events and during rehearsals this week.

When the audience began applauding and cheering, I raised my head and saw the three of them making their way to me.

"That was so amazing," Faith gushed to Billie and Ryne once they were officially off-screen. "I always watched this show at home and thought everyone seemed so nice, but they were even kinder than I expected."

"You just like that the audience cheered the loudest when they were asked if you would win the competition," Ryne muttered, rolling his eyes.

"Green isn't a good color on you, cowboy," Faith teased while Billie laughed and caught my eye. I gestured with my head to the exit, and she nodded.

As we made our way to the street, each of us were stopped at least once by members of the crew and audience to ask us to sign something for their friend, child, or parent. Each time a stranger approached, I would grit my teeth and swallow the words I wanted to say.

As Faith was stopped when we were just about to pass through the door, Billie took one look at my face and told the others, "We might go to the next stop without you guys, if you don't mind catching up in the contestant bus? The Marine team have been asking us to join them anyway."

"Sure, we'll meet you there," Faith cheerfully agreed before turning her attention back to her fan.

"I'll keep an eye on this one," Ryne said, before catching the eye of a female fan eagerly watching his every move and waving.

"Thanks," I replied softly before nodding at Brian and finally making our way to their car.

Once we were outside, Billie whispered, "So, did you have fun backstage?"

"It was thrilling," I replied dryly, and she laughed before leaning against my shoulder. "Where to next?" I asked, bracing myself for another mindless hour of staring at my phone.

"Apparently we're to go to Santa Monica. We're meeting with some music producers at the head office of Platinum Music Group to discuss our debut song choices."

"Platinum is supplying all the contestants with singles?" I asked, shocked. My record label must have fought fiercely to get those rights.

"Yes, sir," Billie responded, biting her bottom lip. "I heard rumors that if they don't like you, they only give you terrible songs they know won't sell."

I wanted to chuckle, but I knew she was seriously freaking out. "Babe, Platinum's entire slogan is they only support and produce platinum-selling records," I told her, bumping my shoulder into hers. "They've signed up this year because they know with the show's current ratings, it won't matter what song you guys select. They'll all sell a million copies easy."

"I do believe you told me a story about vomiting in your signing-bonus car after your first recording session at Platinum," Billie responded, raising an eyebrow, "and yet you tell me to relax?"

"You remember that, huh?" I laughed as I opened the door to our car. "The moral of that story wasn't don't ever step foot in the door at Platinum Music Group. It was don't drink the shots in celebration."

"Welcome to Platinum. Would you like a tequila shot?" a young assistant gushed. "It's our little tradition for our new family members."

Billie stared at the white liquid on the tray as if it were a contagious disease. "Thank you, but I think my nerves aren't a good mixer with tequila," she replied.

The assistant giggled. "Mr. Bone?"

"Maybe later." I was too busy enjoying the way Billie's eyes had enlarged the moment we stepped through the grand glass entry doors. She was like a deer in headlights staring at the eclectic decorating of Platinum Music Group, part distressed and part hypnotized. From the pretentious gold chandelier hanging in the center of the room to the white cushions and ottomans that graced the red entry rug, Platinum's lobby was known for its eccentricity. It was if their decorator was trying to marry all of the styles of music together but forgot things like practicality and comfort.

"I'll bring the tray into the meeting with Mr. Anderson," the assistant continued. "I wanted to let you know I'm such a big fan of you both. I watch *Superstardom* every Thursday with my mom. She thinks you're going to win," she whispered to Billie, causing her cheeks to flush red.

"That's very sweet," she replied.

"They actually told me you would be traveling with the two other contestants. Are they on their way?" the assistant asked, her excitement clearly making her a little jittery.

"They got held up by some fans. They should be here any—"

I hadn't even finished my sentence when she looked past our shoulders and let out a feminine sigh of appreciation.

Ryne walked in, whistling through his teeth. "Now this is a life I could get used to."

"Hell yes," Faith squealed, approaching the giant vertical garden that ran the length of the hallway and pressing her face into the palms. "It smells so good."

"Hi, I'm Mandy," the young assistant greeted, her tray of tequila wobbling a little as Ryne moved closer. She sounded breathless when she explained, "I'll be escorting you all to the conference room."

"Lead the way, little lady," Ryne drawled, making Billie roll her eyes at me. I had to grin.

Mandy led us down the narrow hallway. There had been some renovations since I had been there last. I avoided coming to the main office as much as possible. As far as I was concerned, dealing with contracts was Donny's gig; I preferred recording my songs in my own studio.

"Your albums and concert posters are taking up the entire hallway," Billie whispered beside me as we moved closer to the glass doors of the conference room. "How does that make other artists feel?"

"No clue. They might have put them out because they knew I would be joining you. The hallway could change when Carey Leigh visits."

"I doubt it," Billie murmured, pausing to stare at the album that had launched my career.

It was a black-and-white photo of me sitting on a replica 550 Porsche wearing jeans, my shirt open and a cigarette dangling from my mouth. "Modern-day rebel," the press had called me, "with the voice of a fallen angel." Total marketing scam.

"If your album eclipses mine in the billboard charts, they'll pull mine down and replace it with yours," I told her, nudging her shoulder. "I would bet fifty bucks on it."

She snorted. I just shook my head. She still didn't see how far her talent could take her.

When we walked into the conference room, I was surprised to find nearly the entire crew of *Superstardom* in the building. I had expected the camera crew, but I hadn't anticipated Claudia lounging on a chaise with a glass of champagne and Russell leaning back on his chair, taking a tequila shot from Cindy, who was holding another tray of clear poison. Connor Graves was also whispering to the show's director with disgust in the corner of the room.

It amazed me.

It took a hell of a lot of people to promote one person from ordinary to celebrity.

"Ah, the stars of the hour have finally arrived," Graham Wright,

Platinum Music Group head honcho and one of the smartest men in the music industry, announced. He was one of the few men who worked in this building who I didn't dislike.

He approached me, chuckling. "I heard you decided to hang with the cameraman this morning. How was it being behind the camera for a change?"

"Well, if the music thing doesn't work out because the people here screw up my distribution, it's always good to have a backup plan," I told him, shrugging.

"I'll tell Caroline that you said that about distribution. She won't let you come to dinner with us again or play with the kids." He winked at me before demanding, "Now, introduce me to your better half. God knows I'm going to need to give a detailed description over dinner tonight."

I laughed and felt Billie freeze beside me. She knew she stood in the presence of music royalty.

"Billie, meet Graham. Listen to everything he says and then make him believe it was your idea. He'll have forgotten between flights from Heathrow and JFK and will pay you double for being so clever."

Graham chuckled. "Not bad advice. I'd be insulted about the memory thing if it weren't true. Why they insist I constantly travel everywhere is beyond me."

"You're the boss," I reminded him.

"That's right." Graham sighed. "At least being the boss means I get to be at moments like this. Billie, Faith, Ryne, you all ready to select the song that will be played across the globe?"

"I've never been great at making choices," Billie confessed to the room.

"Darling, that's why we're here," Claudia chimed in. "We're here to help you work out your style. We'll all read the lyrics to some of the songs they've short-listed for you and see if we think it fits your vibe."

"Narrative," Russell announced. "As long as a song tells a story, girl, it'll be a hit."

"I was hoping for something that had a little girl-power twist to it," Faith responded confidently. "I have a few original songs I'd love to share if that's allowed?"

"Of course it is, girl." Graham grinned. "You're a songwriter. That's why the audience has chosen you. We won't be forcing you to be something you aren't."

"Any country love songs short-listed?" Ryne asked, staring at Mandy, the assistant, who blushed. Faith and Billie looked at each other and rolled their eyes.

"Definitely," one of the producers announced. "Most of them are love songs. Only a couple are about heartbreak and infidelity."

"I wouldn't mind singing about heartbreak," Billie suddenly announced, causing them all to look at me with curious eyes. I just smirked.

"I actually had one in mind for you," Graham admitted. "It's a bit of a power ballad about the strength of a mother called 'You're Always There.' A favorite artist of mine wrote it a while ago after going through some family hardship, but refused to sing it themselves on one of their albums. Too personal. After hearing you speak about your relationship with your mother, I thought it would be a perfect fit. It starts softly about the cruelty of life but then builds to the chorus about how during all the ups and downs—"

"You're always there," Billie finished, her eyes lighting up. "I would love that. You sure they wouldn't mind a *Superstardom* contestant singing it?"

Graham handed over a copy of the music sheets. "I'm sure I can persuade them to let you sing the song."

The entire room watched as Billie read the lyrics silently. A single tear fell down her cheek. "It's perfect," she murmured.

"Did someone get that on camera?" Connor Graves asked, reminding everyone in the room that they were part of a television show. "Linda, I thought your vision was for me to hand each of them their final songs?"

"We haven't started filming yet," Linda informed him as if he were an impatient toddler. "Once the contestants have selected their favorite songs, we'll recreate this moment for the audience. And yes, Connor, you will be the one handing out the lyrics."

It took another two hours of decisions, edits, and filming before all the contestants were in their own recording booths practicing their semifinal song as well as the one they selected to be their debut single should they win the competition. Brian had accompanied Billie. I decided to hang back in the conference room with Graham.

The moment we were alone, I turned to him and asked, "How long have you had that song ready to give away? You didn't think you should have asked before offering it up on a silver platter to a *Superstardom* contestant?"

"Was I wrong? Were you going to perform that song ever again?"

"I wasn't, but a warning would have been nice."

"You wrote it for your mother, but you might as well have written it for that girl. Part country, part soul. Sure, your latest song, 'Strong Enough Alone,' was good, but that was your pent-up anger fueling the lyrics. This has always been your masterpiece. It's the best thing I've heard since 'I Will Always Love You,' and you had it sitting on a shelf, refusing to let anyone record it."

"I had my reasons," I huffed.

"You had fear. Why do you think I made the suits fight so hard to get those contestants in this building? The moment I saw her and watched her audition, I knew she would be the one person you would let sing that song."

"You are the smartest bastard in this whole industry," I told him reluctantly.

"And here I was thinking you'd stayed behind to let me know you were still pissed at me for not being able to convince the board of directors that your being a judge on a television show was a waste of your time," Graham teased.

"You know I'm glad I did the damn show," I confessed. "She's special."

"I know it. But if you don't bring her around for Caroline to meet soon, I'll deny ever saying that out loud. I believe I might just end up calling her a groupie not worth our time."

"Always afraid of your wife, Graham?" I laughed.

"One day you'll know the same feeling," he stressed. "A day that's coming sooner than I think you realize. Unless of course you screw it up and someone moves faster than you."

"I won't be letting that happen," I insisted.

"Then why are you hanging with an old man right now and not watching that girl sing your song?" he challenged.

It was enough to have me sighing and heading to the door. Sometimes it was annoying spending time with Graham.

Always the smartest man in the damn room.

CHAPTER
EIGHTEEN

She deserved better

Zach

“I t was just a song,” I overheard my momma tell Michelle while sipping from her wineglass and relaxing on the back porch.

“I don't know, Cora. It looked like there was something more between them during that duet. The way she touched him while they sang together. I've also never seen her look at a boy like that before,” Michelle replied. “And those photos from before the live shows and now that one in the little Mexican restaurant? It makes me wonder if she's falling for him. Hard.”

“Singing together and holding hands does not make a relationship. If it did, Zach and Billie would practically be married. And those paparazzi people edit celebrity photos all the time to make them more interesting. If there is something really happening between them, I'm sure it wouldn't be the worst thing in the world, and it won't be worth worrying about until the competition is over,” my mother remarked. “They eliminated four contestants last night, and she wasn't one of them. She's wonderful on that stage, but the fact that he's a celebrity judge and people are curious about their relationship surely doesn't hurt Billie's chances. Plus, she'll always have the story of how she once dated Jax Bone. I wish I had a few more daring stories in my past than being duped by my childhood sweetheart."

"You're forgetting he's a rock star, Cora, not just some everyday celebrity television personality. Rock stars aren't usually known for their belief in monogamy. And he's nineteen with millions of girls around the world lining up to be with him. He could break her heart, and we're too far away to eat ice cream with her. I don't want my daughter to have to go through heartbreak with the entire world watching and without someone to reassure her about all the other fish in the sea."

"Do you really think she'd be foolish enough to fall in love with a judge on *Superstardom?*" my mother asked Michelle softly.

"At eighteen, weren't we foolish enough to—"

I didn't hear the end of Michelle's statement. I couldn't listen to any more of their late-night discussions about Billie and Jax. Since their performance and the elimination, it was all they and anyone from school could talk about. How *hot* it was. How *intense* it looked. How *great* they were together.

Everyone, even our mothers, apparently thought Billie and Jax were an item.

I grabbed the keys to my truck and headed for the front door. I didn't think about where I was going, just got in and drove on autopilot, my mind replaying that damn duet.

As I pulled into the parking lot beside the gym, I nearly laughed. Of course it was where I took myself automatically when I was trying to avoid discussions about Billie. I'd spent every minute in that gym since I got back from LA.

I wished it wasn't so late. If it were only a couple hours earlier, I could have called Coach. He would have driven over and unlocked the doors for me, and I'd be able to shoot hoops, run laps, and calm down. Focus on drills and forget about the way Billie looked at some other guy when she sang to him.

It was the same way I'd been trying to forget our conversation.

The same way I'd been trying to forget our kiss.

It was as if Coach knew what I was going through, because he didn't say a word or ask any questions. As long as I called before 7:00 p.m., he would unlock the gym and let me stay as late as I needed while he did paperwork in his office.

I sat staring at the gymnasium, trying to picture my favorite game from last season. Remembering the free throw that won the game. Billie screaming my name on the sideline. The pit in my stomach ached. Every good memory I had involved her in some way. I used to think Billie felt the same. Until now.

My phone vibrated in my pocket. I thought about leaving it there. I'd refused to answer the calls Billie had made to me since I left LA. Yet, after the second ring, I pulled it out to stare at Billie's name at the top of the screen and the photo that looked like her face was squished against the glass. I thought about answering. Acting like I had no problem with everything that had happened between us. But as much as I hated the rumors, I couldn't face the truth.

I couldn't listen to Billie tell me that she had thought about being with me and decided that a guy she'd known for a couple of months was who she preferred.

I trusted Michelle was right. Once *Superstardom* was over, Jax the rock star would cheat on Billie, and I would be here waiting for her to return. Ready to accept her apology and give her a shoulder to cry on. I'd be ready to play this season, get a scholarship to Duke, and start my journey to the NBA with Billie by my side.

I just had to survive the next few months.

If they were together, at least it was in Los Angeles, and as long as I stopped taking her calls and watching the show, maybe I could handle this period of her life. The idea that she would experience all the firsts with him that I thought would one day be ours killed me.

But I'd let go of now for tomorrow.

When my phone alerted me that I had a new voice mail, I thought about not listening to it. But I remembered who Billie was. She knew how I felt about her. She would never tell me she picked Jax Bone in a voice mail. Maybe she just wanted to tell me how much she missed me.

I pressed Play, and as the recording started, my eyebrows furrowed at the sound of two men's voices.

"*Whatever works, Jax. The label needs to believe the public thinks it's real or there's a real chance we lose the deal on the table. If they don't, we've got to start thinking about how we go bigger.*"

"*What's bigger than a duet? You want me to do a home visit with her next? Change this damn show from a singing competition into one of those dating shows where I propose at the end?*"

"*That's not a bad idea. The record label would likely double their bonus.*"

When the recording stopped, I played it again. And again. And again.

As I listened to Jax Bone tell some guy he planned to propose to Billie for some record deal, my stomach sank. I was prepared to wait. Let Billie live in the fantasy land that Hollywood offered. I figured she'd remember how important we were to each other eventually.

I wasn't prepared to watch him exploit Billie's feelings for some damn business deal. Have the first time she was ever proposed to be for some television rating scam.

She deserved better than that.

Now and tomorrow.

I called Coach.

"It's after seven," he grumbled before sighing and reluctantly asking, "You need me to come unlock that gym for you, boy?"

"Actually I wanted to let you know that I might miss our first game of the season."

"You've had more practice sessions than all the boys on the team combined and you tell me you're not going to make it to the first game?" His voice was gruff over the phone.

"Yes, sir. I'm heading to LA to see Billie Bishop."

"Thank Christ. You don't come back until you're head's ready for the game. Also, my wife wants me to tell you that she'll leave me if I spend another night in the office, so I guess I also have to say good timing, Montgomery."

"Thank you, sir," I told him before hanging up and driving home. I needed to pack.

I called the show on my way to the airport. They booked me on the first flight available to LAX. I didn't tell them I was coming to reveal what a d*ck Jax Bone was or that I knew about the proposal; I simply dialed our original contact for the first live show and let them know that Billie had been calling me a lot and I wanted to support her through the final shows.

They didn't question it, offering me a room at the hotel again and a seat at the next two shows. I requested it not be a surprise this time. They agreed. All I had to do was sign a waiver in case I appeared in any of their behind-the-scenes footage.

Billie would be rehearsing around the clock for the semifinal and grand finale shows. They told me she finished at eight most evenings these days. However, I would be able to see her after the show or during rehearsal. They said they would leave all the identification and passes I would require for access at the hotel lobby.

Before I boarded the plane, I decided to do something I hadn't done in a couple of weeks.

I messaged Billie.

Missing you, B.
Zach, I miss you too. You can't stay angry with me, okay? I have so much going on I need to tell you about.

I worried she was talking about her relationship with Jax Bone. I wasn't sure I could read messages about how amazing he was without telling her the truth. However, I also knew she wouldn't listen to the truth if we were still fighting. I messaged her again.

I'm sorry I've been ignoring your calls. I just needed time to sort my head out.

It's okay. I know this singing competition business is a little overwhelming. I really want to talk to you about what's going on. Can we chat later tonight?

Definitely.

I gave my boarding pass to the flight attendant and tried to work out what exactly I was going to say to my best friend before I told her all about how the guy she was spending so much time with these days was trying to manipulate her for money.

The studio was bigger than I remembered. Last time, Michelle and I had been ushered directly to the auditorium and then Billie had led us to her dressing room. I hadn't been able to get my bearings enough to find my way quickly to Billie's door on my own.

I wandered aimlessly for half an hour amongst crew and production teams before I saw anything that seemed even slightly familiar. I felt like I was in some army barrack as I passed more security guards than production crew. When I finally found a hallway I remembered, I asked the mammoth guy standing guard by the first door, "Do you know if Billie Bishop's dressing room is close by?"

"You have crew ID?" he grunted.

"No, I'm a close friend," I let him know. "I have a pass from the show for access."

"This way," he muttered, then led me down the hallway and into a small room. It was empty except for a small table and chair, like an interrogation room from a cop show.

"Should I have a lawyer with me," I joked. "Or has Billie's decorating style changed after spending all this time in Hollywood?"

"Who are you?" the guy asked without a trace of humor.

I pulled out my cell phone and showed him a photo of Billie and me together on my display screen. "Her best friend," I replied, raking a hand through my hair.

"This some Photoshop sh*t?" he growled.

"You know how to Photoshop images together?"

"No," he spat out.

"Me neither." I chuckled, trying desperately to lighten the mood. "If you want, I can wait here until you call someone to confirm that I'm her best friend. I'm a patient guy."

"I'll make a call. You stay here."

"Yes, sir," I muttered and leaned against the table. I didn't want him to think I was intimidated by this mess. I thought about sitting in the seat, but I worried it might lead to more questions.

When he left, I thought about texting Billie and letting her know I was here, but I decided against it. Surely someone on the show would let him know who I was, and then I could spend our time talking about Jax rather than the crazy security for this show.

When the goliath man entered the room again, he said, "He said you're fine. Her room is the first on the left."

"Thanks," I replied, exiting the room.

"My employer, Jax Bone, told me to tell you he looks forward to meeting you properly this visit," he informed me as he followed me to Billie's door and took his position as her guard.

"Great," I mumbled through gritted teeth.

When I knocked on her door, Billie called out, "Brian, I'm nearly dressed. Two seconds."

"Accompany a lot of guests to her door?" I asked curiously.

"I am Miss Bishop's personal security," the giant soldier replied with an edge to his voice.

"Ready," Billie called out, and I decided to ask why she needed personal security from the source.

When the door opened and Billie saw me, her mouth dropped open.

I thought she might be angry or start demanding I turn around and go home. However, she threw her arms around me.

"You're here," she whispered against my neck. "I'm really glad you're here."

When she squeezed me, I squeezed back. *Damn, I missed her.*

She eventually stopped hugging me, and I used all my willpower to let her go. Thankfully she pulled me inside of her dressing room and locked the door. We were going out of earshot of Jax's goon, and I was more than ready to tell her everything she needed to know about the recording I'd received.

I took a quick look around her dressing room and froze. It was spotless. The makeup and brushes that had been scattered around her table the last time I visited were all sealed in bags and containers. Dresses were all neatly hung on racks with locks over each zipper. It was a museum.

"B, how come you have your own security guard?" I asked, suddenly very tense. The guard, her enthusiasm to see me even though I'd been ignoring her calls, and the pristine room were creeping me out. None of it was making a lick of sense.

"It's what I've been trying to call you about. I wanted to talk to you first before any tabloids found out." Billie groaned before sitting down in the middle of the floor. "There's been a couple of incidents."

"What do you mean, incidents?" I asked softly as I joined her on the floor.

"I have—" She took a deep breath. "—a stalker. First it was just notes. Harmless. I thought they were from you and Jax. They were silly single lines about being hurt or something coming to an end. Then someone tampered with my last live show outfit with poison ivy. I had a bit of a reaction and had to go to the hospital. I'm completely fine now, except for a rash on my stomach that's being stubborn, but they still haven't caught whoever is behind everything."

"Are you kidding?" I swore. "How come our moms haven't said anything to me?"

"I haven't told them. I don't want them to worry when there's nothing they can do except try and convince me to come home. Zach, it's only two more weeks of taping, and between the show and Jax's security, I'm surrounded by guards. I just really wanted to talk to you about it. I've really needed you to tell me I can handle all of this like you usually do."

"So the mini army barracks this has turned into is because of you, and you've tried to reach out to me, but I haven't been picking up because I'm sulking over a damn kiss." I wanted to break something. I closed my eyes, furious with myself.

Billie must have read my facial expression, because she quickly began reassuring me. "Zach, I'm not angry at you. Please don't be angry at yourself. I've been perfectly safe. Jax has barely let me out of his sight."

"Jax is protecting you?"

"He's organized the personal security you must have seen at the door," she informed me, rolling her eyes. "And there's another one who's gone to get me a snack. At first it made me uncomfortable. I'm sure it must be costing him a fortune to hire two ex-Marines. But I have to admit it makes me feel safer. I've also been staying at his place because some of the notes I received were at the hotel. Jax's house has this massive gate you have to get through to even reach the front door. I don't think anyone will be able to reach me behind those doors."

I thought about the things I was going to tell her about Jax Bone.

How I was going to play the recording.

But he's been keeping her safe for the remainder of this competition.

F*ck.

"I was thinking about staying in LA until this show is over. Now I'm certain I will be. You can't get rid of me until you're safe," I told her, my tone unwavering. "Coach agreed. I won't tell our moms about the stalker unless you get another note. Don't even think of trying to change my mind."

"I won't," Billie assured me. "I'll be selfish and even confess that I'm glad you're here. I know we ended things awkwardly last time. And I still can't give you—"

"B, don't even worry about it. You have enough going on that you need to focus on. I was wrong to try and make you choose earlier." I squeezed her hand. "We'll discuss my last visit when the competition is over."

"Are you sure?" she asked nervously.

"Completely. Now tell me, what am I going to get to see you perform for the semifinal? Is it going to be better than the year that girl dressed like Britney Spears and carried around a snake that bit her halfway through the chorus?"

Billie laughed. "Unfortunately I'm not nearly as creative. I was planning on singing Miranda Lambert's 'The House that Built Me.' Jax convinced me that if I was going to get voted off the show, I might as well go out with one of my favorite songs."

"Finally singing country." I smiled, avoiding her comment about Jax. "Is it bad of me to hope that you singing about coming home might get you closer to sitting on that airplane beside me when I go back?"

Billie smiled softly and admitted, "I've practiced it a couple of times now. The song reminds me how much I've changed during the course of this competition. It will sure be different when I do eventually go home."

"Things and people don't change that much," I told her, gripping her hands in mine. "Your place will always be with your family."

"I hope that's true." She laughed softly. "Anyway, enough serious talk. Let me show you all the wonderful things you can get with a *Superstardom* backstage pass."

"You're just taking me to the vending machine, aren't you?"

She giggled. "You know it."

CHAPTER
NINETEEN

I wasn't sure I could win

Jax

I watched Billie laugh on the stage during rehearsal as Zach tried to convince her to perform some childhood dance routine. He was lounging in a front row seat with a bag of candy in his hand. He had clearly made himself at home, letting everyone on set know he wasn't leaving any time soon. I had been staring at them for a few minutes from the shadows, and each time he made her laugh, something inside of me twisted up.

"If it makes you feel better, I don't think she's ever thought of him as her boyfriend," Faith told me softly from the side of stage.

I didn't know when she'd approached, and it annoyed me a little that someone caught me staring. "I didn't want to disrupt her rehearsal," I muttered, offering an explanation for a question that wasn't asked.

Faith continued as if I wasn't losing my mind. "Until he kissed her, I think she thought of him as a twin brother. She doesn't get that far-off look when she talks about him like she does over you. And she doesn't smile at her phone when he texts like when you do."

"They have a history. Billie told me they've known each other since birth, and she doesn't have many stories without him in them."

"Well, then I guess you need to convince her that living with you in the future is better than living with him in the past." Faith shrugged.

"At least I'm better-looking right?" I grumbled as Zach raked a hand through his golden hair.

"Umm...." Faith chuckled. "Even though you're my judge and you could say something this evening that might inspire people not to vote for me, I'm not going to lie to you. That tall Southern gentleman is *hot*. He's a Ralph Lauren advertisement, but instead of belonging on a yacht, I believe Billie said he belongs on a basketball court."

I groaned.

"But remember, lots of girls turn down that small-town boy for a rock star," she told me, winking.

"I don't want her to choose me because I'm a damn celebrity. I want her to choose me because she likes me more than him."

"Then you're going to have to wait until she decides." Faith shrugged. "Now you know how it feels to be on the other side of the judging table. Other people deciding your future sucks." She patted me on the shoulder and walked away.

Left in the shadows by myself again, I tried telling myself it wasn't that big a deal waiting to hear Billie tell me she was in love with me and that Zach was just a friend.

I watched Zach's mouth move and heard Billie laugh again.

I swore.

Damn it, I had signed up for a new competition.

And I wasn't sure I could win.

I was waiting out in front of the studio for Billie. The Marine team sent me a message letting me know they would be exiting the building in five minutes. I was relieved that we were finally heading home.

It had been a long day of press interviews and contract discussions about the next season. I didn't plan on returning as a celebrity judge no matter how much money they offered. My new contract with Platinum would be signed in March, which meant when the next season started filming, I would no longer be obliged to revamp my image on a reality television show. The endless rehearsals I had to attend only to stand around and provide some motivational speech was a waste of my time.

I explained to Donny that if he wanted me to be writing and recording songs, I couldn't be spending so much time at the *Superstardom* set. He reluctantly agreed, though I knew he was planning something to get me to change my mind. He just didn't understand why I wouldn't want to have cameras constantly in my face promoting my new album.

When I saw Billie walking to me, her blonde curls catching the wind, I forgot all about my day. She was in a pair of vintage blue jeans, a black tank top, and a brown leather jacket. I fantasized about running my hands underneath her shirt and helping her take it off. She was stunning.

She smiled at me, and I watched as her teeth scraped against her thick bottom lip nervously. Now all I wanted to do was kiss her.

Before I could pull her into my body and do just that, her best friend stepped out from behind her, all six feet of him, with a smile on his face that didn't reach his eyes.

"Hey, man. I'm Zach," he drawled, holding out his hand.

F*ck.

I forced a smile and shook his hand. "Hey, I'm Jax," I muttered.

"I know who you are." He chuckled. "Sorry we didn't get to meet last time I visited. I like your music. I do believe I was the one who forced Billie here to appreciate your song 'Living for Now.' She was a little unimpressed, but I got her to dance to it at least once." The bitterness in his eyes let me know he was trying to cut me down.

"She has mentioned she isn't a fan a time or two." I chuckled back.

This guy thought he could get under my skin by insulting my music, but I'd had too many trolls online try to get at me by telling me my songs were horrible. It didn't faze me if someone didn't like one. "She did show me that she knows all the lyrics to 'Strong Enough Alone.' I'll take what I can get," I replied smugly.

I looked at Billie and noticed her expression was somewhere between fear and hope. I figured she probably wanted us to get along, not stand out front of the studio in a pissing contest.

"Do you need a ride to the hotel?" I asked reluctantly.

"Actually, Zach wants to stick close to me," Billie began pleading with me. "I explained to him that you weren't comfortable with me at the hotel. I was hoping you wouldn't mind if Zach crashes on the couch."

"Brian and Corey have been sleeping on the couch," I reminded her.

"Well, maybe if we both stay in the same hotel room, then Jax won't be worried about your safety," Zach suggested. "Brian and Corey can get a good night's sleep on Jax's couch before protecting you every other waking moment."

Billie looked at me with pain in her eyes. Our nights together were the only time we were completely alone. She then looked at Zach's eager expression with confusion. "Maybe Zach has a point," she conceded. "They do stand around all day watching me. If they aren't sleeping well and something happens, maybe their reaction time will be slower."

"Ma'am, we can assure you that we will respond without haste with no sleep if necessary," Brian stated firmly.

"Look, how about Brian and Corey move to the guest rooms," I said between gritted teeth. "We don't know if the person doing these crazy things is an employee at the hotel, and I'm not willing to take the risk. We can all stay at my house."

"Sounds great," Zach replied tersely.

Billie smiled at me, and like one big happy family, we climbed into the car.

"Thank you so much for letting him stay here," Billie whispered to me late at night. I could hear the guilt in her voice, so I wrapped an arm around her waist and pulled her back into my chest.

"You're in my bed right now," I whispered, my eyes closed. "Nothing else matters," I continued trying to convince her and myself.

"I promised him we were just sleeping," Billie confessed. "I didn't want him to think you were taking advantage of me. I mentioned that the windows in your room were the only ones in the house that were bullet-proof. This is the safest room in the whole house. He understands."

"You can tell him whatever you want," I murmured softly as I squeezed her body tightly against mine.

"We just need to get through the semifinal and the finale without an incident. Then I'm sure he'll go home," Billie muttered as if calming herself. "I'll also explain to him how I feel about you."

"So you won't be joining him on the plane home?" I asked softly, opening my eyes to stare into the dark.

"I thought you promised me that once this competition was over, you were going to give in to your urges," she whispered, pushing her backside against my groin.

I swallowed my groan and leaned down, moving some of her curls and kissing the back of her neck, "I'm counting down the days."

I heard her sharp intake of breath, felt her shift, and released her body to give her the space to turn her hips to get comfortable. She surprised me when she kept turning until we were chest to chest.

"Then I guess I have a reason to stick around after the finale," she returned sweetly, looking deeply into my eyes. I felt my chest get tight. She then burrowed into me.

I thought about kissing the top of her head and telling her how great that sounded but to focus on finishing the competition. Yet the temptation of her lips so close to mine and her soft words still replaying in my ears was too much. There was also a big part of me that wanted to remind her that unlike that guy downstairs or anything she was saying to other people, we weren't just friends.

I lifted her chin and claimed her mouth. It wasn't a sweet kiss. It was a hungry one that let her know how long I'd been dreaming about her lips. The taste of her was like honey straight from a beehive. I wanted more. I felt her fingers slide through my hair and then hold on tightly as I nipped her bottom lip.

"Are you sure you want to wait until the competition is over?" She sighed against my mouth when we finally broke apart.

"Yes," I gritted out. "Which is why I need you to turn back around and close your eyes." My control was snapping.

Thankfully, she giggled and followed instructions.

I took a deep breath and then kissed the top of her head. "The faster we fall asleep, the closer we get to the damn semifinal and this all being over so I don't need to be wearing boxers right now," I muttered.

She laughed softly and murmured, "I can't wait."

I felt her body go limp in my arms when sleep finally took her. It was another five minutes before I could settle my body down and join her.

The end of this competition could not come soon enough.

It was fifteen minutes from my call time for the filming of the semifinal. The show's hairstylist added more product in my hair to make it appear messy, and the makeup artist lathered oil on my arms to make my biceps glisten under the lights. Once they murmured their satisfaction to each other, I thanked them and they made their exit. I took a hard look at the outfit Michael insisted I wear tonight, the exact same one that had my album being purchased by fifty-year-old women who hated my music. I was definitely sick of wearing a ripped wifebeater and showing off the lion tattoo I got on my shoulder when I turned eighteen. I was desperate to remind myself that I wasn't a cog in the music machine, but a leader of a pack. My leather pants put way too much of my body on display. I felt ridiculous. I was contemplating taking off the pants when Donny let himself into my dressing room.

"Oh good, you're still here," he said. "I wanted to give you something before you went out on stage." He put his hand in his pocket and pulled out a small blue jewelry box. He placed it on my dressing table and leaned back with a big smile on his face.

I swore. I didn't need to look in the damn thing to know what it was. Donny and his damn schemes. "You've got to be kidding me. I thought I was clear with you about turning this singing competition into a dating show. It isn't happening."

His smile slipped. "Now, Jax, you don't have to do anything. I just thought it might help to have it on hand in case you decided that you wanted to help your girl out," he stressed. "Now I picked the ring out myself. Didn't even send my assistant to do it for me. Its existence is only known by you, me, and the jewelry store, where every employee of course signed a nondisclosure agreement. They understand the risk of this leaking."

"How big of you, Don," I clipped. "I also don't see how proposing to Billie will help her when she might have a crazy fan of mine stalking her. If the idea of us dating puts her life at risk, I can't imagine what would happen if we were engaged."

"Look, we have Brian and Corey keeping guard, and now her best friend is here. The girl is never alone. I don't think you need to worry about the stalker. And were you to do this tonight, you basically guarantee your girl wins the competition. I do believe it would make a bigger statement at the end of the finale; however, if you do it tonight, it benefits you both," Donny explained.

I picked up the box, opened a drawer in the dressing table, and hid the damn thing.

Donny grimaced. "Jax, that's a very expensive ring. You might want to keep it on you or in a safe. It's a beautiful blue sapphire with two diamond halos—"

"Did I pay for the ring?" I interrupted.

"It's not like I can exactly afford four carats," Donny mumbled. "And you're you. The people wouldn't believe it was real if it was only two. When the new signing bonus comes it'll practically pay for itself."

"Four carats," I repeated and winced. "Look, I don't give a sh*t. If it's mine, I'll do what I want with it, which means hiding the thing here and returning it the first chance I get."

There was a knock on the door, and someone on the other side informed us, "Mr. Bone, you're needed on the stage now."

"That's my cue, and a damn good excuse to ignore all this," I muttered and turned toward the door.

"You aren't trying to avoid the ring because you're afraid the girl will say no, are you?" Don asked as his eyes slid to the closed drawer. "I know you met the small-town best friend, but while he's good-looking, I'm certain she wouldn't want him over you."

"He's sleeping on my couch and she's still in my bed," I snapped. "I'm not worried."

"But all you're doing is sleeping and protecting her until after the competition" he noted. "Her best friend has been telling everyone who gives her a sidelong glance that fact. If you're not sure she'll want you more than the country boy after this competition, it would be understandable if you haven't sealed the deal."

I stormed out of the room.

I wasn't proposing because it was a sh*t scheme Donny came up with to make more money.

If she doubted how she felt after the competition, I planned on reminding her how good we were together.

No matter what her best friend thought he needed to tell everybody.

Billie walked on stage, and I heard Zach whistle from the front row. The sound grated on me, but I tried to block out my unwanted houseguest and focus on her performance.

She was wearing a black long-sleeved sheer lace dress that hugged her body and flared at the bottom. There was a single spotlight that shined down on her, illuminating her blonde curls and making it feel like there was nobody else here except for her. She grasped the microphone on the stand with her left hand and began to softly sing "The House that Built Me."

I thought it was the perfect choice for the semifinal. Finally we were getting to hear her sing a country song from one of her idols, and she wasn't losing her individuality. When she told me it had to do with going home after changing into someone different, which would complement her finale song perfectly, I agreed completely, even though I hadn't heard it myself.

When she started singing about going home, the five screens behind her began showing black-and-white photographs of her past. They started with her pregnant teen mother, then her mother teaching a young Billie how to ride a bike, Billie singing in the school talent show and eating her mother's cooking with Zach by her side. When she began singing about turning into someone different, they started showing photographs of her time in the competition and in LA. They even used some of the paparazzi shots of her and me. My smile faded. It was as if she was telling a story that she *needed* to go home, that being with me was dangerous for her. And I wasn't completely sure it was just a song. I worried I was being selfish convincing her to stay.

When she finished the song, the crowd went wild, the room erupting in cheers and whistling.

Claudia and Russell both came to their feet clapping, and I felt like an idiot sitting in stunned silence. I just wasn't sure my legs would hold me. Claudia looked down at me with a grimace and whispered, "Get up."

I shook my head of the crazy places it was going and joined in on the standing ovation. When Connor joined her on stage and walked her closer to our table to listen to our comments, we all sat back in our seats, and I looked deep into those big blue eyes.

"You were phenomenal," Russell called out, making her gaze shift to him.

"Breathtaking," Claudia continued.

"It was a great way to start the night," I agreed, relieved when her eyes came back to me. "I can't imagine Ryne and Faith are sitting backstage eager to follow that."

Billie laughed nervously. "Thank you so much. Your opinions mean a great deal to me, and honestly, if this is my last night singing here, I want you all to know how much you have each helped me."

The entire audience went "Aww," and Billie blushed.

Connor Graves chuckled and then quickly led her off stage.

I felt like Faith's and Ryne's performances went by in a blur after that. Faith sang an acoustic cover of Christina Aguilera's "Beautiful," wearing a white suit with the word brave painted all over it in black. The entire audience was crying by the end. Ryne made every girl in the room swoon with a rendition of Blake Shelton's "God Gave Me You." Still, I didn't worry about Billie's chances of winning the competition. I didn't know if it was because I was biased, but I felt like nothing compared to her on that stage in the spotlight.

When Connor started encouraging viewers at home to vote, I let my eyes roam to where Zach had been sitting in the front row. His seat was empty. I had no doubt he had snuck out the moment Billie's song had finished to spend some time alone with her.

He knew I would need to stay onstage for the entire performance. I didn't doubt that he enjoyed that fact. Almost as much as I enjoyed knowing that tonight, when we said goodnight, Billie would follow me up the stairs and leave him in the living room.

Again.

CHAPTER
TWENTY

Responsible

Billie

"**O**h great, you guys are already here." Faith giggled as she entered my dressing room. Zach and I were gossiping about the photos the production crew could have utilized during my song. Thankfully, they didn't ask for any pictures of my awkward puberty years. My stomach was sore from laughing so hard.

"What are you up to?" I asked skeptically when Faith winked at Brian standing guard in the hallway before locking my door.

"I just thought we should make this our little tradition," Faith confessed before pulling out a bottle of tequila with a big red bow on it and shot glasses from her purse. "You did an amazing job, I did an amazing job, and we're no longer just two girls sitting in a convention center taking selfies. It's time to celebrate."

"With tequila?" Zach looked at me and laughed, "I thought you swore off the stuff since that homecoming party?"

"I did, but Faith hasn't seen me puking my guts up enough to know I hate the stuff," I groaned.

She pouted. "You had some last time. And platinum artists always drink tequila."

"Last time there were extenuating circumstances. We had just done a duet with a celebrity on national television, and I had just agreed to go on a date with Jax Bone." I felt Zach prickle beside me. "I'm fine to pass on this right now."

"Well, if you aren't going to be any fun, I'll just party by myself until Ryne joins us. The cowboy is always up for a good time." She chuckled. "One shot won't hurt until he arrives."

I rolled my eyes at Zach as Faith filled one of the glasses. She had barely taken her first mouthful before she was squeezing her eyes shut and grasping at her throat. When she opened them, she was crying.

I immediately knew something was wrong. "Go get Brian and Corey," I yelled at Zach before gripping Faith's hand.

"It burns," she struggled to say. Her breath had become ragged. "So stupid," she gasped. "Found the bottle in my dressing room addressed to us. Figured it was safe." Her mouth started turning red. She began coughing, and her tears began getting heavier.

"Don't try and talk," I told her. "Someone will be here to help any minute."

Before I could even finish my sentence, Brian and Corey arrived with the show's paramedics team.

"I think she's been poisoned," I said between shaky breaths.

"Move. I'll get her to the hospital," Brian demanded before helping Faith onto a stretcher. "You can follow with Corey in one of the show's cars."

I nodded and got out of their way.

I feared this had something to do with my stalker. I should have gone home the moment I was hospitalized. I should have thought about someone else getting hurt.

I would have to tell Faith this was all my fault.

My tears began to fall.

I paced the hospital waiting room like a madman, stopping only to wipe my eyes and blow my nose. I refused to talk to anyone, even though the entire crew from *Superstardom* was standing with us. As soon Faith and I disappeared from set, her condition traveled the gossip grapevine. One after the other, production assistants, Ryne, all of the judges, camera crewmen, and producers all walked through the hospital doors. It was clear by this waiting room that Faith was loved by everyone she met. I felt responsible, so I struggled to meet anyone's eyes.

I suddenly understood how Jax felt when I was behind those doors and didn't begrudge him demanding answers from the doctor as quickly as he did. If Jax's fame could get us answers, then I wanted all of them.

Thankfully, the same doctor who helped treat my poison ivy approached us solemnly. Jax moved to hold my hand. Zach also came to stand by my other shoulder. It didn't matter how close they stood, I still felt so alone.

"Miss Randall is in stable condition. The tequila bottle you brought in seems to have been tainted with a cleaning product. The lab is still testing the bottle to determine exactly what was mixed into the alcohol. Thankfully, you got her here in record time. We immediately performed gastrointestinal decontamination and pumped her stomach. Her breathing has stabilized, but she still has burns to her mouth and lips. Your friend is extremely lucky to be alive because of your men here," he explained, nodding to Brian and Corey. "If only we all had Marines guarding us."

"Will she be able to sing next week?" I asked softly, daring to hope for an answer that would make my guilt feel less heavy.

"I'm sorry, but Miss Randall will likely need to remain in the hospital for the next week until we can be certain of the poison she ingested. There may be delayed side effects."

Jax squeezed my hand. "Thank you, Doc, for all your help. Can we go in and visit with her?"

"It's in Miss Randall's best interest to rest for the remainder of this evening. However, first thing tomorrow I can arrange visitor passes," he stated before a nurse approached him and whispered in his ear. "I'm terribly sorry, but I need to see to another patient." Then he left us staring at Faith's door.

"Did you want to go get food from the cafeteria?" Jax asked softly. I was relieved that he knew without asking that I planned on staying in this hospital until I could see for myself that she was okay.

"It might be best if we left the hospital for food," Donny muttered. "There's a great deal of press outside. Faith's condition leaked on social media. If we stay any longer, the fans and press will be allowed to enter the building. It is a public hospital, after all, and Jax, you remember the last time they mobbed you in a shopping mall. It'll be pandemonium."

"I'm not that hungry," I murmured to Jax. I watched the pain enter his eyes before they shifted to Zach. He knew I intended to stay, even if he couldn't.

"You okay with staying with her here?" Jax asked Zach. "With Brian and Corey standing guard?"

Zach nodded solemnly.

"Okay, I'll head home, lead the press away," Jax clipped. "The moment you're ready to join me, just let Brian know. I'll be there waiting."

"Thank you," I whispered.

He squeezed my hand again and left the building.

"There won't be an elimination evening tomorrow night," Donny stated. "I know you probably don't care about that right now, but I thought I should let you know. No need to attend rehearsals or go to the studio. The producers already contacted the judges' agents to let them know that the finale schedule would be the same, but they would give you and Ryne some time to recoup after today's incident. With Faith being injured, you and Ryne are automatically the two finalists."

Ryne and I made eye contact over the crowd. Neither of us was smiling.

"I don't think I want to be on the show anymore," I began. "Ryne can be the winner."

"Let's not talk about this now," Zach interrupted. "Billie is worried about her friend, and the finale is a week away. Can we just focus on Faith right now?"

"Of course," Donny murmured before gesturing for everyone to join him in leaving.

Everyone headed out until only Ryne, Zach, Brian, and Corey remained with me.

"You don't need to stay, Ryne," I muttered. "I'll let her know you were here."

"Billie, I'm not going anywhere until I know she's okay," he snapped. I was shocked. The country gentleman who was always easygoing and laid back suddenly appeared ready to hit someone. I didn't realize he cared about Faith at all. All of us contestants were going through a unique experience, apparently.

I shrugged "Okay." I found a chair tucked in the corner and sat down. Ryne walked to the nearest wall and leaned against it.

"It's going to be a long night," Zach muttered before finding his own chair.

I didn't care how long the night would be. All I cared about was seeing with my own eyes that I didn't kill my best friend in this competition.

She looked more fragile than I imagined. Her skin was pale, and there were big yellow circles under her eyes. I tried to remind myself that it could be worse. I could be looking at her in a damn coffin.

My breath caught on a swallowed sob.

She must have heard me, because she opened her eyes and reached for her glasses on the side table. When she saw it was me, she smiled, and I wanted to cry all over again.

"I'm so, so sorry," I told her as I rushed forward and hugged her. "This is all my fault. I should have told you some crazy person was tampering with my stuff. You never would have touched that damn bottle. I should have gone home. I risked your life for a damn singing competition."

"Billie, I knew you had a stalker," Faith croaked. "Everyone knows. Your guards aren't exactly subtle. Don't blame yourself for my stupidity." Her face showed the pain she must have been in to say those words.

"Please don't try and talk. I just want to let you know that I'm quitting. Ryne can have it, or they can reschedule for after you're better. I don't deserve to win."

"Don't be silly," Faith squawked. "You love to sing. Don't let some crazy a*hole ruin this for you. For us. Remember, if I can't win, I want to be able to tell people I knew Billie Bishop before she was famous."

A tear ran down my cheek, and she wiped it away.

"I don't want to do this without you," I muttered.

"Forget that. Do it *for* me," she hissed. "Promise me you'll pretend you're me and love every minute you get on that stage. Make people cry and dance and it'll be like I won." She closed her eyes, clearly exhausted from trying to talk.

I exhaled roughly.

"If that's what you want. Okay," I told her. "I promise."

She opened her eyes and smiled, squeezing my hand.

Before I could say anything else, Ryne stormed in the room. "It's my turn," he demanded, causing Faith to blush.

I looked at the two of them and suddenly felt very awkward standing between them. I eyed Faith quizzically, and she shrugged.

"Then I guess it's my turn to go home," I told Faith. "I'll visit during the week, let you know how your rehearsals for the finale are going."

She winked at me before I softly closed the door behind me.

Jax was waiting for me in the entryway to his house. He didn't say anything to me when I walked in the door, just reached for my hand and pulled me into his body.

I was so exhausted I forgot that Zach was behind me.

I leaned into Jax and felt as if my problems became lighter. He bent his head and brushed his lips over my lips. "Sorry that your day has been so horrible," he whispered. "And I'm so sorry I couldn't be there for you. All I ever want to be is by your side."

"Feels better now," I replied honestly.

"What are you going to do about the competition?" he asked, and him just knowing that this might change my feelings had my heart leaping.

"Faith made me promise to win the thing."

"Good. Her fire and my song, no way you won't win," Jax muttered softly, kissing my head.

I froze. "Your song?"

"Sh*t," Jax muttered. "Look, I thought about telling you I wrote "You're Always There" but I didn't want you to say no to a song you loved because of me. It's perfect for you. I wrote it for my mom when my dad died, but it just never felt right when I would sing it."

"Is this the only secret you were keeping from me?"

Zach started coughing behind my back, and I was reminded that we had an audience. I thought about ending this conversation and waiting, but I needed to know the answer.

"You're in my bed every night, and we basically spend every waking moment together," Jax replied. "I don't have time for any other secrets."

Zach swore, but I kept ignoring him.

"And you really think I do the song justice?" I asked nervously. "This isn't some act of pity?"

"Billie, you are the only person I want singing that song," Jax whispered to me. "I'm a jerk about my music, just ask Donny. I would have told Graham to find a different song for you, if your recordings hadn't been amazing."

"I don't know what to say," I confessed. "Thank you doesn't seem enough." I heard Zach sigh.

"You don't need to thank me, if you hadn't loved the song it would still be sitting in Graham's office. I was never going to release it. Honestly, the song is more yours than it has ever been mine. I should never have called it my song, but I should have told you where it came from. I'm sorry."

"It's okay," I told him softly.

"Now, do you need me to fix you some food?" Jax asked.

"That would be great," I returned, suddenly feeling so much pressure about the finale.

After dinner, I started moving directly to the staircase like a zombie. I needed to sleep. The last twenty-four hours suddenly felt like an elephant sitting on my chest, weighing me down. Jax encouraged me to go to bed without him while he cleaned up our dinner plates.

As I started to take my first step toward Jax's bedroom, Zach approached me.

"You're still going to sleep with him in his room knowing he lied to you?" he asked, his eyes piercing into mine.

"It's just a song, Zach, not an affair."

"He can really do no wrong in your eyes, can he?" he grumbled. "I've never lied to you. Not once."

"Not everyone has known each other from birth and trusts each other with every aspect of their life. It takes time. I've kept bigger secrets from people I've only known a short while."

"He only cares about himself and promoting himself. I was okay to stand by as long as it kept you safe, hoping that once this was over, you would see him for what he truly is. But the longer I see you together, the more I know he's brainwashed you."

"Zach, it's been a very long day. Get some sleep. We don't need to be discussing my relationship with Jax or comparing it to yours and mine right now," I begged. "I promised you once the competition was over we'd hash everything out."

He looked like he was deep in thought before he nodded at me and stomped into the other room.

I was too tired to follow him.

CHAPTER
TWENTY-ONE

Are you in love with Jax Bone or Jax Bone's song?

Billie

The finale rehearsals had been grueling. The tabloids alternated between releasing articles about possible foul play in Faith's mystery illness that had her dropping out of the competition and the likelihood of my relationship with Jax succeeding after the show.

Zach still wasn't talking to me. I watched his eyes follow Jax constantly as if he were a lion ready to pounce on prey. He was constantly disappearing and reappearing. I figured he wanted to uncover some information that would have me disliking Jax but at the same time be there for me every step of the *Superstardom* way.

Meanwhile, I kept telling anyone who would listen that I was ready for the end of this competition.

I was sick of the attention. The lack of alone time.

However, now I was standing at the side of the stage and was one song away from it being over. I would no longer be Billie Bishop, *Superstardom* contestant. My whole body was shaking I was so scared.

Michael approached me, whistling. I tried to smile.

"That dress is my *pièce de résistance*." He sighed. "The blue sparkles match your eyes. A little Dolly Parton with the sequin fringe to pay homage to your country roots, but something that is uniquely Billie with its conservative sheer sweetheart neckline."

I chuckled. "It's pretty fabulous."

"You look like a star. You're going to knock 'em dead, sweetie," he murmured, and I nodded nervously. There were seven thousand audience members this evening, including my momma. I wasn't sure I was going to do anything.

Ryne exited the stage with the crowd still roaring, and Steve, the stage manager, gestured for me to enter.

I took a deep breath and walked to my marker.

The song went by in a haze. The lights came on, the dancer they hired to perform a contemporary routine to "You're Always There" floated around me, and my lips moved of their own accord. It was exactly as I had rehearsed. I hit every high note and moved my body just as I was told to. However, I felt as if my mind had left my body. It was as if my brain couldn't process the fact that it was me standing on the stage for the season finale of *Superstardom*.

When I felt like I finally came to, my cheeks were wet and I realized I must have cried during my performance. The spotlights and smoke special effects faded away. My heart was still pounding. It was like I was in shock.

"That was fabulous," Ryne whispered to me as he and Connor joined me on stage for our final feedback session with the judges.

I wiped some of the sweat off my forehead and grinned at him. "I don't remember any of it," I whispered back.

"Me either." He chuckled. "I went on autopilot. I never understood the endless rehearsals until now. Thank God for them."

I just nodded, unable to say anything.

Connor posed in the middle of the stage and forced Ryne and I to shift to his left as we looked at the judges. "Well, what an amazing song from Billie Bishop. Can you tell us how you convinced Jax Bone to let you sing such a personal piece of music?" he asked, the venom hidden behind smiles and forced laughter. "From the lyrics, it seems to be about his father's tragic death. You thought you were prepared enough to convey such an important message?"

My mouth gaped for a second. I didn't realize the show was going to share this information. "Actually, after I found out Jax Bone wrote the song, I told him he should sing it. I thought I couldn't possibly do it justice. But after our fellow contestant Faith got injured during the semifinal, she made me promise to do everything I could to not only win this thing but to love every minute I got to spend on this stage like she did. I've never loved a song more," I returned honestly.

"You're in love with Jax Bone's song or with Jax Bone?" Connor teased, and the audience laughed along with him. "Billie Bishop, you are making miracles tonight on this show."

I wanted to vomit.

"Well, in just a short few moments, one of you will be singing your original song again, but this time as the winner of *Superstardom*." Connor turned to the judges. "Before we announce the winner for this year's season, do any of you have any final words or advice you'd like to impart to Ryne or Billie?"

Claudia smiled at us both. "Look, guys, this is just one step on a long ladder of success that you're both beginning. I have no doubt you will have amazing futures in the music industry and your hometowns will be erecting signs with your names on them."

Russell laughed. "These kids won't just have hometown signs erected. They need to be prepared for giant billboards in Times Square and on the Las Vegas strip, because I don't think they're going anywhere but to giant recording contracts and sell-out stadium tours."

The entire audience cheered in agreement, and I felt the pit of my stomach drop even lower. A stadium tour seemed like a crazy idea.

Connor turned to Jax, and the audience went eerily silent.

"Well, Jax, we all know you'll likely talk to Billie in private after this competition is all over." A few people in the audience laughed, while I noticed Jax grit his teeth. "And no doubt Ryne is relieved that the judges don't get to vote for the winner this evening. But before we find out who our latest superstar is, is there anything you would like to say to either of them?"

Jax nodded and looked intently at us both. "You're extremely talented musicians, and each of you command the stage like professionals. I'm glad I got to witness both of your journeys through the competition, as well as Faith's, who couldn't be here tonight. I'm also glad we don't pick the winner, because I honestly know there isn't just one. Sure, for television purposes, one person will be crowned tonight and someone will get to sleep in tomorrow while the other begins a giant press tour. But the world has seen how gifted you three are, so there are no losers tonight, just different roads you'll take to one day be sitting side by side at this table."

I think no one imagined Jax would say something so profound. The audience was shocked into silence, and Connor seemed at a loss for words, but thankfully Ryne smiled and responded, "Thanks, man," and suddenly the room roared.

Everyone's cheering seemed to snap Connor back into his on-camera persona. "Well, with those kind words, it's time for us to open the envelope."

Ryne gripped my hand.

"And the winner of this year's *Superstardom* is… Billie Bishop."

The crowd started screaming, and my entire body got goose bumps. Ryne pulled me into a hug and whispered, "Faith and I have known since your Vegas audition that none of us had a chance. It's been great getting to share a stage. Congratulations." He then made a subtle exit off stage as we both had rehearsed, and a microphone was rushed to my hand in order for me to sing.

Connor turned to me and pretended to wipe away a tear, then wrapped an arm around me and stated, "Well, Billie Bishop, it looks like it's time for us to hear that beautiful song again." He started to leave but stopped abruptly when he saw Zach barge on stage, the Marine team close behind.

"Zach?" I asked, shocked.

"Sorry everyone for the interruption, but I've got something serious to ask," he told the audience. I was surprised to see that he was mic'd. He then turned to face me. "Billie, I know life is changing for both of us. I know you won this competition and are about to start the celebrity lifestyle that you've always deserved. But I want to be there for the best and worst moments, whether you're a celebrity or a small-town girl. I don't want you standing in a room alone with strangers ever again without me. You're the most important person to me. So I want to ask you to spend the rest of your life with me." He then got down on one knee, pulled out a little blue box from his pocket, and opened it. I couldn't even look at the box. I just kept staring at Zach's face. "Billie Bishop, will you do me the honor of becoming my wife?"

"What are you doing?" I whispered, trying to turn my back to the audience. I felt a single tear fall across my cheek.

"I'm proposing," Zach murmured nervously.

"On national television? Have you lost your mind?" I stared at the backstage staff, unable to look directly at him any longer without tears falling down my face.

"I was going to tell you. This was always in the works. You were going to be proposed to at the end of this show. You wouldn't listen. You've turned into another one of Jax Bone's groupies, and you deserve better than that," he replied, raking a hand through his hair.

My gaze darted to Jax in his judging chair. The lights from the stage made me unable to see his eyes or read his body language. I was too far away. I had no idea if what Zach was telling me was the truth.

"So you bought a ring? To what, beat him to the punch? You thought that would make things better? If it was you embarrassing me on stage, then it's all okay?"

"The show bought the ring. It was in Jax's dressing room." The audience gasped. "It's a sapphire, and it matches your eyes. Can you just look at it? If you hate it, I'll get a different one. A better one."

"No. I can't. Just because some show is buying me an engagement ring doesn't make any of this okay."

"It was him or me, and I wanted it to be me. Billie, choose me," Zach pleaded, his voice shaking. "I've loved you our entire lives. I know I promised to give you time to think about us, but I also already knew I would be asking this question one day, I just needed to speed up my timeline if I wanted to be the first one to do it. Billie, I want to spend the rest of my life with you, and I want that life to start now. I want to forsake all others and my dreams if it means I get to be a part of yours."

"You didn't think we needed to date first?" I hissed back.

"We went to prom together," Zach murmured, causing the seven thousand audience members to sigh in unison.

"As friends," I snapped, and he flinched.

"We've slow danced to your favorite songs," he continued.

"As friends, Zach," I repeated, my heart ripping just a little more as I watched him flinch again.

"We've kissed," he returned adamantly. "And it wasn't as friends."

"You kissed me," I reminded him and watched his heart break.

"Marry me, Billie," Zach pleaded, and the audience gasped. "I dare you to."

And with those words, my heart broke.

I stood frozen, the spotlight blinding me. I shut my eyes to stop the pounding in my head. I desperately wanted to run and hide from everyone's eager facial expressions.

I willed the band to start playing again.

"So are you going to answer the boy?" Russell asked from the judges' bench, chuckling.

I turned to stare at them in confusion.

Is no one going to stop this from happening?

"Maybe she needs to hear him repeat the question." Claudia laughed. "Girl's having a big night."

The most beautiful guy I'd ever met, inside and out, touched my shoulder and, for the second time this evening, looked deeply into my eyes and asked softly, "Billie Bishop, will you make me the happiest man in the world and marry me?"

If only I felt more than friendship.

"I'm so sorry. This is the first dare I can't agree to, Zach," I replied before I ran off the stage.

I pushed past assistants and camera operators, running through the halls of the theater as quickly as my feet would carry me. Brian and Corey followed, but when I reached my dressing room, I demanded they give me space and wait in the hallway. I closed the door behind me, collapsed on the floor, and let the tears flow. The sweet scent that filled the room from the bouquets of flowers was a harsh reminder of what tonight was meant to represent.

I didn't know what I was going to do. As the tears kept running down my cheeks, I started doubting my actions. Did I just give up my best friend for a competition? Did I just end an eighteen-year relationship for a guy I've known for less than six months? I considered fixing my face and returning to the stage and saying yes.

A future without Zach was unimaginable.

My eyes became like leaking taps; no matter how many times I rubbed them, they kept dripping and covering my cheeks in streaks of water. I tried to squeeze them closed and saw Zach's devastated face again.

This wasn't just some guy. Zach was the person in my life who had been there for and supported me through everything. I never thought of him romantically; he was like my twin, a part of myself that I neither questioned nor fantasized about. He just was. If my blood had boiled or butterflies appeared when we held hands at least once during our time together, I might have been able to say yes. After all, I knew a future to-gether would be one filled with unwavering support.

I decided I needed to go find him and discuss my decision. Maybe I had been too hasty.

When a knock sounded on my dressing room door, I sighed in re-lief. This was why I always felt like he was my twin, my other half. He always knew my mind before I said a word.

"Just a few more minutes," I begged, trying to wipe away the mascara that had smudged beneath my eyes.

When the door cracked open and Cindy slipped through, I couldn't fight the weight of disappointment that landed on my chest. *He's not com-ing after me.*

"Look, I know they probably need me back on stage, but I can't yet," I muttered, the tears falling again. "This evening has just been so over-whelming. If you could go back to whoever sent you and tell them I look like a mess…. They wouldn't even want me on stage right now. If they could give me five minutes, I should be able to pull myself together." The weight on my heart become heavier.

When Cindy let out a high-pitched laugh, I couldn't help but blink twice. "You know what I find amusing about this whole situation?" she rasped out. Her voice was deeper than I had ever heard before. "Even now as you trample on more lives and hearts, you're still playing the vic-tim. It's almost entertaining."

"Huh?" I looked at the blonde pixie, who had always been smiling and helping everyone, now standing in front of me with venom seeping from her eyes. She leaned back against the door, barricading me in, wear-ing her usual denim skirt and her white-blonde hair neatly braided down her back. When she jerked and moved closer to me, I instinctively stood and took a step back.

Gone was the sweet intern, and in her place was a psychopath. "I mean, look at you. Crying and hysterical. You just won the damn com-petition and a good-looking guy proposed to you in front of thousands, yet you're acting like you just got evicted from your damn home." Before I could respond, I felt the sharp slap of her palm across my cheek. "Always the bitch."

The force of her hand had my face whipping to the side. "What the f*ck?" I yelled, touching my cheek.

Cindy just kept ranting. "You destroy lives. You're like a brain cancer, infecting people's minds and slowly killing their dreams. I've watched it. First Connor, then Ryne, then Zach. No doubt Jax will be next. Every guy just can't wait to fall in front of you, and you just step all over them to get what you want. God, I was pissed when Faith got hurt instead of you. It took me weeks to plan that."

She took a step toward me, and that time I moved to meet her. The shock of the evening had worn off, and I was ready to throw my own punches. "It was you," I hissed. "You've been sending me notes trying to scare me. You tampered with my wardrobe and put Faith in the hospital trying to get to me. What is *wrong* with you?" I pushed her backward. All this time I had been imagining some forty-year-old muscleman coming after me but it was this five-foot-nothing nobody. I wouldn't even need Brian or Corey to intervene. I could handle this girl.

She laughed hysterically before her eyes narrowed to slits. "You think something's wrong with me. I'm the only one in this whole damn place who isn't blinded by your f*cking tits." Her eyes spewed crazy as she sneered.

The sting of my cheek couldn't compete with the boiling anger that stirred inside of me. "You're so done. I haven't destroyed any lives, but you can bet I will use any power this show might have given me to destroy yours. You need to get the hell out of my dressing room and probably the state before I tell everyone what you've done. Faith deserved to be here, but you don't," I spat, acid dripping from my tongue. I took another step forward, ready to push my way through her to the exit, when she pulled out a knife.

The light glinted over the sharp silver blade and disappeared into the thick black handle. The anger coursing through my body froze. I had grown up my whole life listening to my mother warn me about her kitchen knives. The stories of accidentally cut arteries flashed through my mind.

"Not so tough now, are you? I'll have you know that before you came along, it was going to be my year. Connor had promised me he'd do everything he could to pull some strings and get me on the show. And if you hadn't ruined his career and gotten him on probation, everyone in that audience would be talking about *me* right now." She grabbed my wrist and let the blade hover an inch away from my skin. "I've been picturing this moment for quite some time. At first I was going to use a gun, but I decided I wanted to make you bleed slowly for every dollar Connor and I lost."

"You d-don't really want to do th-this," I stuttered out, fear suddenly creeping inside of me. I tried to jerk my arm away, but she tightened her grip. "I haven't done anything to Connor Graves. I barely talk to the guy, I promise."

She moved the knife up my arm and pressed it into my skin until blood welled to the surface. "Don't waste your lies on me. Everyone thinks you're so sweet and innocent. The small-town girl who auditioned all alone and caught the eye of Jax Bone," Cindy murmured softly. "They didn't realize it was you trying to seduce every guy in the room like you're this virginal goddess. Of course Connor took the bait, but he got punished for suggesting you weren't as virtuous as you pretended to be." I tried to lean backward, but she pulled me forward once more. "You keep moving, I'll push it in harder and we won't get to chat anymore. It would be a shame for you to not know why you're being punished."

I exhaled a shaky breath. "I'm listening. Connor said something during my audition and it's my fault," I clarified, trying to calm the crazy out of her.

"He predicted that you'd be jumping into someone's bed, and they told him they wouldn't be renewing his damn contract," she growled. "You set out to destroy him and me."

I felt the pressure of the knife deepen and watched her smile.

The pain and seeping blood pissed me off. She wasn't going to listen to reason. And if she was going to keep cutting me, I needed to start making her work a little harder. "Bless your heart, you think I care at all about you," I drawled and watched her eyes flare. I braced my body to fight her.

"Cindy, I need you in my office—" Connor said as he stuck his head in the door. His eyes bulged when he saw the knife in her hand. "Cin, what the f*ck are you doing right now?"

His entry distracted her enough that she loosened her grip and I yanked my arm away. The edge of the blade dragged along my skin, but I was able to move backward. The farther I got away from her, the better I felt. I tried to look around the room for anything that could be turned into a weapon.

Cindy hissed. "There are two of us now. You won't get past us both. You aren't leaving this room alive."

The reality of her words made a knot form in the pit of my stomach.

"Cin, what are you talking about?" Connor cried, staring at the blood running down my arm.

Cindy rolled her eyes and shut the dressing room door.

"Connor, stop making noise before someone hears you. I don't want you ruining what we've talked about for months. I'm finally teaching the wannabee a lesson," she replied, waving the knife around, demonstrating that she was a total lunatic. If she had been teetering on the edge of sanity before, the b*tch had just completely fallen off.

I watched Connor stare at her and the knife in horror. "Where did you even get the knife from? There's security everywhere."

"I stole it from the caterers upstairs. They've prepared a whole after-party for the newly crowned superstar. And it should have been for *us*," she screeched. "It isn't fair, and I won't just sit around and talk about it anymore. She needs to *know* how it feels. How she screwed up *our* chances. She should lose her dreams like we lost ours."

Connor looked at her French braid and snarling mouth with critical eyes before slowly concealing the emotions that had been running across his face. He sighed dramatically. "Cindy, you could cut me with that damn thing if you keep waving it around. Put the knife down," he scolded as if talking to a toddler. I was shocked when I saw her pause and lower the knife a fraction. I was even more shocked when I watched Connor change his body language as if posing on camera and tell her, "You're about to make us both look bad, and you'll be as bad as she is if you cost me my sponsor deals. It's like you don't love me at all."

Cindy gasped. I tried not to snort. "You can't mean that, Gravey train," Cindy pleaded. "You know I would never hurt your face." She looked to me with evil in her eyes and muttered, "And I'd never do anything that would risk our futures. Once this b*tch is cut up, we'll be free to live our lives again without problems."

I watched his eyes widen again and then adjust as if unfazed. "You can't do that, Cindy," he replied calmly.

I wanted to cheer but kept my mouth closed and prayed that she'd listen to him.

"What do you mean, 'you can't do that, Cindy'?" she mocked. "This is the only way she'll learn. We both agreed she's a sneaky slut."

I wanted to intervene, to ask what the hell I was supposed to learn by bleeding to death. But Connor seemed to have a scheme, and because the only weapons I could see in this room at my disposal were my finale Christian Louboutin heels, I figured he was my best shot.

"Are you on something?" he asked carefully. "What did you take? I'm worried about your health. Should I rush you to the hospital? This isn't a thought-out strategy, and you're smarter than this."

"Drugs? Smarter?" Cindy scoffed. "You think I need drugs to want to cut up this rock star groupie? I just want to take back what she stole." She waved the knife at my face. "There is no more time for planning. I've been smart and it hasn't gotten me anywhere. Now we act."

"There's always time to adjust a plan," Connor replied cheerfully. "And you've never involved me before, and you know what they say about two heads being better than one."

"How do you think she should be punished?" Cindy growled. "I doubt it would be enough. You should just block the door and I'll hurt the pop princess."

"You're forgetting that I don't care about her, but I care about you," Connor crooned. Cindy paused her antics and smiled. I wanted to puke. Connor continued seductively. "If Billie goes out unscathed, she'll be able to go back on stage and tell everyone about your actions. You'll be famous *tonight*, because millions are tuned in for the finale. Everyone will want to see photos of you and of us. It'll make your career. They'll find those videos you made online for your channel. Now you just need to let the public come to you. I don't care about her. I just want you to get the fame you deserve."

I watched Cindy hesitate, then lower the knife and ponder the idea. "My video channel is good," she muttered. "I just need more people to look at it and notice me."

"Exactly" Connor continued. "But if you cut up her face or body, she goes in an ambulance. They keep her locked up and she never tells our story. And it could take months for your name to be released. You hurt her and she also won't tell them how fierce you looked holding that knife or the awesome way you look in your denim skirt."

"You'll tell them?" Cindy asked me skeptically.

I nodded slowly, afraid that if I spoke even a single word, the strange trance Connor seemed to have over her would be broken.

"See, Cin-Cin? We need to focus on us and our future. Now, babe, just give me the knife and let Billie go on stage," Connor encouraged. I held my breath.

"Her arm is bleeding," she said cheerfully. "They'll notice that and even ask about me. I guess that's enough for today."

"Babe, you're exactly right," Connor agreed, reaching for the knife.

"Where should we be when she announces it onstage?" she asked eagerly, looking at herself in the mirror and fluffing her hair.

"I have to escort her back, because that's my job." He sighed reluctantly. "But you should wait in here. It'll be more dramatic in the dressing room. And the camera crews can move straight from the stage to here."

"You won't be here when the cameras come to me?" Cindy whined.

"I wouldn't want to steal your spotlight. They're going to catch that golden light of your hair if I'm not standing beside you and casting a shadow." Connor grinned, running a hand down Cindy's hair. She purred like a cat.

"Do you see this, bitch?" she asked me smugly. "That's my guy. You tried to destroy him, but he always thinks of others." She handed him the knife.

I watched Connor visibly exhale.

I just nodded again. Whatever game he was playing, I really didn't want to interfere in the fourth quarter.

"You need anything else while you wait for the cameras?" he asked sweetly.

"No, I'll just fix my face with her makeup," she gushed.

"Perfect." He grinned.

When Connor led me out the door and closed it behind us, I collapsed. He looked at me with such sorrow. "You okay to stay here? I'm just going to get the chair from next door so I can lock her in."

"Okay," I muttered, too shocked to process anything else.

"Billie, I'm truly sorry. I was letting off steam in the bedroom. I didn't think she would do this. I knew she had gotten a little obsessed with me and being famous, but I thought it was like the other *Superstardom* groupies. I thought she was an assistant who looked good naked, not a sociopath with a love of knives."

I just shook my head. I didn't need an explanation or apology. I just needed to sit down.

CHAPTER
TWENTY-TWO

Everyone had dreams

Jax

left my judge's seat to go find Billie. They were replaying her winning song on the screens and launching fireworks to distract the audience from the fact that the star wasn't on the stage. I knew they would drag her out here any minute, but I wanted to check for myself that she was okay.

I saw Zach approaching me and stopped in my tracks. I didn't hit the guy like I wanted. I knew Billie would want to make things good between them eventually. They had too much history for this moment to destroy them. And If I broke his nose, I feared I would become the bad guy.

I flexed my hand and took a deep breath. "The ring wasn't bought by the show," I clipped. "Put it back in my room so I can return the damn thing. Otherwise, I'll make Donny send you the bill."

"You're just pissed I beat you to the punch," he muttered.

I took another calming breath. "You didn't beat me to anything. I would never have done that to Billie. This is a once-in-a-lifetime moment, and she worked hard to get here. I never would have made it about me and my feelings."

Zach took a step back like I'd hit him. Then he shook his head and told me, "You can lie to Billie all you want, but you can't fool me. One of the production assistants told me all about your plans and even where to find the damn ring. If you were so damn pious, there wouldn't even be a ring and no one would know about it."

"No one *was* meant to know about it," I growled. "It was Donny's idea, and I told him no." I thought about what he said, and it was like a freaking lightning bolt through my body. "Which production assistant knew something about Billie and me that no one was meant to know about?" I asked, feeling the rage inside me boil.

"The blonde one," he murmured. "She's little and usually fetches everyone for the stage."

"Cindy. Have you seen her at all tonight?"

"Before I went on stage," Zach choked out. "I thought I saw her follow Billie when she ran off. I thought it was the show trying to convince her to come back."

I turned and started walking to Billie's dressing room. I didn't care if Zach followed or not as I thought about all the times Cindy had been around, slipping in and out of dressing rooms and fittings. When Corey started calling my name, I began to run.

When we got to Billie's hallway, I saw her slumped on the floor against the wall while Connor Graves held a chair underneath the door handle of her dressing room. The door was shaking.

"What the hell?" I asked before Billie's face turned to me. My heart stopped. There was blood all over her outfit.

"Don't worry, it looks worse than it is," she whispered.

"I promise you I had no idea she was this crazy," Connor explained as he held the door closed. "I sent one of your Marines to get the cops and the other to get you. I figured we'd wait and make sure she didn't get out."

"Cindy?" I asked before reaching for Billie. Both she and Connor nodded. Billie then carefully got to her feet, but before I could pull her to me, Zach stepped in front of me. She blinked in confusion.

"You came for me as well," she whispered to Zach.

"Of course I did. My best friend's life is at risk, I'm coming to find her. Even if it's just after I proposed on stage like an idiot," he muttered.

"Sorry to interrupt your do-over," I said to Zach before turning back to Billie, "but I need to know, how bad are you hurt? And is she still armed?"

Billie took a look at Connor and then turned to me. "She had a knife and made some superficial cuts. I won't need stitches. Connor convinced her to give the knife to him before she did any more damage. She doesn't have anything else in there."

I looked at Connor skeptically. "Why would she listen to you?"

"Because we're f*cking, okay? I knew some of her dreams. Didn't realize a freak in the sheets was just a plain freak." He groaned.

I took a step in his direction and flexed my hand.

"Don't be angry with him," Billie pleaded. "I wasn't joking. If it weren't for him, I wouldn't just have surface injuries."

"I doubt he's blameless," I murmured, and Connor's face flushed.

"Can I go home now? Can you take me home?" Billie whispered. She looked stricken.

"I'll call Donny. He'll handle the show people. Let's go home," I agreed.

"Zach too?" she begged.

I looked at the other person who'd tried to take Billie away from me tonight. "Zach too," I replied between gritted teeth.

The executive producers were furious. The fans began exiting the auditorium confused until the cops arrived and started interviewing everyone about what they saw before Billie was attacked. Suddenly, it was the most interesting end to a season in the history of *Superstardom*. Social media was going crazy over Billie winning, the proposal, our history, and the attack.

I got a phone call from Donny informing us that the director only agreed to let us leave without a lawsuit if Billie assured them that she would sing on a morning television show first thing tomorrow and explain what happened. They specifically wanted her to tell the world that she had a stalker who sent her notes, the show moved her from the hotel to protect her, and Connor Graves was her savior.

I hated the idea that Connor would turn into the hero of the story because I doubted he was blameless. He made offensive comments about Billie to all of us, then spewed that sh*t to a psychotic assistant he slept with, who he had convinced she could be a star. I wasn't giving the guy an award anytime soon for picking up a knife he'd basically helped the girl sharpen. But Billie needed to go home, and she was grateful to him for his actions, so I would leave it alone for the time being.

When we got back to my house, Billie went to the bathroom to shower and wash away the blood. I'd suggested she have her cuts looked at, and she informed me stubbornly, "No hospitals. Not again so soon."

I agreed. For now.

As she turned on the shower tap, I walked outside to breathe in fresh air. My hands had been shaking since I saw her curled up in a ball. I needed to calm down.

My cell started buzzing in my pocket.

"Hey," I answered.

"My baby," my mom murmured. "You okay?"

Trust my mom to know to call me. She had been in the audience, and it was surprising she didn't storm the stage when everything went down. "She's okay."

"Didn't ask about Billie, baby. That's all over the news. I know the girl is safe. I want to know if my boy is okay after watching the first woman he's fallen in love with get proposed to by another man and then attacked."

I exhaled. "She's in my house."

"That all you need?"

"That's all I need," I told her, hoping I was speaking the truth.

I walked inside and found myself staring at Billie and Zach sitting on the couch, deep in conversation. She was in her pajamas and he hadn't changed since returning home. I thought about walking away and giving them privacy, but considering their conversation might impact me, I decided to hang back and listen to what they were saying.

"The way you're acting, I feel like I barely know you." Billie groaned. "What you did today makes no sense to me. Is it just jealousy, Zach? Have I turned into a competition that you want to win? Are you fighting over me like a basketball?"

"It has nothing to do with jealousy or some bullsh*t competition, B. It has everything to do with the fact that I love you," Zach explained.

It took every ounce of control I had to stay where I was and not interfere.

"You love me?" She scoffed. "Even though you've never mentioned it in eighteen years."

"I'm not joking. I love every part of you. I love it when you're nervous and when you're confident. I love it when you laugh and when you cry. There isn't a moment I've spent with you that I can't recall what you wore and how you smiled at me. I haven't ever said the words to you before because I didn't want them to lose their power. I wanted you to know when I said them to you the first time that it wasn't out of friendship."

I watched tears glisten in Billie's eyes and stilled myself for her response.

Thankfully, Zach continued. "If I said them before today, would they have been more powerful? Would you have said them back?"

"I don't know what I would have done if you had told me before this competition. We might never know. All I can tell you is that today, I'm angry and I'm hurt. I'm more upset about you coming onto that stage than a crazy woman coming after me with a knife, Zach. You embarrassed me and threatened our friendship by turning a proposal into a dare. And before that lunatic stormed into my room, I was about to come to you and say yes because of that ultimatum. Your friendship means the world to me."

Zach smiled.

My heart twisted.

"But after that woman cut me, it wasn't your arms I wanted to run into," Billie continued slowly. "It isn't fair to either of us if I chose you just because I'm afraid to lose our friendship."

I felt the breath I was holding release.

Zach looked stricken.

"I wish things were different. I wish I could give you the answers you need," Billie sobbed. "I just can't go there. I don't know if that's because I'm starting a life here that I want to focus on, and you remind me of home and a safety net I need to pretend doesn't exist."

"I'll go home, then," Zach replied, wiping away her tears. "I'll wait for you to make your career and realize you can have both. You can be with me and live here. You're the new winner of *Superstardom*. It won't take long for you to be on the radio now."

I shook my head. Some guys refused to take a hint.

When Billie shook her head, I almost cheered.

"You shouldn't be waiting for me. It isn't right for you or me," she explained.

"Do you love him? Is Jax why we can never be together?" he snapped.

I felt my heart leap into my throat. My neck muscles tensed. Everyone had dreams, and apparently tonight was when we all found out if they were coming true.

When Billie started talking, it was as if the room disappeared, "Jax is a part of this world. He understands the things I feel before I step on stage, during a song, and after a performance. Each night he's entrusted me with information that he knows I could share with dozens of articles for hundreds of thousands of dollars. He's protected me.

"He's so different from you. Zach, you never confuse me. I've always known who you were and why you did the things you did. And I've always relied on you knowing me, challenging me to be better and do more. You've been there for me so many times, I couldn't even count them if I wanted to. And Jax, he's frightening. I'm scared when I'm with him, and I'm scared about never seeing him again. I can't explain it. He's told me things, but there is so much more I don't know. I never know when he'll ask to spend time with me, and if he does, who he'll be when he sees me, the teenager or the rock star. Maybe I'm a little in love with him because his two sides are like the two parts of myself I don't always understand. Or maybe I don't love either of you, and my feelings have gotten mixed up with the competition and drama.

"But I do know I'm not the girl you deserve. The one who wants to marry her childhood sweetheart and start a fairy-tale family straight away."

Zach looked at Billie for a long time before muttering, "Your momma warned me that convincing you to leave might mean you wouldn't come back."

"That's the problem with our mommas," Billie returned. "They're usually right."

They started hugging, and I knew I needed to stop watching them. I had also heard everything I had to hear.

Walking up the stairs to my bedroom, I realized I lied to my mom. Billie in my house wasn't all I needed. I needed to know she wasn't leaving now that the competition was done.

It was late when Billie climbed into my bed.

"Are you sleeping?" she whispered.

"After the day we've had, you think I could sleep without you?" I whispered back.

"No," she replied with a touch of smugness in her tone.

"I heard what you told Zach."

"I know. I heard the door open when you came inside."

"I want you to know I'm a little in love with you too," I admitted nervously. "But I could also be confused with all the drama that's been going on."

She giggled. "I guess we'll work it out in time. I plan on staying as long as you'll have me."

"How about forever?" I suggested, making her laugh.

"Forever sounds appealing," she murmured. "Although there is just this one thing we need to do."

She pulled on my hand until we were out of my bed. I was standing there just in my boxers, and she was wearing only my shirt. I felt guilty for just a moment that while some cried over broken dreams, we stood together living ours.

I took a closer look at the shirt she was wearing and realized it seemed liked she didn't have any panties on underneath. It made all of the blood in my head rush to more excitable body parts.

She started tugging me to the door, and I managed to get enough brain power to ask, "Where are we going?"

"To your recording studio in the basement."

"You want to write a song right now?" I asked, shocked.

"No," she replied coyly. "I want to have the after-party we discussed once the competition was over in your soundproof studio. I don't want us waking up any of the other men currently still sleeping under your roof or being interrupted by any of your alarms." She looked at me nervously, biting her bottom lip with her teeth. "I hope you only forgot because I was attacked by a crazy woman and my best friend tried to marry me and not because you changed your mind."

I blinked twice as understanding dawned. "Billie Bishop, are you trying to seduce me?" I chuckled softly.

She leaned forward, laced her fingers with mine, and kissed me. Her tongue swept across mine. "Jax Bone, rock star and teen idol, are you seducible?" She wiggled her eyebrows.

I pulled her body tight against mine. "Definitely."

EPILOGUE

Next season

Billie

Three Years Later

"**T**his feels so strange, y'all," I said out loud, running my fingers across the judges' table. "You sure you don't want me to try and call Jax instead? I'm sure I could convince him to get his butt back in this chair. Or maybe Faith. She and Ryne don't start their tour for another month."

Tim, the director of the new season, smiled and shook his head. "We want contestants to see how far they can go following this competition. You're the embodiment of all their dreams come true. In the three years since you won *Superstardom,* you went on to a sold-out major arena tour, were awarded a Grammy for best pop song on your debut album, and we've heard pretty strong discussions about how Disney is asking you to be the star in their next movie musical."

"I can't comment on that," I replied, blushing. It was all still so foreign to me. It didn't feel real.

"You can't even confirm it with your best friend?" Zach probed as he joined the room. He was dressed in jeans and a simple button-up shirt, but the show's stylist had his hair like Connor Graves used to wear it. The only similarity between the old and new show hosts.

It suited Zach better.

I had to take a sip of the water they provided the judges to keep the goofy grin off my face while staring at my best friend, appearing so relaxed in front of the cameras. Who knew the public would fall in love with a small-town boy who proposed and got turned down on national television? It also didn't hurt that Jax whispered in enough ears to have people question Connor's recognition as a savior during my ordeal. I feared in the beginning that Zach gave up basketball and accepted *Superstardom's* offer to show me that he could understand my new life and convince me to leave Jax. However, from his time on the show and in LA, it's been clear that he truly loves encouraging people to step out of their comfort zones and shine. And Jax and I have never been closer, even when Zach comes over to watch the latest episodes with me on the couch.

"Not even for you," I told him smugly. He laughed and winked at me. "Now, do y'all just chat now, or am I going to get to judge my first contestant?" I laughed.

"Welcome to the big leagues, kid," Claudia told me as her makeup assistant applied the final touches to her flawless appearance. "Where we just sit around trying to look pretty until we change someone's life forever."

The idea that I could change someone's life freaked me out a little bit. I took another sip of the glass of water the crew provided and tried to appear calm.

When Jax walked through the doors holding his favorite acoustic guitar, my brows furrowed. He was wearing the outfit he wore as a judge during my season that he'd avoided wearing since, leather pants and a loose white T-shirt.

"Hey, I'm Jax Bone, and I would like to audition for the role of Billie Bishop's future husband."

My eyes widened. I immediately looked at Zach, and his big smile told me he knew what was going on.

"What—"

"Sweetie, we don't interrupt the audition until the end," Russell Conway informed me tongue in cheek.

Jax started singing John Legend's "All of Me," and my eyes filled with unshed tears. I could barely see. Jax usually refused to sing anyone's music but his own.

When he stopped singing and the entire room was standing and applauding, I struggled to get to my feet.

Jax came up close to me and whispered, "I never thought I was a dreamer. Not like you were when you entered this competition. I got unlucky in life and then lucky in the music industry. And then you walked in through those doors and my life changed. I started to have some wild dreams. Not just about singing sold-out concerts with you or being there to kiss you as you accepted your first music award. I dreamed about a future that is constantly beyond my imagination. And now I'm auditioning and going after all my wild dreams. So, what do you think? Want to make them all come true?"

He smiled at me and my shock disappeared, replaced with this feeling of warmth and certainty.

"I think you should sing something upbeat," I teased. "Just to show your full capabilities as my future husband."

The crew, along with Zach, Russell, and Claudia, chuckled in the background.

"Okay, then." Jax winked at me and turned to go back to his spot in the audition room before I giggled and grabbed his hand.

"I was kidding," I told him solemnly. "No more audition rounds needed. You've won my heart, Jax Bone." I kept hold of his hand, rounding the table until I could wrap both my arms around his shoulders. I looked up at the man who kept changing my life in unbelievable ways and smiled.

"If it's official and I've got the job, could I bring in my cheer squad?" Jax asked, rolling his eyes.

"A cheer squad?" I repeated, confused.

Zach opened the door and Bambi, Cora, and my momma stormed

in the room holding glittering signs that said JAX & BILLIE 4 EVA, SUPER*LOVE*DOM, and SAY YES THIS TIME!

I burst out laughing. Jax just sighed.

"The signs were Bambi's idea," my momma whispered in my ear as she hugged me. "She wouldn't be convinced otherwise."

"I can't believe you're here," I choked out, trying to keep the tears away.

"I might have been a fool a few years ago, but not any longer. I'm not missing any more life-changing moments," Momma replied softly.

"I hope you don't mind me tagging along," Cora stated nervously. "You're like my own daughter, and Michelle said she thought you'd want me here."

"She was right. I love that you all came," I replied, looking at each of them.

Bambi kissed me on the cheek and then turned to her son. "So, did she make you sing at least two songs? Or were the leather pants enough?"

The entire room burst out laughing.

"You surprise me, Jax Bone," I informed my fiancé later that evening as we cuddled under the blankets. "I never would have thought with how much our lives are in front of the camera that you would have wanted your proposal aired to the world."

"The footage won't be used in the show," he confessed as he ran his hands over my body. "The only people who will get to see me audition are our families and future kids. The show agreed to the deal."

"What did it cost you?" I laughed as he kissed my collarbone. He kept moving south with every kiss, and my breath quickly turned into pants.

"You're a celebrity judge this season, and next season Jax Bone returns to the celebrity judge couch with you." He groaned.

"You must really love me," I murmured, pausing running my hand over his chest to stare at the one carat rectangular diamond sitting on my left hand. Jax chuckled at my need to look at it constantly, even if it meant interrupting our celebratory activities. It was understated, romantic, and nothing like the attention-grabbing ring that was bought before for media purposes. It reflected us perfectly.

"I love you more than anything," he whispered as he kissed the side of my breast. "I wasn't lying earlier today. You are the dream I never knew I had that I have no plan on letting go of."

I sighed, moved Jax's face back to mine so I could kiss him seriously, and then helped guide him inside of me. I never knew what was more beautiful, singing one of Jax's songs or feeling him move inside me. It took me years to be confident with him in the bedroom, always afraid I might not compete with the celebrity girls he'd been with before. However, he constantly let me know that our lovemaking was just like our duets everyone demanded we perform.

Incomparable.

Later that night, I fell asleep curled in Jax's arms, amazed how a childish dream had provided me with a magical life.

THANK YOUS

I am forever grateful for the women and men in my life that help support me and my writing.

Chantal Fernando, this book is dedicated to you, but those words still don't express the full extent of how much I appreciate your guidance, our speed writing sessions and your inspiring words.

Claire Hielscher, there is no one like you and I am so very grateful for our friendship and your help.

Amy English, thank you for always offering your time and advice. Your love for this genre and passion for authors is unparalleled.

Ari at Cover It! Designs, thank you for my wonderful cover and your enthusiasm in making it beautiful.

The fabulous team at **Hot Tree Editing**! I always sleep a little easier knowing such clever women are examining my words.

Love Affair with Fiction and Wildfire Marketing Solutions! Thank you for everything you have done to promote my work!

Rose Tawil, your belief in my writing has made a huge difference in my confidence and perseverance. I cannot thank you enough.

And Jake, you continually show me that your dreams are all about helping mine come true. I love you so much.